Richard Dee is a native of Brixham in Devon, England. He left Devon in his teens and travelled the world in the Merchant Navy, qualifying as a Master Mariner in 1986. Coming ashore to be with his growing family, he flirted with various jobs, including Dockmaster, Marine Insurance Surveyor and Port Control Officer, finally becoming a Thames Pilot over twenty years ago.

He regularly took vessels of all sizes through the Thames Barrier and upriver as far as London Bridge. He recently returned to live in Brixham, where he has taken up food writing and blogging. He retired from pilotage in 2015.

The Rocks of Aserol is his third Science Fiction novel; his other titles, *Freefall* and *Ribbonworld* are available in paperback and electronically. He is married with three adult children.

The Rocks of Aserol

Richard Dee

4Star Scifi

All rights reserved.

Published in 2016 by 4Star Scifi

4Star Scifi, Brixham, Devon, England

www.richarddeescifi.co.uk/4Star

I.S.B.N. 978-0-9954581-0-9 (ebook)

I.S.B.N. 978-0-9954581-1-6 (paperback)

Copyright © Richard Dee 2016

This is a work of fiction. Any similarity between the characters and situations within its pages and places or persons, living or dead, is unintentional and coincidental.

Cover by Avalon Graphics

For Isaac and everyone who pushed my pen.

Chapter 1, Aserol

The doors hissed open and a fine mist of steam and water drops entered the carriage. Horis was standing by the door, ready to disembark when the spray from a poorly maintained seal soaked his trouser leg. As he stepped from the carriage the wet fabric stuck to his calf. Muttering to himself he jostled his way onto the platform, dragging his cases and Ministry bag through the unyielding throng.

The air smelt of coal dust and unwashed humanity, it was a different smell to the well-scrubbed human odour of the capital. But even though the tang was different, the steam was the same, and the coal dust was the same. In fact his whereabouts could be defined by the unusual clarity of the air, and that the late afternoon sun shone more strongly. And where he normally shrank from large crowds – due to his short, wiry frame and shy nature – the urgency of his mission made him bolder as he elbowed his way to the exit.

"Aserol! Aserol!" a rail-master cried. "All alight here! This is the end of the line! Move along now! This is Aserol! The end of the line!" And indeed it was, thought Horis, the end of the line; it could have been the end of the world, to a lot of folk, it still was.

The carriages loomed over him, their brass-works shining amid the dull steel and brown livery of the Rail-Ryde company. There was a seating level and a recessed passageway on the roof. This was manned by soldiers armed with gas weapons against the brigands that infested the countryside, and the Drogans whose dive was an ever present threat. Horis had been guiltily hopeful that they might have an adventure on the journey and had spent the whole time gazing through the windows. Sadly nothing untoward had happened and the official papers he had intended to read had remained in his bag.

Reaching the barrier, Horis showed his Ministry pass to the ticket collector, who touched his grimy cap with a set of nicoweed stained fingers and waved him through. There were the usual crowds of small children gazing through the metal fence at the gleaming locomotive, no doubt dreaming of one day driving such a beast. A team of mechanics were attending the engine, oiling and greasing the pistons and other moving parts, or polishing the gleaming flanks.

Another group were cleaning the large ram fitted to the front of the locomotive. Nicknamed the bovine shredder by the popular press, it was designed to clear a passage for the Ryde, dislodging any objects from the rails before they could cause a problem. There were stories of Rydes arriving with whole beasts impaled on its blades, hence the name. This time it seemed to have only caught a few branches.

Past the ticket barrier there were groups of disabled sailors begging and selling sundries. There were entertainers juggling, tumbling and balancing. There were cages full of exotic animals. And everywhere was the hiss of steam. Steam drifted across the concourse like small clouds. Horis stopped and gazed out at the scene, so different to the cityscape he was familiar with.

The Rail-Ryde terminus was situated on a high point, and looking towards the sea, Horis could see the town of Aserol spread out below him. Compared to the capital Metropol City, it was a small place, but important due to the mines in the vicinity, and of course the Rail that carried its produce and people to the centres of the country. There were smoking chimneys below, but not as many as he might have expected. On the other hand there were a lot more Bal-towers; clearly the town was closer to Bal than the city was.

Priests were becoming a rarity in the city and worship was declining, being replaced more with the religion of science. Horis knew that the further you went from the capital, the more resistance there was to the scientific advances that city dwellers took for granted. He shuddered to think that he might not be able to find some of the small comforts that city life afforded him. In his opinion science was more relevant than Bal; at least the science was generally predictable.

"It's quite a thing, isn't it?" The voice came from a man at his side. Horis turned and recognised him from the Ryde; he had been sat in the same carriage.

"I'm sorry," Horis replied, still looking around but not wanting to appear rude, "do you mean the Ryde, or the place?"

"Oh both," replied the other, a tall man dressed in dark suiting. "Do you realise that a little more than five years ago, it would have taken four days of travel over rough roads, through mountain passes and subject to the whim of surly equines to reach this outpost of civilisation."

He had the way of speech of an educated man but the knack of stating the obvious. He sounded like a government spokesman. Horis was intent on his purpose but did not wish to give offence.

He nodded. "And we were safe and comfortable all the way, with a meal as well."

"Indeed," the man continued. "Now, thanks to the determination of the government of Norlandia, and the brute force and skill of its people, it's a mere six hours from the capital. Times are changing."

He was right of course, civilisation had advanced and as usual, conflict had driven the process. In the quest for superiority Norlandia had developed many things, but not all were general knowledge. From his place in the Ministry of Coal, Horis knew of all sorts of innovations that were both thrilling and secret.

"They certainly are," agreed Horis, remembering a document he had seen at the Ministry. "And who knows, in another five years we may be able to journey between towns through the very air, like the birds and the Drogans do." As he said it, he realised that he might have said too much, the document had been marked Secret in large red letters.

But the man clearly thought he was overly optimistic. "That's a fascinating idea," he mused, "but I fancy there will be all sorts of obstacles to flight, why the weight of the boiler and the coal alone would be a problem." Horis was about to tell him more of the document when he stopped. Perhaps this man was a foreign agent, or an undercover Watchman testing his fealty. He changed tack.

"Are you a military man?" he asked. "You seem to have knowledge of the mechanics of flight."

"No," the other replied with a grin, "just a mere functionary in administration." He held out a hand. "I'm interested in many things; Lewis Morgan at your service."

Horis shook it. "Horis Strongman," he replied, "from the Ministry of Coal."

"What brings you to Aserol then, Horis, or do you live here?"

"No, I'm staying in a hotel, the Provincial," Horis hesitated to tell the man more, continuing his visions of spies and secret police. He was about to utter "Ministry business" when they were joined by another, who clearly knew Morgan. "Good after, Lewis," he greeted him, nodding to Horis. "I have the vehicle readied."

Horis caught a look of frustration from the man Morgan, as if his arrival had spoiled an opportunity.

"Excuse me," said Morgan to Horis, "it was pleasant to meet you; I hope your stay in Aserol is fruitful."

As they left, Horis realised that he had given his occupation but the man Morgan had revealed nothing.

Glancing around at the throng, Horis saw that there seemed to be a lot more people wearing swords and dart pistols on the streets here, and their overall dress was gaudier than the restrained, formal styles in the capital. Bright satins and polished leather mingled with shiny black suiting and feathered hats.

Horis carried a compressed gas pistol in a holster on his hip even though he had been told that the area was not known to be generally lawless. He suspected that in many ways the locals would also lack the sophistication and manners of the city. Perhaps, being on the coast the population felt less safe, despite the recent treaty with the Western Isles, there could still be raiders that would not yet have learned of the peace. Horis knew that there was a naval base just a few miles up the coast, and while there were also Drogan attacks, since the navy's expedition to the nesting sites, these had reduced, so that now they were no more than a nuisance.

Not that a sword or a dart pistol would be much use against a Drogan in full flight. Even his gas pistol, the latest invention and presently only available to government employees, would be of little help in that situation. Glancing up, as if half expecting to see one of the beasts, he noted the web of fine netting strung over the station entrance, and the gas balloons that floated gently on the breeze.

He knew that they carried armed balloonists in their wicker gondolas, their long telescopes keeping a watchful eye on the skies and the seas. They were flying, he thought, all they had to do was control their motion.

Also, Horis noticed the absence of masks and breathers on the faces of the people. It must be because the air is so clean, he mused. Indeed every breath almost hurt him, so sharp was the effect of the clean air on his lungs. His own mask hung around his neck, redundant.

It had recently rained and the cobbled roadway ran with grey rivulets, coal dust washed from the air and the road. It had the effect of making the view sharper and after the closed vistas of the capital and the limited view from the carriage window, the sight opened out in front of him gave Horis a glimpse of the enormity of the world.

And he inevitably thought of his country's place in the world. Norlandia was one of several countries that had benefited from harnessing coal and then coal gas to produce power, and whose machinery of metal gave them dominion over the less enlightened kingdoms and territories. There seemed to be a perpetual struggle between the world's industrial powers for influence over the others, and over the disputed parts, as one gained an advantage it would briefly rise, until it was caught in achievement by the others.

The overall effect was a rapid scientific advance, but espionage and warfare were the continual gifts of the race for superiority. At the moment, Norlandia was supreme, and with the peace that had

5

recently been agreed with their neighbours came hopes for a long period of stability.

They had a new and popular monarch, and government was stable and apparently uncorrupted. Although pirates and opportunists occasionally caused problems on the coast, the navy, with its superior equipment, generally kept order.

He knew that Aserol had expanded as trade had increased, for now that the capital could be reached in a day it was worth producing more food and catching more fishes than could be used locally. And of course the coal that was dug here could find its way to the factories and steam-generators more easily.

But the populace were struggling to keep up with the advance of civilisation. Indeed there was a lot of resistance to progress in places like Aserol, despite it being a bustling port in the most powerful country in the hemisphere.

Looking to his left, he saw an aerial beltway, which strode across the countryside from a point between two hills in the distance. Its metal framework towers and clanking rollers spoke of power, the power of man over the land, and of the power of technology. From its end, it was discharging coal into a large yard attached to the terminus; a fine mist of water was spraying over the lumps of coal from a metal pipe at the end of the belt, damping the dust and reducing the chances of fire.

Mechanical shovels were piling the coals into lines of Rail wagons, all bearing the name "Waster Mining and Metals" on their sides. Exo-Men swarmed around the shovels, assisting in the operation, their steam lines forming a tangle of pulsing knitting on the ground, damp with water from vented pressure. Waster Mining was the company Horis was coming to see, and from the size of the operation, and the number of workers, he could see that it was a force in the area.

Horis had not seen many Exo-Men in the flesh, so to speak, and he was as impressed by the sight as any child would be, ten feet tall in headless human form, they had articulated arms and legs, driven by steam pistons. Attached by hoses to their generators, they were moved by a man, strapped to a metal frame, with wires attached to his joints. As he moved his arms and legs, so the steam flowed through pistons and moved the Exo-Man's limbs, enabling work to be done.

To his right he could see the harbour, filled with a variety of craft, large metal steamers, a few wooden sailers and the usual collection of fishers and work-boats. Cranes bobbed and dipped as cargo was moved. A naval vessel was cruising past the harbour entrance, all flags flying, in a show of strength to the population, probably patrolling against pirates.

As Horis walked across the concourse, past a couple of magickers who were making objects borrowed from the crowd disappear and reading minds for small change thrown, a fight broke out between two men waiting in a queue for a refreshment stand. Horis put down his bags and stood, watching.

The wheeled wooden hut was selling hot drinks and various snacks. Painted in gaudy colours, it had the image of a smiling porker on its canvas awning. The smell of oil-fried foods and coffee drifted in the air, as the mood changed in the crowd, which backed off and made a circle around the two men, one in an army uniform of grey, and one in the naval blue. Both of the men were huge and heavily muscled, the sailor's arms were tattooed, and the soldier had a shaved head and half an ear missing. Their caps and uniform jackets were off; shirtsleeves rolled up, they faced each other.

They were engaged in a shouting match, something about a girl whose honour had been questioned, and their insults escalated in severity and volume, until the point was reached where violence was inevitable. They started to move, each looking for a weak point in the other's stance, throwing exploratory punches and kicks, neither doing much damage as they tested reflexes and speed, cheered on by the crowd, who seemed to favour the sailor, which was not surprising, given that this was a navy town.

But the soldier had his backers; a regimental party had formed up around the edge of the informal ring and were cheering their man on. At the rear of the throng, a shady looking individual in a greasy suit was taking bets; notes and coins were passed and pocketed. A few dubious looking characters stood by the roadside, trying to appear nonchalant whilst scanning the road for the Watchmen's arrival.

A number of smaller scuffles were in progress where the two sides' supporters met, adding to the confusion as the main protagonists wrestled. The soldier had a lock on the sailor's neck, and he was choking in its grip. In desperation, he swung his booted feet at the legs of the soldier, who danced out of the way, keeping his lock firm. The soldier was so intent on his victim and avoiding the flailing feet that he failed to notice the kerb stones and tripped. His grip released and the sailor fell to the ground wheezing. The soldier stumbled into the crowd, who pushed him upright and he turned to see the sailor still on the ground. With a grin the soldier stepped confidently towards his foe and swung a boot at the sailor's face. The sailor must have been shamming, as he grabbed the swinging ankle and pulled. Now it was the soldier's turn to fall, and the crowd cheered. As both men rose to their feet, the sailor drew a knife from his boot and lunged at the soldier, who backed off quickly until his retreat was halted by the throng. Unfortunately he had retreated into that part of the crowd containing the sailor's backers, his arms were grasped by his sides, and despite his struggles he could not free himself.

The sailor advanced, holding the knife in a casual, familiar grip, with the point steady on the soldier's stomach. Horis turned away, sure that the man was about to be gutted, this was a sailors' town; the army had no friends here.

"Stop!" rang out an authoritative voice. The crowd hushed and parted as a Watchman strode into the gathering, tall and black uniformed, his cap badge and cane ferrule gleaming brass.

He approached the sailor. "Give me the knife, laddie," he commanded in a tone that, whilst soft, carried the unmistakable sureness of command. Everyone stood still and waited.

He looked to the soldier, who had got free and was trying to creep away. "You stop there," he ordered. "I will want a word with you as well." There was a low growl from the crowd, like a wave breaking on sand as the Watchman repeated his request, holding out his hand towards the sailor. "Come on, laddie and give it to me, before things go too far."

The sailor wavered, and whilst the Watchman was looking at the knife, the soldier saw his chance and made a run for it. The crowd dissolved as he pushed through them.

The Watchman saw him move, reached into a pocket on his quip-belt and withdrew a small ball, which he threw underarm at the disappearing soldier, it bounced between his legs, and metal bars sprang out from it, tripping the man and leaving him sprawling.

"I told you to stay there." He sounded exasperated and turned his attention again to the sailor. "Now you, please give me the knife, and don't make me take it."

The sailor wavered, reversed the blade and handed it over. The Watchman took it and put it in his backpack. Producing cuffs he fitted them over the man's wrists. Walking to the fallen soldier, who had wisely decided to stay down, he pulled his hands behind his back and cuffed him. "On your feet," he demanded, as a Watch-Wagon arrived in the concourse, pulled by two glossy black equines. Both men were placed in the rear of the wagon, and then turning slowly the Watchman surveyed the scene. "Any of you fine gentlemen care to enlighten me to the cause of that disturbance?"

The Watchmen, Horis knew, were totally impartial, and would single-mindedly pursue the truth, they could not be bought, or put off, and resistance only made them stronger. "As honest as the Watch" was a compliment in business and in life. No-one in his right mind would dare to fight with a Watchman; there was only one punishment for that.

The crowd thinned; clearly there were no takers for the request. Horis, who had not been close enough to hear anything, picked up his bags and resumed his walk toward the town. There were flags and bunting hanging from every available surface, and everywhere was decorated with flowers and the fruits of the Harvest. Of course, tonight was the festival of thanks for a good Harvest. It would be celebrated in the cities, but as they were less connected to the soil, it was muted, and mainly an excuse for a military parade. Here there was likely to be a more earthy ritual.

Chapter 2

As Horis walked away from the Rail-Ryde and down the hill, his case bumped against his leg with every step. The crowds thinned as he got further from the terminus and he wondered why the omnibus halt was so far away.

He was starting to perspire, and he felt as though people were watching his discomfort when he found himself at the halt. There were several long queues for the various routes, and no obvious means of telling which one he should choose to reach the hotel arranged for him.

He asked a man standing close to him, but the answer was delivered in such a thick provincial accent that it left him none the wiser. Politely he bowed and thanked the man anyway, all the time looking for an inspector.

As in the capital, the omnibuses were guided by a metal shoe at the front, which was held in a single track laid in the cobbles. There were wheels to steer across the intersections and provide stability. Unlike in the capital, the omnibuses in Aserol had a single deck, and were drawn by pairs of giant equines, blinkered and resplendent in leather. As soon as one arrived, the crowd swarmed towards it, jostling for spaces. There was a number on the front, but no details as to the places on the journey.

With his bags, and his small stature, Horis quickly realised that any journey would not be pleasant. Hoping that Terrance would understand the extra expense, he turned away. He felt very out of place, a stranger in his own land.

In desperation, Horis made his way to the mobile stand, where he soon found himself at the head of the much shorter queue for a steam-mobile.

The latest adaptation of technology, it was a form of equineless carriage, driven by a coal boiler heating water to drive pistons, much like a Rail-Ryde locomotive, only much smaller. The driver sat outside at the rear, atop the boiler and furnace, with a coal bunker behind him.

Gravity and a belt fed the powdered coal into the furnace, where water was heated to drive the pistons and propel the mobile.

The passenger compartment was at the front, below the driver, and above the water tank. They were still only used over short distances, or in urban areas; for no decent roads connected towns, and there were few places to refuel with either coal or water. The machine vibrated with an alarming motion as the pressure was vented from the boiler, as ready as a racing equine to do his bidding.

Its brass and steel frame and fittings were dulled and grimy, and the wheel rims caked with mud and coal dust, which did not inspire confidence, but he was next in line and for good or ill, this was his conveyance. Horis opened the door and placed his bags inside, then looked up at the driver, masked and leathered, sitting hunched over the controls; he turned to Horis and grinned, showing a set of metal false teeth that shone. "Where to, Guv'nor?" he asked.

"Provincial Hotel, good sir," Horis answered, and almost before he had a chance to seat himself and shut the door, he was swept back into the deep velvet cushions of the seat as the machine accelerated away, scattering the urchin children that played and begged around all such places. Horis squawked into the speaking tube that connected him to the driver, "Have a care, man!" but there was no answer. Horis remembered tales of the first of these machines, how in the rush to make ever smaller boilers the thinner construction had resulted in explosions and deaths. Also the dry coal dust was known to be particularly combustible. He hoped that this one was well built and maintained.

Opening the grimy window, Horis could see the mountains that encircled the town, mountains that were covered with tall trees, and which contained the reason for his visit. The summons had come the day before, and as the most junior in the Ministry of Coal he had been singled out for the job. In truth it was close to the public holiday, and none of the others had wanted the disruption; as Horis was single he had been everyone else's choice for the journey.

He had left his lodgings early this morning for the long Rail-Ryde to Aserol, with no knowledge of how long he might remain away, and only a vague notion as to his purpose.

His superior, Terrance, whose family owned the mine, had given him little intelligence. "See what Mr Obley is up to," he had said. "I would go myself, but..." He waved his arms about. "...It's Harvest and I am required at official things. Reassure him and solve his problems, you have my authority to do what is reasonable. He has called like this before; it will probably be a trivial matter. And see if there is any talk of the mine in town, Obley has strange ways of dealing with his 'problems'."

As he was carried along the cobbles, the mobile bucked and rattled and Horis thought of his fast-breaker, a rather splendid piece of haddock and boiled new potatoes eaten on the journey. It was more than he would normally break his fast with but was included in the price of the ticket. At the time it had seemed a shame not to indulge. The springs on the mobile were tired and gave a motion like a ship in a squall, and Horis silently prayed to Bal that the meal would not make a reappearance.

Buildings and people flashed by, and the machine tilted violently as it cornered. It overtook many equine-drawn vehicles, and Horis wished that he had taken the more sedate option of a carriage ride. He noticed that the equines seemed unperturbed by the machine, even though in many ways it would be their nemesis.

After what felt like an hour, although it had only been a few minutes, the mobile wheezed to a halt. Horis could see that he was outside a somewhat faded building that was barely clinging onto past grandeur. It was one of several joined in a long curving terrace, facing the harbour. The driver's voice squawked through the speaking tube.

"Provincial Hotel, sir, I hope you enjoyed the Ryde, the old girl does her best, but spares is hard to come by."

"It was fine," gulped Horis, his stomach was still fighting with gravity for control of his haddock. He looked at the fare shown on a clockwork and opened the door. Climbing out onto the pavement, he rummaged in his pocket for coins. Handing the driver half a Sol, he muttered, "Keep it," and started to drag his belongings from the mobile, which shuddered and spluttered, dripping steaming water into the drain ditch. There was a rattle from the coal bunker as more fuel was fed into the furnace down the belt.

"Bal blesses you, sir," said the driver, looking at the coin. He touched his cap in salute, and Horis saw that his hand was made of polished wood, the fingers frozen in a claw-shaped position that fitted the controls of the mobile. "I hope you enjoys it here in Aserol."

"I'm on Ministry business," he replied, but with a roar the machine had gone; only a wisp of steam remained.

Chapter 3

Close up, the buildings were grey and dust stained, with pock marks in the brickwork, Horis knew that the coal dust and water made an acid that ate bricks; it was a constant job to repair. In the city, there were gangs of convicts out continuously with their buckets and trowels; here it seemed that the job had not been done for a long time. The state of the brick was not helped by proximity of the Local, the steam and gas generator for the area. Not thirty yards away, its stack belched thick black smoke. A queue of steam-lorries waited outside, filled with coal for the boilers.

A porter, in a tired uniform, came slowly towards him, the man had the lower part of his left arm missing, the sleeve of his shirt was pinned to his chest. He had a row of medal ribbons over his heart, faded and grease stained, but he held himself tall and there was life in his eyes. And his shirt and trousers were well cleaned and pressed; while his braces and boots were of polished leather.

"Good after, sir, and welcome, let me help you with those." He attached one case to a hook slung on a leather loop over his missing arm and hefted the other, showing dexterity for his injuries. With a cry of, "This way," he led Horis into the hotel.

The corridor was lit by coal gas lanterns, the wicks needed trimming and the glasses were covered with oily stains. The whole effect was to throw shadows and leave the corners in darkness, although the corridor was in general well-appointed. After a short walk Horis entered the main lobby.

A huge metal framed glass dome gave the room a stark, bright look after the dull corridor, and the late afternoon sun shone on an area filled with comfortable looking leather chairs and settees, arranged around low tables. Small groups were sat taking afternoon char and chatting happily. A piano in the corner was being softly played, and everywhere were tall plants and ornaments. A large ornate clock filled one wall; its surround carved with scenes of Drogans in flight, together with images of Bal. Small birds chirruped and flitted among the foliage, and off to one side was an ornamental pond with lilies and fountains. It was like an indoor park. Horis and the porter approached the desk.

A stout, stern-looking woman manned the reception desk; she eyed Horis as all large women do when faced with a smaller man. The name board on the desk said Sayrah Faith, Horis immediately christened her "Sour Face".

"How may we help you?" Her voice rose at the end of the sentence, as did her eyebrows.

"I have a room booked by the Ministry of Coal," Horis squeaked nervously, "in the name of Strongman."

She grinned, trying to associate him with the name and deciding that it was Bal's joke on the poor wretch. Consulting her ledger she made a note and reached for a key. "Can I see your Ministry card?" she asked. "And will you sign the register?" Horis did as he was bid, and with a reluctance that he could feel, she handed him the key.

"It's the garret room," she informed him, returning the pass. "Maloney will take you." Horis suspected that the choice of room revealed her thoughts about men in general; being short he had had a continual battle to assert himself. But he had grown a thick skin, and took little notice of insults, preferring to allow others to underestimate him.

"Thank you, madam," he said meekly as he followed the one-armed man towards the lift.

"Don't mind her, sir, she treats all males the same," the porter Maloney told him with a smile. "Her man went to sea and never returned."

Horis tried to appear sympathetic. "Poor woman," he replied. "Was he killed in the wars?"

"Oh no," said Maloney with a grin. "He tired of her continual nagging and joined a tramp steamer, somewhere abroad he got involved with a bar girl, he sends her postcards telling of their happiness."

Horis could see his point of view. The thought entertained him all the way up in the lift, which seemed to take forever. The lift stopped at the top floor, opening onto a long, thin corridor with a worn carpet. Skylights gave illumination; there were gas lanterns set in the wall, but these were unlit in the low sunshine. At the end of the passage was a door, Maloney opened it with the key and they entered. They were clearly in the eaves of the building; the ceiling sloped dramatically to the window. Horis looked at Maloney questioningly. "Is this the only room, then? Or is it merely another sign of madam's displeasure?"

"We are very busy, sir," replied Maloney. "As you will be aware it is Harvest, and there are celebrations planned, all the rooms have been booked for weeks, and it was only thanks to the Ministry's influence that this one was obtained for you."

The room was simple and clean, if a little threadbare. It had its own washroom, set off to one side; and the window, set in the slope of the roof, gave a good view over the town and the seas beyond.

Maloney put Horis's cases gently down in the corner. "Will that be all?" He raised an eyebrow.

Horis passed him a tenth Sol. "Thank you, Maloney. Tell me; how does one get to the Mines of Waster from here?"

"You can take the omnibus, sir; the number 14, it passes right in front of the hotel twice an hour, but why would you wish to go there?"

"Ministry business," he answered. "Nothing of excitement."

"Beggin' your pardon, but there's been rumours, sir," said the porter. "About unnatural things found at the mine."

At that, Horis was alerted, remembering his instructions. He kept his voice bland.

"Really, what sort of things?"

"Well I call them kiddies' stories, sir, flying things and suchlike, I don't take any notice myself, but Mrs Maloney she gets into one of her states, sir."

"Do you mean the Drogans?" Horis asked.

"Oh no, sir, not them, we are used to them, lots of places have nets to protect us outside and the balloonists are very good; these tales are of things in the ground, that the miners have dug up."

Horis was concerned, although he tried not to show it, news obviously travelled, and while he knew little of the reasons for his visit, clearly rumours were circulating. "I'm just here from the Ministry for an inspection," he said, trying to sound both innocent and convincing, "purely routine, now please would you excuse me whilst I sort myself out; twice an hour you say?"

"That's right, sir," replied the man. "Although the offices may well be closed by the time you could get there."

Horis unpacked his cases, he hung his evening suit up carefully, he had brought it with him on the chance that he might have to attend a formal meal. Cut in the latest fashion it had cost him a month's salary. His washing gear he placed in the washroom, and then he turned his attention to preparations for visiting the mine.

Chapter 4

When Horis left his room to return to the lift, his appearance had changed completely. Gone was the smart suit with the woollen waistcoat and gold chain, replaced by workmanlike overalls of brown cotton, clean and pressed but obviously well used. His overjacket was of the same material, but with leather patches on the elbows and across the shoulders. Sturdy boots, shined to a mirror polish, completed the outfit and he had a pair of thick gauntlets tucked into his belt. He wore a knapsack over his shoulder, with the Ministry crest embossed on the tongue.

The water-powered lift deposited him back in the reception area, where the stern woman had been replaced by a younger, friendlier faced girl of perhaps twenty-five years. Her green eyes surveyed Horis beneath a tumble of curls, escaping from a bone ornament on one side of her head. She had a fashionably pale face adorned with freckles, and she smiled broadly at Horis as he approached. Her gown was low-cut and mauve, brazenly exposing freckles and more. Horis felt himself redden; it was not like the city here. His experiences with women were not few, yet he felt out of his depth in this provincial outpost.

"Good after, sir," she greeted him, seeming not to notice his discomfort. "How may I help you?"

The sign on the desk now said "Grace"; it suited her, she was indeed graceful, and every movement she made was fluid.

"Good after, madam, may I use your speaker?" he enquired.

"Of course," she replied, passing him the instrument on its long wire. Horis saw that it was sound powered, which meant that he would have to use the exchange. In the capital, you could dial directly between many of the speakers. This was another sign of provincial sloth, he decided.

Horis cranked the gearing furiously for a few seconds, lifted the handset and waited:

"Aserol Exchange, what destination please," the operator's voice crackled from the handset.

"Waster Mine please, Mr Obley."

"Just one moment please, sir." Horis looked up from the speaker, to find himself the subject of scrutiny. Blushing he looked away, but could feel the green eyes burning into his very being.

The speaker squawked again. "Waster Mine, this is Mrs Grantham; Mr Obley's secretary is speaking." To Horis it sounded like an older woman, and one who was used to having a position of authority. He imagined her to be the twin sister of Sour Face.

"Good day, madam; I am Horis Strongman from the Ministry. As requested I have arrived in Aserol and would like to come to the mine."

"Very well, please wait for a moment while I consult Mr Obley." The line went dead, and as Horis waited he realised that Grace was still gazing intently at him. He was glad when Mrs Grantham returned, but puzzled that Obley himself had not picked up the speaker.

"Mr Obley is presently indisposed," she continued, "but is glad that you have arrived safely in Aserol. He will be grateful for official guidance; however, it is late and thinks that perhaps it will be best if you were to come up in the morn. Do you wish us to send a mobile for you?"

Horis was surprised, in the Ministry he had been told that the matter was urgent, now that he was here and talking to the instigator of his visit, or at least his secretary, it seemed less so. Perhaps that was the provincial way, but as the junior he felt unwilling to press to speak to Obley directly.

"That won't be necessary, madam; I can get the omnibus, but surely it would be better to come up immediately."

"Oh no, sir, you must be exhausted from your travels, the situation is presently under control and a good night's rest will set you up for a busy day's work, matters will keep till the morn. Anyway," she continued, "transport may be difficult this evening, due to the Harvest celebrations."

In truth Horis was tired, and only too glad to be offered the chance of a rest before his work started. "As you wish then, I will arrive promptly tomorrow morn."

"Very well, we will expect you." The line went dead and Horis replaced the handset in its cradle.

"Thank you," he said to the receptionist as he handed it back.

"I'm Grace, sir." She smiled at him and her freckles danced. "And if there's *anything* that you need, you just ask."

Horis could feel himself flush again. People here were different to those in the city, he could tell that much, even though he had been told that he was bad at reading female emotions her meaning was clear.

"Tell me, Grace," Horis summoned up all his courage, "Where might a man with a night to himself go for entertainment in this town?"

Looking him straight in the eye, she smiled. "Meet me at eight; I will be waiting outside, on the step."

Chapter 5, Northcastle

That same day, several hundred miles to the north, the subject of the document that Horis had seen was being tested in the wilds around Northcastle.

Here the government ministries had taken over a large part of the moorland and coasts for their research and for the testing of all things scientific. In conjunction with the companies which many senior government officials had interest in, they had been mainly responsible for the mechanical revolution which had swept the globe. All manner of machines had been and were being developed here, before production in the factories all over the country.

The complex had its own coal mines and steel foundry, a port and an internal Rail line which connected all the facilities. There were many large buildings, shaped and painted to blend into the surroundings, and part of the valley of the Gudrun River had been covered over, to hide the things underneath it from anyone who was not supposed to know.

Because of the continual threat of espionage, which could never be completely removed, the whole area, some hundreds of square miles had been fenced and were regularly searched by soldiers in steam-mobiles. Naval ships patrolled the seaward approaches. Agents also posed as scientists, reported conversations and watched all the while for treason. Balloons hung in the sky, watching over the surroundings.

The bright red air-mobile stood at the end of a long wood and metal ramp, pointing down the valley of the Gudrun River. Scientists and engineers had been working on flying machines in secret for some time and this was the latest version. In true scientific fashion it had various names: rocket, air-mobile or for some unknown reason, plane. It all depended on which expert you spoke to. Whatever you wished to call it, it was fixed to a wagon, mounted on rails set along the ramp. Men moved around it, readying it for flight. They were dressed in faded uniforms of brown, with the red stripe that showed their convict status. There was a ready supply of criminals for the workforce, and enough volunteers for the technical posts, given the pampered living conditions. The wages that the artisans earned were good, although few of them had ever been allowed out to spend anything.

Even though the place was a well-guarded secret, stories of what went on here were well known. Very often, truth and fiction mixed, but public spirits were buoyed by the tales. It was true that the balloonists trained here, the darlings of the age in their gas balloons, floating high over the land and masters of the skies. The green uniforms were the ticket to free meals, drink and more when worn around the towns and cities of Norlandia. Less well publicised was the high mortality rate, and the fact that a lot of balloonists simply blew away on the breeze and were never seen again. The flyers of these new air-mobiles were drawn from the balloonists and called pilots, as they directed the craft rather than were moved at the elements' mercy.

The river here was wide, and the banks at each side were steep. It was early afternoon, and the autumn sun had just cleared the hills to the south, lighting the purple heather and yellow gorse on the hillsides. A few small clouds drifted in a blue sky, where gulls wheeled and cried. A line of gas balloons each attached to a tripod of mooring lines floated above the valley, marking the line of the river towards the sea. Each was manned by spotter balloonists, their job was to watch the flight of the craft and signal its progress. They would be helped by its red colour, making it easier to see in water or on land. A side effect of the colour was to make recovery of the pieces of crashed craft simpler.

Behind the ramp and the craft was a hole in the cliff face, extending into a large cavern, filled with workshops. The air-mobile was facing into the wind that blew up the valley; and even though it was secured to the wagon by heavy hooks and chains, its wings rattled and vibrated as if it was trying to be free to soar.

Made of wood and canvas, it was little more than a tube with wings and a tail, with a small opening above the wings containing a seat for the pilot. There was a glass screen just in front of this hole to help shield the pilot's face from the wind. Two pressurised steel canisters, one in each wing, held gas which was fed to a fierce burner situated just under the pilot's seat. The whole of the fuselage was taken up by a steel tube, containing this burner.

Forward motion down the ramp forced air into this tube; here it was compressed by a series of vanes and baffles. This compressed air passed over the burner and was rapidly expanded by the heat. Being unable to go in any direction except out of the rear of the pipe, the result was to push the craft forward. As speed increased more air was pulled in, and the process became self-sustaining. High speeds were theoretically possible, but the process could not start from rest.

At the rear was a large funnel-shaped opening where the heated air would exit. The steel pipe weighed more than the rest of the craft and the pilot put together, and was the result of years of testing and development. In theory it was too heavy for flight, only the forward motion over a certain speed, and air flowing over the specially shaped wings kept it in the air. It was as different to the gas balloon as it could be, yet the balloonists were keen to try and master it.

The pilot was walking around the craft, moving with difficulty in the thick wool and leather overalls that would keep him warm when aloft. Over the top of this, he wore a bright red cork jacket, which he hoped would keep him afloat should he find himself unconscious in the water.

He was carefully inspecting the surfaces of the wings and the movable portions that were designed to control the craft whilst it was in the air.

The air-mobile in front of him was exactly the same as the one that he had practised on, except for the engine. He had spent hours in the wind chamber, where a large fan, powered by the waters of the Gudrun, had blown air toward the practice craft. It was held in place by two strong steel springs, but the airflow over its wings was the same as if it was in motion. Thus its pilot could safely make it rise and fall, turn and swoop, whilst never leaving the spot. He had also spent time learning how the gas burner worked, and how to control it.

Ralf, the pilot, was a veteran of the flying tests; he had completed many trips from the ramp, more than most others had. He put this down to a through system of checking, and of cultivating friendships with the engineers and the convicts who built the craft.

He helped them out, passed them small comforts, and generally made sure that they thought well of him. He was sure that other flyers, those who affected a superior air, were not so well liked or looked after; they seemed to have a higher crash rate than was good for them. That was a problem with the system, he decided.

When Ralf was happy with his inspection, he was helped up a ladder into the open cockpit of the craft. He put on goggles and a thick woollen hat, which he pulled down over his ears.

The artisans moved around the craft, disconnecting the gas hoses that had been charging the tanks built into the wings, and releasing the chains that held the craft to the ramp. Now it was held only by a hook on the wagon. The ends of each wing were held by convicts, keeping the plane balanced. He tested his control column, and looked around him to see that it was working correctly. His feet danced on the pedals that controlled the rudder, he could see it move in the mirror by his left elbow.

A hatch was opened in the belly of the craft and a flame was applied to the burner, lighting the gas flow. The pilot worked a control and the flame grew and shrank. Satisfied that all was in order with the igniter the hatch was shut. After a final check the engineers backed out of the way, the burner was turned to maximum and the brake released. Gravity started it moving down the ramp, forcing air into the combustion chamber. The men holding the wings ran with him, until the speed was too great for them. With the burner at maximum, hot air was expelled from the pipe at the rear, in a shimmer of heat and burnt gas.

As the speed built up down the ramp, there was an increasing roar that could be heard above the sound of the wind and the craft leapt forward, straining to rise. Before it had reached the end of the ramp, Ralf pulled a lever by his side and the hook holding him to the wagon fell away. Free now to move on its own, the pilot pulled back on his control column, and was airborne, climbing into the wind.

The pilot felt the resistance in the control column, like an animal trying to escape his clutch, and as he pushed it one way and another the craft banked and rolled. Remembering his instructions, he reduced the gas flow to the burner, to conserve fuel, but the speed barely faltered. Exulting in the sensation, he turned his attention to flying down towards the sea, and the waiting ship. In his mind he would be home for supper.

The craft flashed past the balloons, whose occupants waved and hoisted flags, these passed the message downriver: "Successful launch". The message outran the craft until it was received by the waiting warship, in the wide river mouth. Here preparations were made to recover the pilot if they could, and more importantly the craft, after his flight. A small boat was launched ready to assist in the recovery, and bobbed alongside the warship, poised for action.

Ralf spotted a flock of birds ahead; at this speed he would hit them in a matter of seconds. He hauled on the controls, kicking the rudder with his feet, and the plane tilted violently.

The birds had sensed his approach, and scattered, one thumped into his wind deflector and another hit the mesh guard covering the pipe. The manoeuvre had caused his speed to reduce and with the nose up it was close to stalling. Ralf could feel the wings vibrate as the flow of air over them faltered. His stomach felt like it was rising into his mouth as he dropped. Remembering his training, Ralf eased the control forward and increased the burner. The nose dropped and the speed built up. As he felt control return he breathed a sigh of relief.

If he could have seen below his feet, he would not have been so confident; the motion of the craft as he had turned it had loosened the control valve on one of his gas cylinders. The flame from the burner was, at that instant, travelling up the gas line back into the tank in his left wing. This tank was nearly empty, but still contained enough of the flammable gas to cause an explosion.

The watchers, having signalled a good launch, looked on with dazed familiarity, as the blast ripped through the craft, breaking off one wing. Unbalanced, the remainder spiralled down towards the ground, the impact breaking it into a thousand pieces. Burning fragments from the wing fluttered to earth, setting light to the gorse bushes on the hillside.

In the cockpit, the initial explosion had shaken Ralf out of this reverie. However, the force of the blast had removed all the burning material and to his surprise and relief his arms and legs still worked. He knew that he had to get out to stand any chance of survival. It was either certain death here, or hope that he survived the fall and landed in the river. Training took over, and without thinking he undid the belt securing him to the seat as the remains of the craft threw itself around the sky, plummeting in its death throes. He was disorientated by the motion, his stomach heaved, but by using the strength born of desperation, he pushed himself out of the doomed machine.

Shaking his head, the foreman engineer turned to his team. "Poor old Ralf," he muttered, removing his cap and clutching it to his chest. "Seems like the gas lines are still not secure enough." In a louder voice, he called for another air-mobile to be winched up the tunnel to the start of the ramp. "Get the next pilot up here," he called, privately thinking: the next poor soul who will try to fly to the sea. Meanwhile, he would try to guess at the fault, and check everything again.

The crew of the nearest balloon saw the pilot fall clear, and watched his body plunge into the river. The flag signal for a man in the water was hoisted, and the boat rowed away from the warship's side, to search for the red of the flotation jacket.

~~~

As he bobbed in the cold water, unable to swim due to the thick layers of clothing and the cork jacket, Ralf mused on the problems of the flying machine. Certainly the wings of this model were more efficient; his manoeuvre to avoid the birds had proved that. He could not understand how the gas tank had exploded, as the supply pipes were fitted with the same flame arrestors that miners had used for years.

Ralf had had the germ of an idea in his head, from time spent on the training machine in the wind chamber. He had seen how air could be moved over it by the fan, allowing it to fly without moving forward, and it came to him that a fan mounted on the rear of the machine would have the effect of pushing it forward, in the same way as a ship was pushed by its propeller.

The thought excited him, for he lived for flying.

He could hear the calls from the rescue boat as the oarsmen drove it through the waves towards him. He was feeling colder and water was starting to seep into his inner woollen clothing, but he raised his arms as a loop of rope was thrown towards him. Shivering, he was dragged into the boat and wrapped in blankets. The oarsmen rowed him upriver to a landing stage under the launch ramp. There was a flask of hot char in the boat, laced with spirit and he had drained it by the time they arrived.

Wasting no time, he went into the pier-master's hut and changed out of his wet clothing, rubbing himself dry with a rough towel. There was a good fire going and some spare clothes, left there for just this eventuality, and he donned them, feeling much better to be warm and dry.

On returning to the workshops cut into the hill, he went to the engineer with his ideas.

"I understand what you say," said the artisan engineer. "It has been thought of many times before. But how can we make the propeller spin fast enough? A steam engine is too big and heavy, and turns too slowly to reach the speed required. And air is thinner than water, young Ralf."

Ralf was ready for that. "We already have a gas burner inside the machine," he explained. "Instead of just heating the air and letting it out, we could use it to turn a fan on the same shaft as the propeller."

The engineer was not convinced. "And how does the air get into the fan?" he asked triumphantly, but again Ralf was ready for him.

"Another fan on the shaft, with the blades reversed would suck air into the combustion chamber. All that would be needed would be a clockwork to start the shaft turning."

The engineer thought for a moment. "Yes," he said. "Once we get it spinning, air will be drawn in and heated. The expansion would drive the shaft faster, sucking more air in; I believe you have something there. Let me work on it."

"One more thing," said Ralf. "We need a single word to describe the machine; everyone calls it by a different name."

Chapter 6, Aserol

Returning to his room, Horis felt a mixture of emotions, both pleased that he had a companion for the evening, and slightly anxious that his failure to go straight to the mine might be viewed with disapproval in the Ministry. He was somewhat fearful of his superior Terrance, but knew that he was only in Aserol because he was the junior man. And anyway, he had been told by Obley, who was also technically senior to him, via his secretary, to wait till morning. He tried to put those thoughts out of his mind, and instead conjured visions of an enjoyable time in Grace's company.

Horis took a short nap, setting his timepiece to wake him in two hours. When the buzzing roused him, he was in the midst of a dream, chasing shadows through a web of tunnels. Repairing to the washroom, he started to prepare for his evening. He took care and extra time shaving his chin and bathed in piping hot water. He decided to put his best suit on, together with a cravat in purple, and splashed some perfumed balm around his neck. Automatically, he threaded the leather holster of his gas pistol onto the belt of his trousers; it lay snug under his fashionably long jacket and hardly disturbed the lie of the fabric after he had tied the holster's lace around his thigh. Placing his polished felt hat on his head, he locked the room, and descended to the lobby. The porter called Maloney was on duty at the desk when he handed in his key, reading a news-sheet.

"Off out for the parade, sir?" he questioned. "You'll not have seen the like in the big city, I'll imagine."

"No I expect not," replied Horis, who had quite forgotten about the Harvest. He felt disappointed; Grace had probably meant the invitation as a gesture to a visitor to show off the local celebrations.

Horis had hoped that it was more of a personal thing.

"People in the city forget the ways of the country-folk," he said. "Harvest is not so important to them, food appears in the shops and markets and modern city dwellers cannot see behind that."

"It's a sad side to progress," mused Maloney. "But here we are close to the earth, and we remember. Enjoy your evening, sir."

Horis walked to the entrance and stepped outside. It was still warm, although the sun had set, casting a rosy glow in the western sky, and a few bright stars were shining in a sky dotted with small clouds. Both moons were visible, one full and one a sickle, in opposite sides of the sky.

Crowds of people were moving slowly down the road, in the direction of the harbour, the few men who were not in uniform were dressed in suits not unlike Horis's, and the women in strange creations of lace, leather and other fabrics unfamiliar to him. The overall effect was one of contrast, between the staid and the abandoned. The air was filled with an expectant buzz of anticipation.

Grace was standing at the foot of the steps. She had changed from her gown into clothes that seemed to be made mainly of polished brown leather; long boots, tight trousers and a fitted jacket with many brass buckles and buttoned pockets. A leather cap, from which her curls tumbled, and flat polished shoes, completed the ensemble. She was taller than he had imagined from seeing her behind the desk, or perhaps that was just an effect created by her slim body in the tight covering, for when she stood beside him, their eyes were level.

"Good eve, sir," she performed a small graceful courtesy. "Your suit makes you look very dashing."

"Why thank you, ma'am," replied Horis, bowing in return. "But please call me Horis. Your attire is… well, it is different to that which I would have expected, although very fetching. Is it some part of the Harvest celebrations?"

Grace smiled at that, as if in despair of males. "Look around you; these are the fashion amongst women in Aserol, particularly for an evening perambulation."

Glancing around him, Horis could see that it was true, whereas on his arrival the women had been dressed in gowns and shawls, now their clothes reflected those worn by Grace and in some cases made hers look formal and restrained. There were quasi-militaristic leather uniforms of all sorts, and outfits that appeared to consist of brightly coloured lace underthings worn as outerthings. Surely it was important that it was not a cold evening. Compared to evening events in the capital, considerably more female flesh was on display than might seem decent. And in a way, the tightness of some garments seemed to be more revealing than their absence would have been.

Grace extended a gloved hand, smelling faintly of oiled leather. Horis took it and they started to walk with the throng.

"Where are we going, Grace?" Horis asked as they wandered down packed streets. The gas lamps shone brightly as the sky darkened, and a light breeze had sprung up. The sky blazed with the occasional blast of flame from a gas balloon's burners, throwing long unpredictable shadows. The cobbles throbbed from the steam pipes buried in the road, and laughter echoed from the high walls of buildings.

"There is a parade on the High Road, we are almost in a good place to view it," was her reply. "And then I will take you to a small inn that I know of, where we can eat and drink a toast to the Harvest."

They reached the end of the road, ahead was a wide thoroughfare, lined on both sides with people. The building fronts had all been decorated with flags and flowers, as had the lamp posts. Horis and Grace squeezed into the crowd until they could get a good view of the street. People were hanging out of the windows and standing on boxes to get a better view.

To their left came the sound of a band, the volume grew and they appeared around a corner, preceded by a group of the Priests of Bal. They were all male and wore long robes with bare feet. Chains hung around their necks under long beards. In contrast, their skulls were shorn and painted yellow, to match the sun. They waved their hands about and muttered blessings as they passed, most of the crowd bowing before them. Horis was not particularly religious but aware of the sensibilities of local custom, bowed along with them. He straightened up just as the band approached.

To Horis's surprise, they were all female, and all dressed in leather uniforms not unlike Grace's, there were brass instruments of all types, and large drums, and the reason for the buckles and hooks on Grace's jacket became clear to Horis. They were the places where instruments were clipped or hung, realisation dawned on him and he leant to Grace's ear, "You are in such a band?" he asked.

"Why yes," she replied, "but tonight it was not our honour to lead the procession, I wear my uniform to show that I am a bandswoman."

Following the band were a convoy of steam-lorries, belching smoke and sparks through high chimneys as they rattled and wheezed along at low speed. The flat trailers were decked in tableau of farming and fishing scenes, complete with animals, plants and dancing children. They resembled moving fields and in some cases fisher-boats had been lifted onto the lorries, with nets hung overside, filled with sparkling fishes. Along with most of the throng, Grace waved at every one that passed, and called to the children, all of whom were smiling and waving at the crowds. She reached into her pockets and pulled out a small flask; taking a sip she passed it to Horis.

"Here, it's local wine, have a mouthful." He did and gasped at the strength of the draught.

After a gap of several minutes came what seemed like a legion of Exo-Men, in ranks of four, striding along at a fast pace, their generators struggling to keep up. The machines were polished and gleaming figures in brass and bright steel, reflecting beams from the gas lamps into the crowd. The operators were flailing in their harnesses to keep in step as they marched along.

"My brother is there, look!" called Grace, pointing to one of the passing vehicles. "He drives an Exo-Man at the Waster Mine. She was waving to a large man who was operating one of the machines, but he either did not hear her, or did not want to lose concentration, as he ignored her calls and kept his gaze firmly on his place in the parade.

"We will meet up with him later, at the eatery," announced Grace. "His name is Divid and you will like him." Horis could hear the pride in her voice, and was revelling in her closeness and vitality; she was unlike any of the city women that he had known. Her laughter and cheering was infectious, and the normally restrained Horis found himself waving and shouting with the rest of them. The crowd had forced them together and Horis could feel the heat from her body where their hips touched.

As the last of the Exo-Men passed, clockwork carts loaded with fruits and vegetables were steered past by farmworkers. They were accompanied by women and children, dressed as animals and trees, who handed out produce to the crowd as they passed. Horis received an apple, and Grace a parsnip, much to her amusement. Horis was about to bite into his apple, when she grabbed his wrist.

"Wait!" she shouted in his ear. "It is not to be eaten now, it's a symbolic gift from Bal, you must keep it in case you have nothing else to eat, it's proof that Bal will never let you go hungry." Horis nodded as he remembered and put the apple in his pocket.

After the carts had passed, the crowd began to break up and drift away. "Is that all the procession?" asked Horis.

"Yes, for tonight," she replied. "Come, now we will eat and dance the night away."

Chapter 7

Horis almost had to run to keep up with Grace as she took his hand and led him through the twisting backstreets of Aserol. The wheezing music of a steam organ grew louder, together with the excited shrieking of a crowd.

After a few minutes, Horis was completely disorientated when they entered a large square. All of one side was taken up by a building shaped like a Local, with white towers and chimneys. Tables were set outside, filled with people drinking and talking, whilst the windows were open and a noisy party could be heard inside. There were flashes of coloured lights and music from the organ and some stringed instruments, with off-key singing to accompany. The sign over the wide door, atop some steps, read "The Drogans Rest" in fancy lettering. He entered with Grace.

She was clearly well known inside, for everyone stopped her to say hello, or peck her cheek, and Horis found himself introduced to so many people that his head quickly filled with names and stories that he could never hope to remember. They ended up at the bar, a long wooden topped affair with many pumps and bottles displayed on it. Behind was a long mirror, and in its image Horis saw a large Drogan circling the room. A model, it was attached to some sort of clockwork, hanging on a wire it slowly traversed the room, and turning to view it directly, he saw that it was ridden by a scantily clad lady, who waved and smiled at all the patrons as she passed over their heads.

Whilst he had been looking, Grace had obtained two glasses of something, and led Horis over to a table, where her brother Divid sat, nursing a large glass of dark ale. His face lit up when he saw her and he rose from his seat to hug her. "Hello sis, it's good to see you," he said, in a warm voice as deep as the hue of his ale. "And who pray is this?"

"Divid, this is Horis Strongman, he's from the Ministry of Coal in the city, and he's come to see the mine."

Horis bowed and Divid took his hand; he had a grip of iron as he shook it. "Glad to meet you, sir. You'll have come to see old Obley then, no doubt he's told you of all the goings on."

Horis was stunned, no-one else was supposed to know of his visit, yet here he was discussing it with a girl he had met three hours previously and her brother. A hotel porter had also known, was everyone in on the secret but him?

"Well Divid, it's Ministry business that has brought me here, and I'm not really at liberty to discuss it."

"Oh don't be a stuffed shirt, Horis," urged Grace, holding his hand and gazing into his eyes. "We are all friends here, and Divid knows a lot about the mine and what goes on there. As an Exo driver he goes all over the mine and hears a lot of gossip."

"'Tis true," replied Divid, "and I hear that a section has been closed due to some problem. See over there," he pointed to a group of women, seated round a table in earnest conversation. "They are some of the wives and girlfriends, their men have been away far past the end of their shift, as there has been no cave-in there must be another reason."

"Well, I don't have all the information," said Horis. "That is why I have been summoned. To be honest I am off duty, in pleasant company and would prefer to speak of other things. Tell me, Divid, how does it feel to drive an Exo-Man?"

"It's the best feeling ever." There was a glow in Divid's eye. "Once you are used to being held in the air, it feels like you are invincible, you can do things that you only dreamed of. Of course, I need my driver to keep the hose slack and the pressure up, so they are as much a part of it as I am, and we take turns at each job as well."

The two men went on to discuss the mining of coal, and the machines used in the mines. Horis thought that Divid was far too intelligent to be an Exo-Man driver, he could have been an overseer, and he told him so.

"I was, once," said Divid sadly. "But alas I am opinionated and it does me no good. My mouth works without my brain's input and I upset people."

A waiter came over with three bowls of steaming food, and more wine. "I took the liberty of ordering some stew," Grace told them, "whilst Horis was mesmerised by Marie atop her Drogan."

It was true that Horis had been stealing glances at the girl on the Drogan; she was now preforming acrobatics on the beast's back, and swinging all around it, using its wingtips and feet as handholds.

The stew was delicious, containing chunks of braised bovine, with onions and roots in rich gravy. There was a chunk of spelten bread to mop the bowl and Horis realised that he was starving. The wine helped cut through the rich sauce, and Horis, who was not used to drinking, soon drained his glass. When he had finished the stew and mopped the bowl, he sat back with a satisfied air. Grace watched him with amusement.

"I think you need more wine," she suggested.

"I will get some," said Divid, he stood and made his way to the counter.

Grace took Horis's hand and looked deep into his eyes. "So tell me," she purred, "do you like it here in the provinces, or is it more exciting in the big city?"

Horis suddenly felt like he was in a dream, the wine was stronger than he was used to, and the girl's perfume was making his head spin, he tried desperately to focus on his intended journey to the mine but the noise and the smells and the spinning Drogan were too much for him.

Chapter 8

He awoke with a groan; where was he? His head felt like the inside of the Waster Mine, and when he moved it got worse. He was in a bed and he realised that he was in his nightshirt.

He got up in a panic and had to clutch at the bed-head to stop from falling. Memories of the previous night came creeping back and he shuddered. He realised that someone was knocking at the door. "Hello," he weakly answered.

"Good morn, sir. 'Tis six of the day, and you asked for a shout." The voice was that of the porter Maloney and Horis vaguely remembered returning to the hotel, supported by Grace and Divid, at about three. They must have removed his suit, found his nightshirt and put him to bed, he realised with a blush.

Horis quickly washed and shaved, then dressed again in his overalls and descended to the lobby.

Sour Face was on duty, and must have heard of his arrival in the early hours, for she regarded him with a look of disgust, and shouted very close to his head that fast-breaker was available in the atrium. Horis, his head swimming, could only nod, and the effort of that brought bile into his throat.

He tottered into the atrium and found a vacant table. Grace was on duty serving; how had she managed to stay sober, and how was she able to look so beautiful?

"Good morn, Horis," she softly called. "Shall I get you some coffee?"

"Thank you, Grace," Horis answered. "I'm embarrassed to say, but I have little recollection of last night's events, past a certain time."

Grace smiled innocently, and set a coffee cup and jug down beside him, it smelt like ambrosia. "And when might that have been?" she asked.

Horis gulped the brew, he could feel the caffeine coursing through his veins, displacing the stale blood and alcohol, and he started to feel better. "Well," he began, "I recall the stew, and then more wine, but after that it becomes hazy."

She laughed. "Then I could tell you anything, and you would have to believe me?"

Horis hung his head, this would be bad. "I take it I did not arouse the Watch?"

She laughed again, her curls rippling. "The Watch would not venture in The Drogan without reinforcements. No, you are quite safe, but you made a stir, what with your dancing and singing and riding the Drogan with Marie…" She stopped, as Horis, mortified, buried his head in his hands, his body shaking.

She could hear him mutter, "The Ministry, if they hear. Oh Bal, what am I to do?"

"Come," she put her hand on his shoulder. "I am teasing you, we merely sang and danced a bit and then you fell asleep. Divid and I brought you back and Divid put you to bed."

She departed, still laughing at his discomfort, returning in a moment with a plate of porker and eggs. "Here, this will settle you, and prepare you for your labours." She also placed a small bag by his side. "It's a few things for a meal, and a bottle of water, in case you cannot get a luncheon," she said in a voice filled with affection. "I would hate to think of you going hungry."

Horis thanked her; he had never been treated so well by someone who he knew so little. He felt flattered by her attention, and not a little affection of his own.

Horis devoured the plate of porker and eggs, and had another cup of coffee, all the time feeling more revived. He could not speak further to Grace, as she was busy with other diners, but she waved her serving cloth to him as he left the atrium.

Chapter 9

Leaving the hotel, Horis crossed the street to the omnibus halt, and stood with a small group of people who were already waiting. He noticed more of the Drogan nets, strung over poles at the corners of the omnibus shelter. Red flags fluttered at the corners, giving it a festive air, although they were probably part of the defence. The net looked fairly insubstantial, but was probably enough to distract a diving Drogan, and it also gave psychological comfort.

Glancing around, he could also see several large towers looming over the streets, as well as the ever present balloons. He knew of the Drogan watchtowers, but like most of the younger city dwellers had never seen them manned and armed. Since the development of balloons, the towers had fallen into disuse in the city, and besides, the city had not experienced an attack in living memory, the beasts had learnt that a warm welcome could be expected and now kept away.

The towers that Horis was familiar with were old and in a poor state, playgrounds for urchins. Those in Aserol however were manned and in good repair, the barrels of gas weapons stood ready.

He was about to ask the man standing next to him about the Drogan threat when the omnibus arrived, with a whistle and a hiss. The noise rang in his head and he realised that the effects of the coffee were wearing off and his hangover was returning.

This omnibus was steam powered but ran in the same track laid in the cobbles as the equine-drawn ones he had seen yesterday. Horis waved his pass at the driver as he entered, then looked for a seat. The omnibus was crowded with school children, all in uniform, attended by several teachers, on what appeared to be some sort of educational trip. Horis moved as far back as he could and clung to a leather strap hanging from the ceiling for balance as the omnibus set off with a rattle. Joining a larger road, it had a special lane for its track and so was able to avoid the queue of steam-lorries heading away from the Locals of the town.

He listened as the teachers explained the structure and workings of the various machines that they passed; all were variants on the steam generator that had been common in Norlandia for several generations.

Fuelled by the plentiful coal deposits that were the basis of the country's wealth, the power of boiling water had been harnessed for many purposes. Mechanical devices almost beyond counting used the power; either from their own generators, or by piped supply, enabling ever more complex applications. Power was also stored in mechanical devices of all sizes by springs, and clockworks of brass and silver enabled delicate applications.

Coupled with the gas lighting of towns, society had advanced quickly, with smaller and more efficient generators and machines being developed in quick succession. Apart from the need to supply coal and water to the machinery at intervals, a lot of physical labour had been removed from man's daily struggle.

There were only two things, Horis thought, that still needed to be achieved to make society perfect. One was to remove the steam from the system, to find some way of getting the power to the devices without the pollution and the constant wetness. And the second was... well who knows, he mused, maybe the second would be solved by what he might find at the Waster Mine.

After a journey of several miles, the scenery changed from the urban sprawl to a more rural setting. Traffic was still brisk in both directions but the omnibus kept up with the flow, turning off the roadway to board and drop passengers. The halts were served with painted wooden shelters and more netting; some had refreshment stands or stalls selling fruits and vegetables. The air cleared of coal dust and fields of crop and grazing animals could be seen from the windows. The number of chimneys decreased as did the frequency of balloons and watchtowers. Unlike the steam powered equipment in the town, in the country machines would be worked by spring power, the converter boxes could be seen at the base of each tower. The power of steam had been stored on large metal springs, ready to run clockworks of any description through the coupling on the face of the box. When the power was exhausted, the spring could be plugged into a steam supply and rewound. Springs of varying size could be harnessed to any application as required.

The omnibus stopped at a junction; there was a track leading up over a low hill on the landward side and the teachers started assembling the children to disembark. Gratefully, Horis approached an empty seat, the motion had made him feel dizzy and his arm was tired from holding onto the strap. Out of the opposite window, Horis could see a large field leading down to the shore. A flock of ovines grazed peacefully. Suddenly a shadow passed overhead, the teachers blew whistles and the children hurried back inside, quickly filling the space. Horis stopped and stood, wondering what had caused this urgency. He was rewarded with the sight of his first live Drogan.

Resembling a mixture of a bear and a large bird but with scaly wings and body in place of feathers or fur, it swooped on the ovines, who scattered under its onslaught. The beast was a dull grey colour, with flashes of red and silver as its leathery wings flapped. The head was atop a long sinuous neck and it twisted this way and that; fixing its prey with beady eyes.

It was joined by another, and then a third, they all seemed to be working together and were herding the ovines into a group in the middle of the field. Horis was unable to tear his eyes away from the spectacle and almost fell as the omnibus jerked into motion. Flailing, his arms grabbed the back of a seat and he knocked heads with the man sitting there.

"Do excuse me, sir," he gasped. "I was engrossed in the Drogans and taken unawares by the motion. They show intelligence in their attack."

The man looked at him, rubbing the side of his head. "Drogans, sir?" he said in a questioning voice. "Are there Drogans about?"

He peered around him, as if one were on the omnibus. "They are a fact of life, have you never seen them hunt before? And they have a certain low cunning I suppose, I pay them little mind."

Horis realised that the events he had witnessed must have been commonplace for the dwellers of Aserol, it marked him out as a stranger. "Why no, sir," he replied. "I have not, in Metropol City the Drogans seldom appear."

The man shook his head and sighed, as if to say that city dwellers knew nothing.

He saw that no-one else, even the children, had been watching the Drogans either. As the omnibus drew further away he could just make out the three of them feasting. They obviously knew where they were safe out of reach of the towers and balloons.

The omnibus driver had been calling out the name of every stop, and people were continually boarding and leaving. The children had remained on board; the teachers had said that they would stay until they were under the safety of the towers of the next town. So Horis still stood; although several times he refused a seat, leaving it to a woman or an old soldier. When he finally sat down, scarce seconds had passed when the driver announced, "Waster Mines." Head throbbing, Horis rose and made his way to the exit. The doors hissed open and he climbed down, facing the sea across a wide, sandy beach.

Chapter 10

He turned, the entrance to the Waster Mine, two sets of imposing, well maintained wrought iron gates on stone columns were on the other side of the road. A dun coloured brick wall extended away in both directions, topped with rusty wire. There was a guard post beside the smaller entrance, with a watchtower attached. Horis watched for a break in the traffic, and scuttled across as fast as he could, to the sound of horns blaring from irate lorrymen.

The gatehouse was manned by a one-legged man in miner's overalls; Horis suspected that he had probably been given the job after an accident. Lorries were diverted through the other larger gate, here was an oasis of calm but it was a while, enough to be annoying but not enough to make a fuss about, before he looked up at Horis, taking in his clean clothes and Ministry knapsack. He beckoned him into the porch, "Come over here, you. Keep out of the lorries' way, what do you want?"

"I'm Strongman, from the Ministry, to see Mr Obley," Horis announced, waving his identity card at the fellow. The miner consulted a stack of flimsy papers on his desk, and then picked up the speaker handset by his side. After cranking, he spoke a few words. Replacing the handset he looked at Horis with renewed interest.

"Ah yes, you are expected. It's a bit of a step up to the office, mind the road, it gets wet and slippery. If you keep to the path, the lorries will not harm you." He moved a lever and to the sound of clockwork the gate opened.

Horis trudged up the slope towards the office buildings, which he could see in the distance, on the hillside across a wooded valley. A large lorry passed him every minute or so, lumps of coal falling from its rear as it bounced over the uneven surface. Horis soon realised that traffic only came from the mine. There must be another road, he thought, for empty lorries to return. If he had known there would be a long, uphill walk, he would have accepted the offer of a mobile.

Behind the buildings he could make out several large holes in the sides of the mountain, they must be the mine entrances, somehow he had imagined there to be holes in the flat ground, with lifts and winding gear, but there was none. Off to one side were rows of cheap looking houses and everywhere the boiler rooms that fed from the mine and returned power to it. A river ran by the side of the road, which would be the water supply for the boilers. Its waters were dirty and steaming.

The day was bright and warm, with a few clouds scudding across the sky, driven by the brisk, northerly wind. Leaves were starting to fall, a sign of summer's end and a prelude to the cold of winter. But even though it hadn't rained for many a day the road was wet, as the guard had warned him; it was unpaved and rutted from the passage of the lorries, which seemed a little strange, and was festooned with lumps of coal of all sizes, so that he had to pick his way carefully.

There was enough coal here to last a family for days, and he wondered at the waste of it all. Then as he rounded a bend and passed through a grove of stunted trees, he saw women breaking up and then collecting the lumps of coal further up the road. They must be scavenging for their houses, he decided, maybe that was a right of the workers, a sort of extra on the wages. With winter approaching it would help them keep warm, for snow was a regular thing, even in this southern part of Norlandia.

His headache had subsided but now his stomach rumbled as he walked, and he opened the bag that Grace had given him, there was a wedge of meat pie, with golden pastry, some sweet biscuits and an apple. He munched as he walked, and gradually felt more able to face the day's rigours.

As he climbed the hill and approached the boiler sheds, the

vibration from the equipment could be felt in his feet, and the puddles of dirty water shimmered with patches of coal dust sparkling in the sunlight. Pylons strode across the yard, holding up rubberised conveyor belts which carried coal to large openings in the roofs of the sheds, where it fell into hoppers. One belt, larger than the rest, pointed in the direction of the coast, probably the one that emptied into the rail-yard, thought Horis, wondering at the extent of the place.

Clouds of steam billowed from the doors and windows. Around the openings stood groups of workers, stripped to shorts and perspiring freely, sweat-streaked with dust in bizarre patterns on their torsos and legs. They wore gloves, goggles and thick boots to the knee, many also had leather caps and all of them showed scars and scalds. Most were smoking nicoweed tubes, a mild narcotic which probably helped them cope with the rigours of the work.

Stokers, thought Horis, what a job. As he passed, a hooter sounded and the men dropped the tubes, turned and moved back inside the buildings, seconds later a different group emerged for their break and stood, a copy of the first.

Through the clouds of vapour, Horis could see steam hoses coming from the walls and fanning out in every direction, throbbing and shaking under the pressure, joints whistling and dripping. He knew that these were the portable hoses, used for small appliances. Safely underground lay the permanent pipes, huge metal things a foot across, pressurised to enormous levels.

Sirens suddenly started shrieking, and Horis looked about him for the cause. The noise came from a watchtower and was echoed around the mine. A group of stokers came rushing from one of the boiler houses and Horis was swept up in them as they ran across the yard. Rounding a corner, Horis spied a large steam catapult, with multiple arrows fitted, and its twin on the other side of the yard. The stokers clambered over both of the weapons in a manner which suggested repeated training and practise. "What in Bal's name is going on?" Horis shouted, hoping anyone would answer.

"Drogan," said one old miner, through a gap-toothed smile. He patted the steam catapult and leered. "Don't you worry; this old girl will see 'em off."

The valve had been opened and steam was coursing through the works of the catapult, a piston extended, pulling back the firing strings, whilst the arrows swung and rose on their carriage. One of the stokers had his ear to a speaker and quietly relayed commands to the man controlling the movement of the catapult.

Horis lifted his head up, realising what was occurring, he had disjointed sight of a huge beast, long necked and scaled in bright colour, flashing past. It was closer to him than the Drogans he had spied from the omnibus and seemed all the bigger for that. His being in the open with the beast stirred a sense of fear in him but he was buoyed by the presence of the miners. They obviously knew what they were about. He heard a loud twang as the other catapult fired and saw a forest of arrows rise into the sky towards the Drogan. Its body twisted as it tried to evade the missiles, but some struck home. Wings flapping as it clawed the air, it turned - now it was coming straight at them.

This Drogan was about twenty feet long and had a thick neck, corded with sinew. Leathery wings, with hooked claws at the ends, flapped as it dove, framing a thick body and whip-like tail. Children's stories gave the Drogan magical powers, such as flaming breath and invisibility, but the truth was they were just a big flying beast with a hatred of people. They may not have the ability to breathe fire, but they could and did snatch small children and animals, as Horis could now testify from his own experiences.

Horis realised he was holding his breath; he felt the ground shudder as the weapon next to him fired. The beast flew head first into its rain of arrows, they clattered against its body, but several found soft points and lodged in its neck and head. Uttering a mournful cry it fell to earth and lay, twitching, on the ground.

The men cheered and Horis could make out shouts of joy as they moved towards the animal. It may have been wounded, but it was still dangerous and it thrashed its head, tail and wings wildly, forcing the miners to keep their distance. One ventured too close and was caught by the wingtip claw. It ripped him almost in two and with a shriek and spurting of blood he fell, dead.

Ropes were thrown and a loop was made over the beast's head, then with twenty people on each side, Horis included, it was hove taut. The animal's struggles became feebler as the air was choked out of it, until it lay still. The men clasped hands and shouted congratulations at each other, the men on either side of Horis, each a good foot taller, lifted him up. "Well helped, stranger, that's one less to carry our babes away," one said. "Was that your first?" said the other.

So that was a fearsome Drogan, Horis had seen the carcasses exhibited in the capital, but before today never a live one.

And now he had seen four in one morning. What a tale for Mrs Hendress his landlady. Except that she would never believe him.

Diplomatically he stole away from the celebrations.

Chapter 11

The sign said "Office" and he entered a different vision of disorder. Leading from the hallway was a series of smaller rooms, all of which appeared to have been vacated in a rush.

Papers were strewn over every horizontal surface, including the floors, and there was the click of clockwork from adding engines, still working even though every room he passed was empty of human presence. Horis moved through the building and eventually came to a room from which a low muttering and rustling could be heard. Putting his head round the door frame he could see a tall thin man, dressed in a frock coat, bent over and searching through a stack of papers on his desk.

He cleared his throat. "Hello, I'm looking for Mr Obley."

"Are you the man from the Ministry? Please say that you are and that I can hand all this over to you." The man rose up and turned, his face pale. On seeing Horis he sighed, "Oh they've sent the junior, the most important thing has happened and they've sent the junior." He shook his head several times.

Horis felt slighted, the man knew nothing of him, apart from that he was small. "That's as maybe, sir, but as I am the man from the Ministry, perhaps you had better explain to me what's happening here that's so special. And I did offer to come up here yesterday, if you recall."

"I did not know you were here yesterday," replied the fellow. "But no matter, Grantham keeps all sorts of things from me." He shook his head, as if to clear his thoughts and continued. "Well look up, man, and tell me what you see." The man, who Horis presumed to be Obley, was so tall that his head nearly touched the ceiling. His movements were jerky, as if controlled by strings, and his gaze bolt-eyed and maniacal. Horis followed his pointing fingers and saw what looked like several dark lumps on the ceiling, almost as if someone had taken sticky mud and flung it upwards.

Obley was gesturing wildly. "Look at them, I found the first of these two days ago, what are we to do? You're the expert, the 'Saviour of Waster Mine', what are we to do." The last words were more an anguished howl than a question, as if the fate of the whole world depended on Horis's answer.

Taking a deep breath, and trying to see the significance of the situation, Horis hoped that by remaining silent and appearing confident he could calm this individual, his presence was making Horis feel nervous. He would not have been in the least surprised if Obley had vanished, or turned into some creature and flown away.

"I don't follow…" began Horis, but Obley reached up and scooped one of the lumps from the ceiling.

"Watch," he advised and threw the lump towards Horis. He moved to catch it, expecting it to fall, but to his amazement it ROSE, and stuck again to the ceiling.

Obley was triumphant, and he turned his gaze full on Horis.

"And what does the Ministry think of that?"

Chapter 12, Metropol City

In the capital, Metropol City, there was an exclusive gentlemen's club, where the rich and powerful met to discuss and control the nation's fate. Far more important than the visible face of government, which they allowed to give the semblance of democracy, they competed ruthlessly amongst themselves for power and influence. No means was too extreme; money, women and patronage all combined within the walls of the Gavan Club, and the most important thing to the members was that the general population was ignorant of its existence. Even the Monarch was only barely aware of its existence and would never darken its doors.

Situated as it was in a terraced house in the poorer part of the city, its appearance from the outside was that of a simple dwelling. It had no nameplate on the door, if you were a member, or were invited by one, well then you knew where it was, if not, you had no business with the Club.

Inside, it was larger than its dimensions, partly because it was three houses knocked into one. There were meeting rooms, for business and pleasure, a dining room and a large saloon. The windows were covered with heavy drapes, which kept the place in gloomy light, even in daytime, whilst the walls had portraits of past members hung in ornate wooden frames. Easy chairs were arranged in groups around small gas-lit tables, each an island in the room, secure and private. Not that anyone would eavesdrop, it was not the done thing. There was a constant low hum from the various clockworks that were in the building, some were fixed machines spewing printed papers with the latest news and financial information, whilst others were in motion containing food and drink, moving among the tables with waiters attending.

Terrance, the senior manager at the Ministry of Coal, and Horis's immediate superior, was a new member of the Club. Membership had passed to him on the death of his father, as had control of the Mines of Waster, which his family owned, although that was not common knowledge. It was he who had sent Horis off to Aserol, on the theory that he was most expendable, and easiest to blame.

He was at the Club that night to report to a man called Cavendish on the progress of things at the mine. When he was shown into the dining room by the liveried waiter, Terrance found that Cavendish was at a table with two other men who he did not know well, although he was aware of whom they were. Awed to be in such company, he was unsure of the extent of their knowledge, so decided to let Cavendish take the lead.

Between them these four men owned mines, boiler houses and transport companies. They owned the workshops and factories that built all manner of machines and clockworks, and with those who owned the shipyards and metal works they could be said to be the real government. The army and the civil police, all except the Watchmen, could be relied on to do their bidding. And even the Watchmen were more open to influence than people realised. Answering to the Monarch, they were in theory inviolate but there were ways of guiding them through influence.

Cavendish introduced Terrance to the others; there was Havers and Barnard, and after handshaking and greetings, a clockwork serving trolley glided to a halt, attended by a legless waiter, sitting in a wheeled chair attached to the back of the machine.

"Good evening, gentlemen, what may I get you?" the man asked.

"Hello, Wilkie," said Cavendish. "My friends and I will have a bottle of the best Malt, kindly leave it here, and ensure our privacy."

The man touched his forelock and produced a bottle and four glasses from his trolley. He leant across and placed them on the table. He opened the bottle and lifted it, but Cavendish stopped him, with a gentle gesture. "It's alright, Wilkie, I can pour."

"Thank you, sir," said the servant. "You're a real gent, you won't be disturbed, I will see to that. If you need another bottle, just press the bell on the table." There was a whirr as the trolley departed.

Cavendish poured each of them a large measure of the amber liquid. "A fine fellow, Wilkie," he said. "He was my Bosun in the navy. When he was injured, I got him this position." They settled into their chairs and Cavendish began. The flickering gas light cast shadows over his thin, cruel face as he spoke.

"Gentlemen, I have here Mr Terrance, he has been controlling events at the Waster Mine in Aserol. Will you indulge him whilst he tells you of the happenings there?"

"Thank you, Cavendish," replied Terrance. "Gentlemen, I am a senior at the Ministry of Coal, and some time ago had reports from the mine about strange things found in the workings. It was claimed that the miners had found objects that were floating up to the roof of the mine tunnels," he paused, "and other things as well."

Terrance sensed the disapproval from Cavendish, and despite the warmth of the room, felt chilled, he realised that he had said too much, hopefully the others had not noticed.

Havers, who was sweating profusely and was at least half drunk, gave a mocking laugh, "Preposterous," he exclaimed. "The man has had too much provincial wine. Floating rocks, whatever next." Havers was a fat man, known to be bombastic and opinionated.

"I'm not so sure," said the second; Barnard was tall and thin, with an intelligent face and a slow, thoughtful way of speaking. "In my travels, I have seen many things, and I really think there is little that could not be real, somewhere."

"Quite," said Terrance. "My agents at the mine assure me that these things are real. They of course moved to keep the find quiet. A team of trusted men were the only ones allowed near this find, the access was quarantined. I thought that I had the situation under control, however there have been complications." He was about to elaborate, but a look from Cavendish made him stop.

"The important thing is not whether it is real, it's how it might affect us and our profits," said Cavendish.

Cavendish was nominally the Secretary to the First Minister of the Government, the public face of the state; in fact he led the

Gavan Club, and therefore the country. He owed his influence in government policy to his many and varied business interests. He was a charming host, but with a ruthless streak that had kept him safe at the expense of many challengers, all now a memory.

"But surely," said Terrance, attempting to rejoin the discussion, "until we know more, they are merely an amusement, a children's game with no real value."

"Clearly you lack a view of the bigger picture," said Cavendish, coldly. "The thing that we have not been able to master, with all our skill and knowledge, is controlled flight. Balloons are all very well, but you cannot say with any certainty where they will go, and the effort required in lifting a boiler and coal into the air is beyond us. Thanks to the discovery in your mine, we may now have the thing we need to progress."

Havers, who had been steadily drinking and refilling his glass, exploded in mirth, "Controlled flight? Pah! Might as well go to the moons, it's about as likely. Leave the flying to the birds and the Drogans. What we need is war, it spurs invention." He subsided into his seat with the effort of such a long speech and sat there mumbling.

Cavendish looked at him in a way that said, 'if you didn't control the metal works I would have no hesitation in turning you into part of a roadway somewhere.' He turned to Barnard. "If these rocks could lift a boiler and fuel, could you build a flying machine around them?"

"Undoubtedly," was the enthusiastic reply. "As you know, my engineers at Northcastle are working on lighter boilers and more efficient engines all the time, this may be just the thing we need. We also have other plans in progress, for a different sort of engine but the problem that keeps coming back is that of weight. Your rocks, if they are plentiful, would be most useful in reducing this as a problem. Terrance, what are your man's instructions when he gets to the mine?"

Terrance leaned forward, ignoring Havers, who was asleep and dribbling, and his whisper drew the other two closer to him.

"Between us, neither Obley nor Horis Strongman are 'my man'. Obley, I have had to suffer for his family's usefulness, whilst Horis is my junior and therefore expendable. As I said, I have an agent at the mine, who has thus far kept Obley under control, and the discoveries away from prying eyes." He paused and hesitated, as if reluctant to say more.

"Go on," said Barnard.

Terrance continued, with a sideways glance at Cavendish, who nodded briefly. "However, recently Obley has become more unpredictable in his behaviour, and it has been harder to keep this secret. He managed to evade our surveillance and found out more than was good for him. In place of our trusted men, he let a group of ordinary miners into the part of the mine containing our discovery. And now he is desperate to tell the world."

He shook his head, as if in despair at the problems he had to face. "My agent has been adding a drug to his food and drink, which has given the appearance of a man losing his mind, but the drug is making his behaviour more erratic as time passes."

Cavendish coughed, and Terrance looked up, a group of men were passing on their way to a table in the corner.

He paused and drank, wiping his lips on a napkin he continued, "I am arranging to transport some of the rocks away from the mine. They will be loaded on board a ship, and be taken to Northcastle, where they can be securely stored in my workshops. Then my men will investigate their powers."

"So that is why you come to us with this now?" said Bernard. "It would have been better kept quiet until we had a clearer idea of what we are dealing with, but no matter."

"I agree," said Cavendish, "but when things started to get out of hand, Terrance had the sense to come to me for advice. It's only because Obley found out what was going on and threatened to make the findings public that events have been moved forward."

"That's right," agreed Terrance. "His call to the Ministry was made behind the back of my agent, and has put the matter in the open. To hide the discovery, I intend to remove him and all the evidence once Horis has got to the mine."

"Indeed the secret must be kept," said Barnard. "Consider if the agents of the Western Isles got to know of it, or the anarchists in our own land. They could cause panic, or spur an invasion. You are correct; this must be kept quiet until we have ascertained the use of these things." He paused as he realised what Terrance's words meant, a grim look on his face.

"So your man is expendable then?"

"Yes," replied Terrance. "He will allay the fears of Obley, who has proved to be weak and has outlived his use. My men are following Horis Strongman and have their instructions; in fact they were on the same Rail-Ryde as he. They will seal that part of the mine, keeping the rocks safe, and blame Horis and Obley for the disaster." He smiled. "The Watch will pick up any loose ends and with them arrested and tried the story will die. Meanwhile, we have the rocks, and no-one else is aware."

Barnard was unconvinced. "And what of the miners?" Cavendish gave him a cold look.

"Unfortunately, there will always be casualties in mining."

Chapter 13, Aserol

Horis was at a loss for words, he had seen magickers' tricks that were similar, but had always thought that there was a wire or mechanism somewhere that would explain the illusion.

Obley was still talking, "This has been a burden on me for some time; at last I can get some peace." Horis was confused, he had only heard of it two days before; his journey had been the response. But the man was clearly at the end of his tether, something was having a profound effect on his mind.

"Show me," ordered Horis. "I want to see these things in the mine, where you found them."

Obley nodded. "Come with me then, we'll get you a helmet."

"Can you explain to me," asked Horis as they left the offices and walked towards the entrance to the shafts, "Why is there such a mess in your offices? And why are so many rooms empty. Where are all your employees?"

Obley seemed distracted, but by what, Horis couldn't tell. "We have cut our staff on Ministry orders," he said. "You are from the Ministry, you should know that. It's also true that now that we have clockworks and adding engines we need less people. As to the rest of the office staff, they are on the upper floors."

They passed a room ankle deep in papers, great piles of them like a frozen ocean. Obley waved at the chaos vaguely. "The things you see are the old papers, which were to be filed; we have not finished the job yet with our reduced staff. And to be honest, I have disturbed a lot of them myself, after recent events, looking for any hint of this in the mine records."

Horis thought that the disruption he had seen was more than one man could make in a day, but he kept that opinion to himself.

He felt unsafe in Obley's company and wanted to do as little as possible to antagonise him. Keeping the conversation bland and neutral seemed like the best plan. "I see, and did you find any?" Horis had never heard of such a find in all the Ministry records and he was sure that anything like this could not have been kept secret.

"Nothing," said Obley, "and to be sure I have asked the retired miners if they know of this, but they also know nothing."

Horis was thinking, what would the Ministry want of him, how should he proceed? He made a decision. "For the present, it would be better if we kept this quiet, what of the miners who have seen these mysterious rocks, have they been free to discuss them?"

"Of course not," said Obley. "They have been kept isolated, even from their families, they are being kept underground, at the site of the find, and no other people are allowed into that shaft, by my orders." Obley smiled. "I said that there may have been a gas leak. Yes, that was my story."

"And who is in charge of the party underground?" asked Horis. "Or are they just left?"

"Oh no," Obley sounded annoyed. "What do you think of us, and the way we treat our men? The foreman is Grieve, a capable and well respected man, he will keep good order and the men trust him."

"I like the leak story, that's a good idea, but it must be quickly told, we need to regain control of the situation, news is getting out somehow; the porter at my hotel knows that strange things are going on here, but not with any detail." Obley nodded.

"That will be the women gossiping, they know that their men are being kept underground, but not why. And they meet people at the market, and on the omnibus. And rumours spread like fire."

As they were walking down the corridor towards the entrance, their way was blocked by an imposing woman, who could indeed have been Sour Face's twin sister. She glared at the pair and Obley quailed under her gaze. "Oh Mrs Grantham," he said, "this is the man from the Ministry; I am taking him down the mine to see for himself."

She shook her head. "But I've made you char, Mr Obley, you must drink it first or it will spoil." She looked at Horis. "No doubt you would like a mug, Mr Strongman." She held out her hand. "We conversed yesterday."

Horis took the hand and, following the custom in the capital, lifted it to his face and kissed the back, bowing. The woman seemed shocked, as though provincials and juniors did not have the breeding and manners to behave so.

Obley was still talking. "You and your char, you are forever feeding me char and making me drain every mug. No, we will proceed and maybe return for a mug later. Now let us pass."

Mrs Grantham looked daggers at the pair, but reluctantly stood aside. "Very well then," she said icily, "carry on, sir." She turned and made her way back to her sanctum, where she sat as they passed.

They left the building and crossed the yard, past the carcass of the Drogan. There were a large group of miners standing around as a crane lifted it onto the back of a coal lorry. On spotting Obley, several of the men slipped away, back to wherever they should have been, leaving only the men engaged in the operation. Obley pointed at the Drogan. "We have had one of these attacks every day recently," he said. "And for the last six months, yet none in the two years before that. I wonder that the habits of the creature might not have changed."

Passing the boiler houses, they arrived at a large shed, full of equipment, again it was manned by injured miners, some missing limbs, others eyes, two of whom fitted them out with helmets and gave them gas lanterns. Obley fitted his own lantern after taking a helmet from the racks with his name on it, but Horis was attended by an old, wizened miner, with one eye and few teeth. The helmet he was given was shiny and new and marked with the word "Ministry" in bold letters. Whilst he adjusted the straps, the miner brought him a lantern. He found that the heavy gas reservoir attached to his belt with a brass clip, its hose leading to the filament and reflector unit, behind a brass mesh screen, the whole thing fastening to the front of the helmet. There was a clip for the hose, which led it away to the rear of the helmet, and down the line of his spine to the reservoir. The miner showed him how to turn the valve and work the igniter, and also where to check the level of gas remaining. When lit, the lamp threw a sharp beam in front of him in the dim of the shed.

"These are safety lanterns," said his aide. "If the flame glows amber or blue, it means gas is present, but it will not ignite." He coughed and spat. "It should give you enough warning to get out."

Horis thanked him, but he did not answer. "Deaf," said his mate. "Explosion."

"Have you been underground before?" asked Obley. "Many Ministry men have not."

"Oh yes," replied Horis, "my father was a miner, and I was apprenticed to be a tunnelling technician, I have no fears about being underground."

"Well then," said Obley, "we may as well get started, it's a bit of a hike." His mood had changed Horis noted, since they had left the office, he seemed calmer and more in control of himself.

They walked towards the mine shafts, following the rails and steam lines. There was a constant stream of carts along the rails, except on the lines to the shaft that they were headed towards. A string of loaded carts would come out of the shaft, pushed by a locomotive, then after a very short while, another followed. There were two sets of rails Horis noted, and the empty carts used the second set to return to the shaft.

"Endless loop," said Obley. "The carts go round all day, and they tip by the conveyor and return, never stopping." It seemed a very neat operation, and closer, the shafts were enormous. Large fans were set in ducting that descended into the shaft, they whistled as they turned, and water dripped from the exhaust pipes where they joined the casing. There was a breeze coming from the entrance as they stepped over the threshold.

"Before we enter I must warn you about the noise, we have not stopped the bucket conveyor, as it is not designed to be halted; we should have to turn off the steam and it would mean a lot of work to restart it. The chamber where we found the rocks is below; we cut into the wall as usual and found a hollow beyond. The floor was a thin layer of coal, and some tar-like substance. As we walked across it, it cracked and the floating rocks were released." He handed Horis a small box, opening it he found a set of ear-corks and following Obley's lead, inserted them.

There were gas lanterns set at frequent intervals along the walls, each with their safety covers, and they gave a good light as they walked into the mine. After about a half mile they came to a large chamber, cut from the rock. Here were the lifts that Horis had thought to be outside, together with a bucket conveyor which tipped the coal into the rail carts. In the confined space, the noise was deafening, even with the ear-corks. What the noise must be like when the trains and the conveyor were in full flow he could not imagine.

They entered the lift, after giving their names to the lift-master. He would record them in and out, and if they did not return, would raise an alarm. The lift door closed and they descended so quickly that it took the breath away. The noise and the light receded above them, and the sight of buckets racing past, which could be seen as dark shadows through the open sides of the lift cage, increased the feeling of speed. Obley turned on his lantern and Horis did the same, its beam illuminating the walls as they flashed past. Openings passed and still they descended. "How deep is this chamber, Obley?" asked Horis, swallowing desperately to keep his stomach in place.

"The bucket system goes down over a mile," answered the other. "The workings do not. We should be there very soon."

Sure enough the lift slowed as he spoke and then stopped. The doors opened on a smaller version of the place they had left, with the bucket system clanking, although slightly quieter, gas lights flickering from the draft. It was noticeably warmer, and, as there was no-one attending the lift, the space was deserted. There were piles of piping and gas lanterns in the area around the lift, and Obley gestured at them. "Ready to light and ventilate the shafts as they are secured," he said.

Horis was impressed with the way the mine was organised. "Well sir, you can light the chamber now, so that we may get a better view of things."

Obley nodded, thoughtfully, and then set off into one of three tunnels that radiated from the chamber, unlike the other two, it had no rail lines in it. "Come on then, it's just down here," Obley called. Horis had to run to keep up. The tunnel was not lit, but there was sufficient light from his and Obley's lanterns to see their progress; the floor and walls were smooth.

After a short distance, the tunnel ended, to one side there was a dark hole with a flickering light inside it. The two men stepped through the opening into a natural cave, with jagged walls. Looking up, Horis could see stalactites hanging from the roof. The floor was sticky, like walking through thick mud, and his boots sank to the ankle. The air was damp and smelt faintly of gas, but the flame of his lantern was steady. There were a group of about twenty miners huddled round a large gas lantern, their movement throwing shadows across the walls. The far edge of the chamber was in darkness, so Horis could not say as to its extent.

"Look down," commanded Obley. Horis did so and could see a pattern on the floor, like a ploughed field, lumps of coal scattered like currants in a bun in the sticky stuff and the grey of the strange lumps. He kicked at the coal and dislodged a piece. Beneath it was one of the mysterious rocks, which having been released floated slowly upwards. Unseen by Obley, Horis grabbed it as it passed and could feel it pull against his muscles. He jammed it into his pocket and buttoned the flap; he could feel it lifting the fabric as he walked.

Chapter 14

Obley had walked to the miners and was talking to the foreman. "Grieve, how are your men holding up?"

"Very well, sir." The man touched his forelock towards Horis. "You must be the Ministry man, what do you think, sir?"

Horis had been wondering how to approach this question, it was beyond him, and he suspected that he would not be alone in that. "I really couldn't say," he started, "but I'm sure that this is a discovery that will have a lot of people interested. Now we just need to manage the situation."

Horis knew that here he was on safer ground; this was a problem that he could deal with. "I'm afraid that you and your men must stay here for a while longer, until I have spoken with the Ministry. I will make sure you have enough food and water, give me a list of your names and I will make sure that your wives or families know that you are safe."

There was a murmur from the group, the foreman Grieve spoke up, "Thank you, sir. What will you tell them?"

"Just that you have been exposed to a possibly hazardous situation, and that you are being quarantined underground for a few days. I assume that you are all feeling well?"

"Oh yes, sir," said Grieve, who was clearly in control of his men. "We are used to being down here and are all in good spirits, as long as we know that our families are taken care of, it's the nature of the job, they will understand. The lift-master has the list of us all, sir."

"Very well," said Horis. "While you are here, rather than sitting around, you would be well employed rigging lighting and a steam supply into this cavern. It will need to be examined in detail by the Ministry and others once news of this discovery spreads." The foreman nodded and turned to his men, splitting them into groups.

"Obley," Horis called, "I have seen enough, we will return to the surface, we have a lot to attend to."

They retraced their steps towards the lift, the noise increasing as they approached the bucket system. The lift was waiting, doors open and they rode in silence to the surface. Horis copied the miners' names from the lift-master's sheet into his notebook before they left the tunnel.

On arrival back at the office, Horis gave the list of miners to a secretary, with instruction to ensure that all families were informed of their men's safety. They were to be told of the quarantine, and Horis hoped that this would reduce the spread of rumours. His final job, before departing, was to see that food and water was sent down to the men. He did not call the Ministry from the office, because of Obley's behaviour he wanted to speak to Terrance from the privacy of his hotel.

Mrs Grantham pressed him to take char before he left, but he declined. Obley, who as the afternoon had worn on had become more lucid, had a mug, and soon began muttering to himself and waving his arms at things only he could see.

Leaving the office, Horis found that it had started to rain and the temperature had dropped. The body of the Drogan had disappeared, and the catapults had been reloaded. Turning his collar up, he splashed towards the gates and the omnibus, as daylight faded. To his great relief, one of the first lorries that passed him on the road stopped and offered him a ride into town, so he was saved the worst of the weather. Even so, he had a walk from the Local back to the hotel and was soon soaked to the skin.

He failed to see the group of black-clad men who arrived in two large steam-mobiles. Two of them went to the office, returning shortly with Obley and the secretary who Horis had given the list to. Together with Mrs Grantham and the rest they all descended into the shaft.

Chapter 15

It was fully dark by the time Horis arrived back at the hotel, the rain had become a drizzle and judging from the lack of wind had set in for the night. Maloney was nowhere to be seen, probably sheltering over a hot meal, thought Horis. His stomach was starting to protest at the lack of food, for he had not eaten since the meal that Grace had given him.

Standing in the foyer, he shook himself like a terrier to try to get rid of the water on his head and overalls, he could feel his boots sticking to the carpet with every step, and shuddered to think of the trail he was leaving. Grace had departed from the desk, and Sour Face was in evidence, she looked at him disapprovingly as he squelched towards her, shivering.

"Here is your key, there are no messages," she growled. "You need to get out of those wet things or you will get a chill."

"I will," replied Horis, "but first I need to call the Ministry, may I use the calling booth?"

She was not impressed with his request.

"You can dry yourself first, and get those boots off. I'll not have you damping the furniture. Come back when you have changed and I will be happy to arrange your call." She quivered with the force of her statement, and despite himself Horis wilted under her gaze.

Sheepishly, he unlaced his boots, and then in stockinged feet, with toes showing through un-darned holes, made as dignified an exit as he could. He looked behind him; there were his tracks, as clear as an animal's across the sands.

Horis rode the lift to his room, dripping all the while.

He unlocked the door to his room and reached for the gas control, turning it so the flame increased and bathed the room in flickering light. Horis let go of the door and it swung shut behind him. Moving into the room, he placed his boots on the floor on their sides and pulled off his stockings. His wet overalls followed. Crossing to the bathroom he turned the faucets on full, and the room began to fill with steam from the hot water splashing into the tub. He poured a good handful of mineral salts into the gushing stream, hoping they would make him feel better.

He soaked away the dust and the aches from his muscles and was starting to doze when a noise from the room roused him. Alert, he looked for his pistol; it was in the other room with his suit. There was no weapon here save the back scrubber, still he grabbed it and held it before him as he wrapped a towel around his waist. He opened the door a crack and peered into the darkness. Someone had turned the gas down. The curtains were drawn back and Horis could see that it had stopped raining. One of the moons was shining in the window and he could make out a shape in the bed.

"Who's there," he called, waving the brush about.

"Hello, Horis." He recognised the voice. "I've been waiting for you to return."

Horis was flustered. "Is that you, Grace?" he spluttered, turning puce. "What are you doing here, how did you get in?" The shape in the bed moved, throwing the covers back and in the white moonlight Horis gasped as he saw a vision in creamy, freckled skin. He stepped into the room, the towel falling to the floor.

Much later Horis awoke; the room was still bathed in moonlight. He looked across at Grace, who laid spread on the bed in total relaxation, a sheet covering her body. Memories came flooding back and he allowed himself a smile. Being small and appearing insignificant had its perks; he was often underestimated, both at work and leisure. And Grace, despite her looks, was not the innocent she had seemed. He had been correct in his assumption; it was different here by the coast.

Suddenly he remembered his call to the Ministry. Oh well, it was much too late now; he would just have to do it in the morn.

Chapter 16

He woke again to the calls of the gulls and of the morning news-sheet sellers, boys hawking the headlines. But their cries sent a wave of anxiety through his stomach as he realised what he was hearing.

"Mine accident, huge cave-in at the Waster Mine, many lives lost!"

Beside him Grace awoke, she leant over and caressed him, sensing his mood. "What's the matter, lover?" she whispered, but Horis was already squirming free of her embrace. Getting out of the bed he stumbled towards his case, rummaging for a clean suit. "I have to go, Grace. Something awful has happened and I must check that things are not what they seem." He ignored her protests and dressed quickly, making himself presentable for the hotel lobby.

As Horis went to the door, there was a click as it was unlocked from outside; it flew open and two large men burst in and grabbed him roughly. They were dressed all in black, as Watchmen but without the quip-belt and cane that all Watchmen carried. Also, unlike Watchmen, they wore no caps, and their faces were covered. Horis struggled but was unable to break free. One of the men held his arms behind his back, whilst the other proceeded to beat him around the head with his fists. Their attack was made all the more frightening by the fact that they remained silent. Horis's lip was split and blood splashed around as his head was rocked from side to side by the blows. The room span and his vision blurred as they continued to beat him.

Unnoticed, Grace had risen from the bed and reaching under it had picked up the chamber pot. She swung it at the man holding Horis; it connected with his head and shattered with a sickening thud. The man released Horis and tottered across the room, moaning. The second man was stunned by this, clearly he hadn't known Grace was in the room, or expected any resistance. He stopped hitting Horis and gazed at her nakedness as she brandished what was left of the chamber pot, looking like some avenging spirit raised up from the depths. Her hair was wild and tousled, falling in great curled waves to her waist. The man took a step back, into the range of Maloney's right arm, which was holding a brass poker. He had come into the room quietly. The poker rose and fell.

"Morn to you both," said Maloney as the man hit the floor, unconscious. "I thought these two were up to no good, so I followed them. Are you both alright?" He crossed to the first man, who was holding onto the window frame and trying to clear his head. Raising the poker, he dealt him a blow that sent him sprawling next to his mate.

"Thank you, Maloney," said Horis breathlessly, his head and shoulders ached and blood was seeping from his nose and lip. "Do you have much trouble with thugs in this hotel?" He held onto the end of the bedstead till his dizziness subsided.

"Never before, sir," said Maloney, "and the town is usually quiet and peaceful."

Grace had gone into the bathroom, now she returned with a wet towel, which she used to wipe the blood from Horis's face. She seemed totally unconcerned by her lack of clothing and it unsettled Horis. He gently disentangled himself and made for the door. "Thank you, Grace, but the news from the street has concerned me, I must call the Ministry." He set off towards the lift.

To his surprise, Sour Face was on duty again, did she have nowhere else to go? She looked through Horis as if he were made of glass, and all his secrets were written in letters of fire; it made him squirm. She made no comment at the bruising that was spreading across his face, nor of his bloodied nose and lip. Perhaps she thought that he deserved it.

"Good morn, madam," he addressed her. "May I have my private call to the Ministry now?"

"You may," came her icy reply. "Kindly go into the booth." She waved her pudgy hand imperiously towards a small room at the rear of the foyer. Horis picked up a news-sheet from the pile on the desk and walked across to the booth. Horis entered and closed the glass door behind him. Lifting the handset, he cranked.

The long distance speaker worked on a different principle to the local system, which was powered by sound. Here the sciences of magnetics and statics combined to send the voice over a longer distance than was possible with sound power alone.

"Exchange, which destination please?" The voice sounded slightly mechanical through the earphone. The speaker operator was sitting miles away, Horis knew, but by the miracle of statics her voice was as clear as that of Sour Face. Horis cleared his throat. "Ministry of Coal in Riverside, Metropol City please, Mr Terrance."

"One moment if you please, sir." The line went dead and Horis, whose understanding of the system was more than just passing, could mentally see her plugging brass connectors into the wooden directory box. Then she would speak to the next exchange operator, who would forward her to the Metropol City exchange, and so on till the destination was reached. He could imagine the operator saying "I have a call from Aserol for you", and Terrance replying "Put it through". The minute stretched into two, then three. Horis studied the wallpaper, how could he explain what had happened?

The line hummed. "You're connected."

"Ministry of Coal, Terrance replying, is that you Lewis? Is it done?" Horis felt confused.

"Bryan, good morn, 'tis Horis in Aserol." There was a silence, broken only by the hum and crackle of the line.

"But Horis, I thought that you would have been," there was a pause, "um down the mine by now."

Alarm bells were ringing in Horis's head; was it just his imagination or had Bryan almost said "dead by now". And who was Lewis? He had heard the name recently, but where? Deciding caution, he continued, as blandly as he could, "I need more time to assess the situation, and now I hear there has been a cave-in at the mine, which may complicate things. I will call again tomorrow." He closed the connection before giving Terrance time to say anything else.

The lift was on an upper floor and he had to wait for its arrival before he could return to his room. He used the time to scan the news-sheet. The account was sparse, merely that there had been a cave-in reported before midnight, just as the sheet was printed. It had happened not long after he had left. It all seemed a bit coincidental.

Horis was feeling confused by all the events that had overtaken his normally quiet life. Was it only three days ago that all this had started?

The door to his room was locked, he knocked and it was opened by Maloney. He seemed very capable for a one-armed man, then Horis realised that he had been fooled by the porter's disguise. He had both arms visible and very much in working order, although he was wearing a glove on his left hand. In the centre of the room were two chairs back to back, with his assailants tied together in a sort of tableau. They were both unconscious and gagged, in addition to the wrist and ankle ties there were loops of cord that bound the whole scene together, around their waists.

Maloney was surveying his handiwork. "Well sir, I knew that the rope would come in handy, they're bound up so tight they can scarce breathe."

"Good work, man," said Horis, relieved to see that his assailants had been immobilised. "I take it you are on my side then? No doubt you will explain yourself in due course?"

"Of course, sir. You'll just have to trust me for a while longer. I've heard stories about the mine, like I said before, and I reckons that all these events are connected." He took the news-sheet from Horis and scanned the front page.

The bathroom door opened and Grace entered, she was dressed in nondescript, working women's clothes and her hair was tied back under a flowery scarf. She carried a small bag and looked ready for adventure.

"Horis," she said, "perhaps we'd better try to find out what these two are doing here, and then you can tell us why they would wish you harm." Grace started searching in the pockets of the nearest man, and extracted a small piece of card. She looked at it and shaking her head, she passed it to Horis.

"Well, well," he said. "See here, this is a ticket for the Rail-Ryde from Metropol City to Aserol. It's issued against a Ministry warrant, and dated two days ago."

"But that's strange," said Maloney. "It says here on the sheet that there has been a problem on the lines, robbers have engineered a derailment. In fact the last train from the capital was the one that you arrived on."

"Strange indeed," said Horis. "The news-sheet gives the time of the mine collapse as around midnight. And I was back here by then." At that Grace nodded, in a dreamy remembrance. Horis flushed at her look, he hoped Maloney had not noticed.

But he had been searching the second man, he brandished an identity card. "This one's a Ministry employee," he said. "His name is Lewis Morgan."

"That's who Terrance thought was calling him, just now," exclaimed Horis. "He asked if it was done." Maloney pulled off the man's mask and Horis gasped. "Him!"

"What do you mean?" both Grace and Maloney said as one.

"He was on the Ryde yesterday, we spoke."

Maloney took off the other's mask. "Do you know him?" he asked. Horis nodded, unable to speak for a moment. "Yes, he was there as well."

"Then I think you are in trouble," Maloney's voice was grave. "I told you that there was talk about strange goings on at the mine."

Horis felt his world falling down around him, he had been followed by a man who had done him harm. Terrance thought he was dead, presumably by the same hand he had shaken not long before. Nothing made any sense.

Maloney was speaking. "I don't like it, sir. This all points one way." Like some sort of lawyer he laid out the facts. "Now, the news-sheet says the mine collapsed around midnight, but you were back here before ten. Not only that but these two seem to have been sent before the accident, on the same Ryde as you in fact, which makes me wonder."

"Wonder what?" asked Grace, her brow was wrinkled.

"I must admit, at first sight, I thought they were Watchmen when I saw them pass me at the porter's desk, but the lack of identity cards and the face masks they must have put on in the lift makes me doubt that." He pondered for a moment and then continued, "Do you know what I think?"

Horis was impressed with Maloney's reasoning. "Pray continue."

"Well, sir, as I said, there's been rumours about strange things at the mine. Now let's just suppose that there was a secret in the mine, and just suppose someone wanted it kept. What better way than to send an inexperienced junior to view it, beggin' your pardon, someone who was expendable, and who could then disappear in some sort of accident."

At this, Grace, whose eyes had been growing larger as the tale unfolded, gasped and put her hand to her mouth. Maloney continued. "After all, you would not be around to defend yourself, all the blame could then be put on you, or on the mine, and the secret's safe. The Watch would investigate, but given the circumstances, would point the finger at you, without question."

The enormity of the situation was beginning to sink in, and Horis felt suddenly weak in leg and stomach. He slumped to the ground. He knew just what the secret was.

Grace had been silent, now she spoke up. "Horis, we should go, hide out somewhere until we can disprove any of this. I know of a place you will be safe, if we can get you there."

Maloney had a glint in his eye. "I will come with you," he announced. "I've missed adventure since I left the service. Anyway, I must confess I am intrigued." He reached up and took off his cap, placing it on Horis's head. "Not a perfect disguise, but it does change your appearance, it's the best we can do. We will follow Grace's plan, but first, we must make sure that we are not observed."

Horis was in such a confused state that he hardly noticed how they had become a group.

Horis threw all his belongings into his cases and closed the lids. Together the three left the room, locking the door on the unconscious pair behind them.

Chapter 17

Despite Grace saying she knew of a place of safety, Maloney was determined to ensure that they were not being followed. He led them away from the hotel and into the backstreets, they doubled back several times, and once Maloney pushed them into a dark corner and they waited, to see if anyone was taking an interest. When he was satisfied, they continued and soon even Grace, who thought that she knew the town well, was hopelessly lost. Eventually, they came upon a small park, with a strip of grass surrounded by late summer flowers. The place must have been quite a distance from the nearest Local, as there was little coal dust in the air or on the ground, a stream ran clear over rocks, and the throbbing from underground pipes was muted and faraway. In the middle of this oasis was a small coffee house, Maloney led them across the grass and they entered.

They sat in a crowded room with Maloney positioned to watch the entrance, drinking the bounty from the Western Isles. Since its introduction, coffee had proved so popular that yearly, the number of steam ships crossing the oceans just to collect this miracle bean had more than doubled. It was fast becoming as popular as char. The climate of Norlandia was unable to support the tree from which the bean came, thus the wars with the Western Isles had threatened the supply, and forced up prices in a way that had helped the resolution of the conflict.

People had complained that they were denied their coffee just because of the generals' insistence on war, and public opinion swung towards a just settlement. After all, trade was in everyone's interest. At last people could see that there may be a better way than continual fighting. Peace meant that supplies could be obtained easily. And the present government was resulting in a decrease of the generals' power.

Maloney professed his opinion that they had not been followed, it appeared that they were safe for the moment. The room seemed to be filled mainly with womenfolk who tended baby carriages and perambulators. Horis and Maloney were just about the only males inside, apart from the barista, who had nodded in greeting to them when they entered. They ordered large mugs of the brew and various pastries to break their fast.

There was a murmur of conversation which muffled their discussion, but in truth no-one was paying them any attention as they ate and drank.

"Now then, Maloney," said Horis, whose head was still spinning from the events of the morning, and it was still early, he avoided the subject of their flight, instead asking the first thing that came into his head. "Perhaps you can explain your missing arm, which seems to have miraculously returned to existence." Maloney smiled and wriggled the gloved fingers of his left hand.

"Well sir, I am employed as a porter it's true, but knowing my background, the hotel also keeps me as a form of security. After all, people pay a cripple little notice, so I can keep my ear to the ground, so to speak. And I have an arm." He removed his left glove and a brass and leather hand, complete in minute detail, became visible. The fingers moved naturally, with the faintest of noises from the clockwork within.

"Well I never," said Horis, too stunned to form a sensible thought.

Grace spoke up. "Mr Maloney, I didn't know, but I did wonder about the glove, and why sometimes your sleeve was pinned."

"Where did you get such an appendage?" asked Horis, who had thought that he was worldly wise, and knew of false limbs, but nothing of this complexity.

"It's a long tale," replied Maloney, replacing the glove. "And one for another time, if we are to get you to safety, we have more important things to consider."

Horis tried another question. "Why help me? You hardly know

me." Maloney nodded, drank a mouthful of coffee and composed his thoughts.

"I'll tell you true, sir. I have been a bit concerned about things at the mine for a time. My wife's brother works there, and Shirl tells me of the things he says, there have been strange goings on, a new crew in a part of the mine that has been sealed off to the regular men. As well as that, Obley has been getting more and more eccentric, and that witch Grantham is running the place. They do say he is suffering from a form of madness, one day he wrecked the offices, hunting for Drogans, which he said were hiding in the furniture."

Horis remembered the chaos in the offices and Obley's behaviour. "I met Mrs Grantham," he said. "She kept pressing him to take char and seemed to be unwilling to let him take me underground."

At this Maloney nodded. "It fits then, what Petroc told my Shirl. He said that Grantham was pretending that all was under control and then all of a sudden, Obley gets her and her men out of the way and opens the sealed level up. Next thing, the men go down and don't come back. Then you arrive, and I'm left wondering what's going to happen next." He smiled. "And now I know."

Horis was amazed to hear the tale, at the Ministry he had no idea of this and he thought that he was as well informed as anyone.

"Then my superior, Terrance, must have a hand in all this," he said and again Maloney nodded.

"Well he does own the mine, does he not? After his father, Bal rest him, passed on, and Grantham is his kin by marriage." Some of this was news to Horis, but made sense, as much as any of the tale.

Maloney continued, "My wife's brother is one of the miners who have disappeared, along with my uncle and some of my friends. I feel like I owe it to them to keep close to you, as you are the best chance now to solve this puzzle." Horis felt the rock in his pocket and debated whether to show it.

"And why you, Grace?" He turned to her. "Why are you with me?"

Her green eyes shone as she looked straight into his. "In my case there is no subterfuge in me, sir. I just liked you the moment I saw you." Her words, and her smile, made Horis blush again.

"So," Maloney said, "clearly, you have found something of significance, and there appear to be those who feel threatened by that discovery. So I thought that you might need a little help. Life had become boring at the hotel and I feel that it's time for an adventure. And like I say, I owe it to my family and friends."

Horis felt emboldened by their help. "Well I can't promise you an adventure, but I can give you a mystery." With a flourish he took out the rock, which he had moved from his wet overalls to his suit pocket when they had departed the hotel. He had it wrapped in his kerchief, and had secured it to the buttonhole of his pocket by means of a bootlace.

"What's that then?" asked Grace, looking at the white bundle, with mud stains leaking through.

"Watch!" And Horis let the bundle go.

Maloney grabbed it as it rose and the force almost pulled Horis's jacket pocket off. "Put it away, sir," he hissed. "There's no need to make an exhibition."

They both looked open-mouthed as Horis returned the bundle to his pocket and closed the flap.

"Now then, the cave which I saw at the mine was full of these, many bigger ones and Bal knows how many more there might be. Obley claimed to have told the Ministry about them the day before I arrived, which was why I was sent. No miners had the chance to tell anyone, so what can we deduce from that?"

Grace furrowed her brow. "There must be someone at the Ministry who knew before Obley and who doesn't want this discovery made public." Horis nodded.

"When I called Terrance, he seemed surprised to hear me; in fact he thought it was someone called Lewis calling him from Aserol. It's as if he thought that I would have been silenced by those two thugs, so he must be high up on the list of suspects. And even more so after the other things I have just learned," he paused for breath.

Grace spoke, "But why would anyone want this discovery to be kept secret, surely it's a benefit to all?"

"Well," said Maloney, "if one man could control the supply and production, it would give him a lot of money and power wouldn't it?" The question hung in the air, and in the silence it was clear that the reality of the situation was sinking in.

"So you think it's this Terrance do you?" said Grace.

"I think it may be him yes," replied Horis. "He has a lot of friends involved in industry, who might benefit from this thing, or indeed from its suppression."

"But although you have got away, they don't know that you have the rock."

"No-one saw me take it at the mine, but that doesn't make me any safer."

"No," said Maloney. "But it does mean that if we can get it to the right people, your story will not seem so far-fetched with this proof."

"So what do we do? We could go to the Watchmen. I'm sure they would take an interest in these developments."

"That's a good idea," Maloney said. "I have faith in the integrity of the Watchmen, they answer only to the Monarch and it seems unlikely that he would be a party to the things that have gone on. If we could only get them on our side then no-one would question them. But if someone high up at the Ministry is behind this, who knows what else is happening. If they have planned this then surely the Watch may have been misled. It may not be safe to involve them."

Grace was trying to enter the conversation, now she had her chance. "I have an idea of a safe place for you, I said so before, but we are here." She shot a look at Maloney.

"Well I thought it proper to make sure we were alone first," he said. "It would be no place of safety if we led them to it."

"Where's this place, then?" enquired Horis.

"Come with me," was her only answer, and standing she took Horis's hand. Bidding farewell to the barista she led him into the park, Maloney following. They stopped in the centre, away from prying ears.

"I realised where I was when we arrived," Grace said. "Although I would never have taken such a long-winded route to get here."

"Again I'll say it, I was taking precautions," Maloney replied. "We would have seen instantly if anyone were following us."

"Mr Maloney, and there was I, thinking you were a hotel porter, not some sort of spy." There was wonder in Grace's voice, and not a little sarcasm.

"Old habits, my dear," he enigmatically replied, and said no more.

"Very well," she said, "now that we are alone we can proceed. Come with me."

They left the park and crossed the street. Ahead of them a news-sheet stand was selling a different edition to the one they had seen in the hotel, this one had Horis's name and likeness on the front page. The vendor was nowhere to be seen. The street was deserted as Maloney grabbed Horis by the arm, the force spinning him round. "Wait over there, in the shadow," he said as he bent to look at the sheet.

"You were right; it looks like the Watchmen are out of the question. Apparently you are a terrorist who caused the mine disaster."

Grace gasped and put her hand to her mouth in shock. "But we know that's wrong, surely there's something we can do?"

Horis felt slightly flattered that Grace had said "We". After all, they scarcely knew each other, yet she wanted to be included in his plans.

"You don't need to stay with me, I will have to return to the Ministry and try and sort this out."

"You're a fool, have you not been listening?" Maloney was almost shouting. "If you don't mind my saying so, sir, just how far do you think you will get? All the Watchmen and the Rail guards will be out to get you, the stations will be watched, and the story against you seems to have been well constructed. You'll see the inside of prison, and the noose, so fast that your head will spin. And no-one will ever believe you. No, you need us, and we'll have to hide you somewhere whilst we devise a plan."

Grace spoke, "I've already said, several times, that I know of a safe place. I'm taking you to the docks. My uncle has a ship, a steamer not a sailboat. He runs all sorts of things around the coast, even to Metropol City. If we wanted, we could use him to get us there, and he may even have some way of helping us to get to the bottom of this."

Maloney looked suitably impressed with this idea. "If we can get onto the ship unnoticed, and if he's willing to help, it would give us a couple of days to come up with a plan."

Chapter 18, the *Swiftsure*

The docks were crowded with people and vehicles, both steam and equine-drawn; the air was thick with smoke from the Locals that supplied steam for the cranes and winches. They had evaded attention on the way from the coffee house by keeping to the back alleys of Aserol, only crossing the main thoroughfares when they had to. Finally they faced a tall brick wall that stretched in both directions. "Here we are then," said Grace as she confidently led the way to a small gate set in the wall. "This one is little used, it's a shortcut for the stevedores to get to the ale house," she said with a grin, "and the guard is a friend of my uncle."

Sure enough, instead of the Watchmen at the main gate, this one was attended by an old man who waved at her and let them through with a cheery, "Good morn." They found themselves in a maze of alleys and sheds; every so often they had to leap out of the way to miss a loaded mobile or wagon, which seemed intent on squashing the party almost before they knew they were in danger.

After a while, the sounds of the sea, splashing water and gulls' cries filtered through and that, combined with the smell of tar and grease overlaid on coal dust, made them realise that they were close to the water's edge.

They turned a corner and found themselves staring at the side of a ship, rust-streaked and riveted, with a mass of derricks and ropes all leading this way and that. No doubt there was logic in the arrangement but Horis, who was a confirmed landsman, could only see chaos. Packages seemed to be moving in all directions and there was a constant shouting in what sounded like a foreign tongue.

Stevedores clad in overalls and boots moved bales and barrels about with hooks and bars, lifting them onto the backs of carts and mobiles. Whistles blew and wires sang and there were shouts of "haul out," and "heads below," as cargo operations proceeded. The three took the opportunity of a brief lull to scuttle to the gangway.

Grace led them all on board and into the accommodation block, past a brass nameplate; very brightly polished it announced that they were on board the *Swiftsure*.

Inside, the din had receded, replaced by a low murmur from the ship's engines. The alleyways were well lit by statics lanterns, the new system that promised an end to gas light. It was a form of energy produced by steam, but instead of moving through pipes the energy was somehow carried along lengths of twisted copper. The light came from glass globes in which wires glowed. Horis knew that there was a lot of excitement about statics, but they were still only practical for ships, the system lost effectiveness over any great distance.

Grace led them to the Captain's apartment, up several decks, and knocked on the frame of the door. The entrance was open, covered by a beaded curtain.

A deep voice boomed out, "If that's the chandler, your food stores are not fit for porkers!"

"It's me, Uncle," replied Grace demurely. There was the sound of a chair scraping back and then a large man with an enormous beard and a beaming smile appeared through the beads, which rustled and swished. He swept Grace up into a hug that must have sorely tested her ribs. "Good to see you, my dear, to what do I owe this pleasure?" He lowered her to the ground, holding her at arm's length and caught sight of Horis and Maloney. "Who are these two?" he asked. "Are they more of your waifs and strays?"

"Uncle, this is Horis, from the Ministry of Coal, he has been wrongly accused of a crime and needs shelter. His companion is Maloney, from the hotel."

"Good day, gentlemen," said the Captain. He wrung Horis's hand then Maloney's with a grip of iron. "My favourite niece Grace has the idea that she can help everyone, I indulge her as much as I can, but I cannot abide dishonesty. And I will not stand to see her used."

His beard seemed to have a life of its own, it quivered as he spoke. "If you are guilty, I'd thank you to tell me now, and then get off my ship."

Horis spoke first. "Sir, I am most certainly innocent, and Grace can vouch for me, as for Maloney here, he is not a part of my problem, merely someone like Grace, who has offered to help me."

Grace nodded at this. "Indeed Uncle, Horis was with me when the crime of which he is accused took place."

"Very well," replied the mariner. "I trust Grace and so will help you. I am Captain Nabbaro, Hector Nabbaro, and I am at your service. You may take refuge on my ship and be under my protection, for the law cannot take you from here without my permission."

He continued, "When we have sailed, you can explain your predicament to me, and I will offer such help as I can. But you will have to excuse me, for I have a voyage to prepare."

A thin, anxious looking man walked towards them at that point, Nabbaro saw him and shouted, "Ah the chandler, now about the slop you call food."

The man looked worried at the verbal assault as Grace led them to a pair of cabins on the next deck, behind the wheel-space. They were marked for passenger use. "I will have this one," Grace said at one door. "You two can share the other." Horis gave her a disappointed look, which she ignored. "I have to do a few things," she said. "Wait here, you will be quite safe, I will return presently." She pecked Horis on the cheek and departed.

"Come on then," said Maloney and they entered the room. It was well fitted with four separate bunks in two tiers, armchairs and a desk as well as clothes hangers and drawers. Horis opened another door in the corner and discovered a washroom. It was better than his hotel room had been, indeed it was better than his apartment in Metropol City. Taking armchairs the two settled down behind a locked door to await departure.

An hour later there was a knock at the door. Maloney opened it a crack while Horis moved into the washroom. There was a muttered conversation and the sound of crockery.

"This is wonderful," Maloney exclaimed, "Come out and look Horis, we had quite forgotten luncheon, Grace has remedied that." Horis emerged to see that a steward had brought them a tray of char and a large amount of comestibles. Horis filled a plate as Maloney poured char, and then they polished off the food in companionable silence. After they had finished the last drop and crumb, Maloney stood and walked to the desk. "Now then," he said, "to business, it's time to prepare my arm."

Horis watched with mounting interest as Maloney removed his jacket and rolled his shirtsleeve above his left elbow. Horis could see that the man's false arm started just below the elbow joint, where it was connected by a leather device that fitted over the stump. Maloney gave the false arm a violent twist and it detached. Part of the leather remained on his arm. "They call it the boot," said Maloney, "though Bal alone knows why." He placed the limb on the table and stood over it, fiddling with his good hand. There was a click.

"There must be a tale attached to that appendage," said Horis. "If you'll pardon my asking, I would be fascinated to hear it."

Maloney was a large fellow, at least six feet tall and wide to match, with enormous shoulders, the fact that one arm ended below the elbow seemed to add to his character. He had opened a flap on the false arm, revealing the workings, all shining metal, glowing with some sort of grease.

"I lost it in the Western Isles," he said, waving the stump in the air, so that the empty sleeve flapped like a flag, "to a foul tribesman, he came sneaking up behind me and lopped it right off, like chopping wood." He smiled. "I suppose he thought he was being clever, cut off my pistol arm and I'm defenceless. Anyhow I fell down, all spurting blood. I was trying to remember where the pressure point was through the pain. Meanwhile he left me and went for my mate Sapper."

"What happened?" Horis asked. His military experience had been limited to his compulsory service, where due to his small size he had been unfit for any active duties. He had spent his two years as a messenger on Drogan watch in Metropol City and had never faced a human foe, or even seen a live Drogan close up for that matter.

"Well, Sapper had been alerted by my blubbing and it had made him angry. We were supposed to be moving quietly and there was I, screaming like a porker. Anyways he was ready for the man's attack. He put a couple of darts through the savage's head and then he managed to stop the bleeding. He put a dressing on my arm and carried me to a field hospital." Maloney said all this in a matter-of-fact voice, as if it had been the most natural thing to happen on a day's work. To him it may have been but Horis was both thrilled and feared at the telling.

He peered closer into the opening in the arm, entranced by the intricate clockworks exposed under the flap. Maloney had produced a key and was winding springs, his stump holding the limb still as he counted the turns in a whisper.

When Maloney had finished winding the springs he removed the key, clipping it into a slot on the flap, which he then pushed back until it clicked into place. "Look," he said, showing Horis the leather and brass thing he had called a boot on his stump. Horis saw that it was studded with small brass contacts, and when Maloney picked up the false arm, Horis could see small brass cups inside the end. Maloney pushed the arm onto the socket, it was a tight fit and when he gave it a final twist it seemed to be as one with the boot. "They fix so tight, they become one," he explained. "And the boot is attached to the bone, so now the arm is as strong as mine once was."

The arm no longer seemed to be a separate thing, the fingers moved and the wrist and elbow rotated, with little clicks and a faint whirring from the inside.

"How does it do that?" asked an incredulous Horis.

"It's beyond me, sir," came the reply. "You'd have to ask Professor Woolon at the army hospital."

Horis had heard of him, he was the head of the Institute of Medical Statics, and a pioneer of the study of the nervous system. Clearly the brass work of the arm acted as the nerves, passing impulses by some means to the clockworks that drove the joints. Horis had never seen the like, and guessed that Maloney was a lucky recipient of a medical breakthrough.

"It can do most things," said Maloney, "but I have to remember to wind the springs once a day, and only punch people with my right hand."

Horis was not surprised that a provincial army man like Maloney would be the owner of such a marvel. In his experience, such things were often tested on the ready supply of maimed men and women that the services and the mines provided, before they found their way to the general population.

The hospitals in Norlandia used the latest medicines, derived from plants found on expeditions to the corners of the world, and major surgery had been made bearable by the development of sleeping drugs from Coal Tar.

The last few years had seen medicine move from the preserve of the rich to the right of everyone who paid taxes, and the health of the population had improved as a result. Whereas in the past the maimed and crippled were a fact of life, now they were mostly old, it was rare to see young people with untreated infirmities. As well as the state, there were philanthropic businessmen who gave of their own fortunes to endow hospitals which provided healthcare to the masses.

And statics were clearly the science of the future, already they had developed from a curiosity to practical applications, such as in Maloney's arm. And new uses were being found every day, as man's understanding of his world increased.

Chapter 19

Horis and Maloney took a turn around the deck outside the passenger suite, listening to the noises of a busy working ship. People called and whistled; there was the constant throb of engines and the squeal of wires over winches. Grace had not returned from her errands. There was an occasional Watch patrol on the wharf but they showed no interest in the *Swiftsure*. Even so, Horis ducked back away from their sight until they had gone past the gangway. "They are the Dock Watch," said Maloney. "They will have started at six of the morn so will not know to look for you yet." Even so, Horis moved back inside, after all the next shift of Watchmen would know of him and he would not be able to relax until they were well away from Aserol.

There was something else that had been bothering Horis, and now seemed as good a time as any to air it. "Maloney, you mentioned a Mrs Maloney, will she not be wondering where you are?"

"No sir, me and the Missus have an understanding, she knows that I do the odd extra job for the hotel, and for others, so if I don't turn up for meals she won't fret. As long as I let her know my whereabouts after a week or so, things will be just fine. My sons will look after her." Horis wondered at her understanding, having a husband away in the wars must have made her used to separation and lack of news, he decided.

Late afternoon there was a knock at the door. Horis, who had been dozing in a chair, woke up and could not see Maloney. Nervously he went to the door. Keeping the chain on he opened it a fraction, despite what Captain Nabbaro had said he still felt unsafe.

A small man in a steward's coat and pressed black trousers was outside. "Good after, sirs." He offered Horis a small sheet of card.

"Here is the Eventide meal menu, Captain's compliments, and would you both join him in the saloon in ten minutes?"

"Is that more food?" called Maloney from the washroom.

The dining saloon was empty; it was a large room with wood panelling and several paintings on the walls. There were several tables arranged around a large central one and they sat at one of the smaller ones marked "Passengers". They had just settled themselves and poured water when Captain Nabbaro entered with Grace, they both made their way to the head of the large table. Seeing Horis and Maloney, Nabbaro waved them over to sit beside them.

"Gentlemen, please sit at my side and eat. Perhaps we can discuss your concerns whilst we do so."

"Thank you, Captain," said Horis. "Not wishing to be rude, sir, but when do we depart?"

Before he could answer, the steward who had called them came over and took their orders, fish featured heavily on the menu, and they all chose fillets of Cyd, with salads and roots. The dining room filled with people as the officers and crew came in to eat; many of them knew Grace and greeted her. Horis and Maloney were introduced as her friends, on passage to the city. By some understanding they were left alone, the others all sat at different tables to eat.

"Worry not," replied Nabbaro when the steward had departed. "I realise that you are fearful, but I have put a man on guard at the gangway. Should the Watchmen appear, he will let me know, they cannot come aboard without my permission and my ship is sanctuary for you. We depart at high tide tonight, at eight of the clock."

"That is good news," said a relieved Horis. "I don't mean to be ungrateful, sir, but my situation is unfamiliar to me, I always believed that the law was just, and that those above me were honest. To find myself manoeuvred into this course is unsettling, to say the least. I will relate my tale to you presently."

At that point the food appeared, it smelt superb, and cutting into his Cyd, Horis found that it tasted as good as the aroma had promised. When the steward departed, Nabbaro resumed.

"I understand your reticence but I am afraid that curiosity has got the better of me, and I prevailed upon Grace to tell me some of your story. Unfortunately, I have had a lot of dealings with the bureaucracy from the other side and I see them in a different light. They will not hesitate to use any means to protect their power." His words hung in the air.

They ate in silence for a while and then Nabbaro spoke again. "Do you have this strange rock, which you took from the mine?"

"Yes I do," confirmed Horis. "But not on my person, I will gladly show it to you after we have left the port."

"That will be an education, I hope," said the Captain. They ate for a while in silence. Nabbaro excused himself, saying he had ship's business to attend to. When they had finished, they all returned to the cabin, locking the door again.

The time passed slowly, Horis paced up and down the small cabin whilst Maloney snoozed on his bunk. Grace watched out of the porthole and gave a commentary on the people she could see and the events taking place on the wharf.

At about seven, the cargo operations were completed and after the holds were closed, the ship fell silent, save for the engine's hum. The wharf emptied of people, and as darkness fell, lanterns were lit on the sides of the sheds. Statics lights came on all over the ship, lighting the preparations for departure.

Promptly at eight, the dock pilot appeared in a steam-mobile and two paddle-wheel tugs made their way towards them from the sea. These were fastened to the ship, and all lines to the shore were let go. With the tugs pulling, the *Swiftsure* was turned, and now pointing out to sea, started her engine. Horis had left the cabin and was standing on the deck near the ship's side and saw the Watch patrol strolling along the wharf. They paid the departing vessel little attention, even so Horis ducked back into the shadows as the distance between ship and wharf increased. His last sight of them, still unconcerned, as the ship increased speed, made him feel that he was at last safe.

As the ship increased speed and they left the calm of the harbour, its motion changed and it started to buck and roll, at first slowly, then with increasing vigour. Horis, who was not accustomed to travel on water, felt sick almost immediately; he went to his bunk and on laying down discovered several straps atop the mattress.

"They are to hold you steady," advised Grace who had followed him, concerned at his green pallor. "And then you will not slide about in the bunk. The best plan would be to stand outside for a while, and get used to the motion. If you stay in here before you are used to it, you will feel worse." Horis stood outside for a few minutes and sure enough his stomach settled. However, when he returned to the cabin, he started to sweat and feel dizzy immediately.

Neither Grace nor Maloney seemed in the least bothered by the motion, clearly it was natural and did not mean that the ship was in danger. The realisation made Horis feel better and he drew courage from their relaxed attitude. After a while he realised that he no longer felt ill.

"It will take us about three days to get to Metropol City," said Grace. "I have made this trip many times; we have to round the Cape of Storms to the east, then stop at Ventis to drop some goods. And now if you will excuse me, I am tired. I will retire for the night." She left the room and they heard her cabin door close.

"Well then," said Horis, slightly worried by the name Cape of Storms. "That gives us some time to decide what to do when we arrive. I suppose that my lodging house will be unavailable, as will all my possessions."

Maloney nodded. "That's right, sir. It will be best if you keep from your old haunts, plenty of room to get lost in that city."

"So do you have a plan?"

Maloney held up a small notebook in which he had been scribbling. "I believe I have the makings of one, yes."

"Do tell."

"There are two parts," began Maloney. "First there is the need to keep you safe, and undetected. That requires a place to stay which is out of the way. I think I can arrange that through my old regiment."

"And the second?" queried Horis, he had visions of sleeping in a barracks, or a stable somewhere, surrounded by soldiers.

"Ah, that is the harder part; I think that we could send an unknown to poke around the Ministry, to drop the hint that he knows of your whereabouts to see who takes the bait, I have some friends in the capital who owe me favours."

"Why go to the trouble on my behalf, someone you hadn't even met three days ago?" Horis was confused as to Maloney's motives.

"It's quite simple, sir. As I said, my wife's brother is a miner, and before I came to work the day we left, we got word that he was in the cave-in that you are alleged to have caused."

"Then surely you must blame me." Horis was suddenly terrified; he had trusted this man and now was alone, on a ship with him, in the middle of the night.

"Not so, Shirl had got word the day before that they were safe but quarantined, from one of the mine secretaries who overheard Obley call the Ministry. That was the call that summoned you."

"Then folk know that the cave-in story was a contrivance?"

Maloney nodded. "We may be provincial, but we are not stupid. As I said, the times do not add up. Shirl will not open her mouth. She has too much sense for that, and who would listen to the words of a grief-stricken, common miner's woman, especially one with no evidence." He paused for a moment then added sombrely, "And you can rest assured that the secretary who told her will be mysteriously unable to repeat her story."

Horis remembered the empty offices and scattered papers. "Does that mean that Obley was played for a fool too?"

"If he was in the cave-in, then yes," was the emphatic reply. "And now I'm following Grace's example and getting some sleep."

Horis was left with his thoughts as the ship ploughed on through the night.

Chapter 20, Northcastle

While Horis was waking on the *Swiftsure*, in Northcastle Ralf the flyer had just finished his fast-breaker, along with the others. Normally they would all be taken to the workshops by steam-mobile, some to train on the model and others to prepare for a flight down the valley. Today, Ralf was separated from the rest and was instead taken to a strip of level ground, where a long, straight path had been laid out and levelled by the convict labourers. The artisan engineer explained that they had a different job for him that day.

"We have been working on your idea," he said, "and here is the first attempt at it. We are calling it a plane."

In front of him stood the new plane, still sitting on a small wheeled wagon. Ralf started to perform his checks as usual, noting the differences in this one, pleased to see his ideas made solid. The breeze blew into his face as he stood behind the plane. Perfect, it would aid in giving him lift as he moved.

This machine was distinguished from the previous one by the wood and brass propeller at the rear. The five curved blades had been carved from wood and fitted onto a brass centre. The whole was polished to a glossy finish. Ralf gave a gentle tug on one of the blades and it spun freely, it had obviously been mounted on fine bearings as it continued to rotate long after his hand left it.

Several of the old engineers were stood around muttering, the general thought amongst them was "it will never move". That and, "how can that small propeller move enough air?" And there was much nodding in agreement.

His artisan came to talk to him. "Take care, Ralf," he said in a kindly tone. "And remember that this is not our only plane. The base is strong enough for a landing on the road or you may make it to the sea, the ship is alerted to your flight." Lowering his voice he continued, "Bring it back if you can but if it's a choice, then of course you must save yourself."

Satisfied with his external inspection, Ralf settled himself in the cockpit and tested his controls. The burner was lit and a strange machine, mounted on the rear of a steam-mobile, was backed into position alongside the craft.

A long rod was inserted into a hole in the side of the plane and engaged on some gearing inside with a metallic click. At a signal from Ralf, the machine started and the rod spun under the power of the coiled spring inside it. Clearly this was attached to the shaft on which the propeller was mounted as it now began to spin. Ralf increased the rate of the burner and the craft vibrated, it wished to move as it rattled against the wedges holding the wagon. The force created by the shaft's rotation must have triggered a release mechanism as the rod shot backwards, clear of the craft.

The propeller blades were a blur as power increased, and Ralf waved the wedges away. Once they were gone the whole machine rolled with ever increasing speed along the road as the heated air spun the shaft and the propeller faster. As it moved, more air was sucked in and at once it was clear that Ralf's idea was perfect.

Quickly Ralf felt the plane's controls lighten; the air flow over the wings was enough to lift the craft clear of the wagon. He pulled back on his control column and the ground fell away beneath him. Free from that drag, the plane shot ahead as it climbed into the sky with a roar.

On the ground the engineers were no longer doubters, indeed they all now said, "of course it would work," "I never doubted it." and other comments as they slapped Ralf's artisan on the back and shook his hand. He was pleased and relieved; he would have bragging rights for his trust in Ralf's ideas.

Ralf reduced the gas supply to the burner and faced up to the realisation that his idea had worked. He knew that somehow his life would never be the same, however he also wondered how he might bring the machine safely back to earth; landing had never been one of his strong points. If his craft survived at all, his landings were a sort of semi-controlled crash. But that was in the future, he looked at the rudimentary instruments in front of him. Installed at his insistence and all based on the science of pressure differences, they showed his height and speed and the amount of gas left. To his surprise he found that the burner had used a lot less gas than he had expected. Hoping this was not a mistake he tapped the gauge with a gloved finger. The needle jerked but did not fall. Ralf could see that there was plenty for several minutes flying before he would have to face the landing question. Banking slowly, he decided to fly over the main buildings, to show his craft to the people there. He levelled out of his turn; the whole camp was below him, tiny in the vastness of the countryside. He pointed the nose of the plane down and headed towards the buildings.

The first that anyone knew of his approach was when the windows rattled at his passing. Running outside they just saw the tail of the plane disappear behind the buildings. After a few seconds it reappeared, climbing till it was vertical and then upside down, finally rolling till it was the right way up again. The engine howled as it dove and passed overhead again, leaving a wind in its passing.

As Ralf climbed back into the sky, he saw that he was not alone. His flight had attracted the attention of a Drogan which had come to investigate. Even though he was moving faster than he had ever flown before, its large wings beat effortlessly as it kept pace with him. The head turned and a beady eye regarded him, the lashed lid blinking. He felt no fear of the beast and increased the burner to maximum, increasing his speed, yet still the beast was there. He spotted the line of balloons far below him that marked the valley where his flying adventures had all started. While his attention had been distracted, the landing strip had fallen well behind. He could return but had a better idea, he would ditch in the water, he just hoped that the plane could be salvaged. He started to reduce his altitude to fly into the valley, the Drogan keeping station just off the end of his left wing.

The watchers could hear a plane approach but could not see it coming down the valley. Then one glanced up and saw the Drogan and plane flying in company and descending towards them. There was no flag signal for that, but the Drogan approaching flag was displayed and gas guns were trained from the baskets of the balloons and the hillside. The telescopes of the balloonists saw that the Drogan was escorting a plane. No attempt was made to fire, for fear of hitting Ralf.

As Ralf passed over the first balloon and turned to follow the line of the valley the Drogan sensed that it was in a dangerous place and peeled off to seek other game. Ralf saluted it as it flapped away. The watchers could see that more control existed in this version of the flying machine as it twisted and turned down the valley. In each balloon that he passed the officer trained his telescope on the plane and by his side, a signaller waved flags in the direction of the next post. Watchers on the hills repeated his message. It raced ahead of the plane until it was received by a naval vessel, wallowing in the low swell, just off the river mouth. Seconds later, the plane itself appeared, banking around the last turn in the valley before streaking towards the ship.

Lower and lower it sank, until it was barely skimming the waves. There was a silence as the engine died, empty of fuel. Slower and slower it went, down the side of the ship, and then as it seemed that it must dive into the water, the nose lifted. Abruptly it stopped and seemed to hang in the air for a second, and then it fell down, landing on the crest of a swell. It bobbed like any other boat as the warship closed in on it, cranes already swinging over-side, as a small boat was rowed alongside it. A sailor clambered onto the wing and attached the crane's swinging hook to the lifting ring just behind the cockpit. Steam filled the crisp air as the plane and its pilot were lifted on board by the wheezing crane. Ralf had completed his flight and the plane was intact. This time he had not even got his feet wet.

Once the plane had been lowered to the deck of the warship, he breathed a sigh of relief, undid his straps and climbed out. The Captain greeted him as he entered the wheel-space. Clapping him on the back he said, "Well done, sir. That was the best flying yet, more often than not we only collect the pilots."

"Thank you, Captain," replied Ralf. "I'm pleased to have kept dry this time. Will we be returning directly to land? My artisan needs to know of my success." The warship had already turned its bow towards the jetty at the river's mouth and soon secured alongside. A flat wagon was waiting to collect the plane, together with the engineers. They had all climbed into a steam-mobile and followed his progress, now it pulled to a halt and they disembarked A round of applause rang out and they crowded round to slap his back.

"I told you," Ralf told his artisan engineer, "it flies like a Drogan."

"I know," replied the man. "We saw you and the beast racing for the coast."

"I was faster, and I have other ideas as well, to make it even better."

"Well done, young Ralf," replied the man. "We will have to see about that, for now bask in your glory."

On their return to the camp they were met by a crowd who cheered at his feat, and his survival.

Chapter 21, Metropol City

Cavendish had heard the news from Aserol and was not amused.

"Perhaps you can tell me what has happened to Strongman?" he asked Terrance. They were seated in an ale house on a back street near the Ministry, and Terrance had come at short notice after being summoned.

The ale house was a dark, dingy place and all conversation had ceased when Terrance had entered. The low ceilinged room was populated by uncouth looking men with large tankards in front of them. They wore workmen's clothes, coal-heavers most likely, and their faces were blackened and sweat streaked. The potman had obviously been told of his summons as when he spied Terrance he jerked his head over to the corner, where Cavendish sat under a flickering gas light.

Terrance walked through a silence that felt solid, like a wall of cobwebs brushing his face. As he sat, conversation restarted.

"What a place," Terrance exclaimed, feeling out of his depth and slightly worried.

"Oh these are all stout fellows," replied Cavendish. He raised his glass. "Your health, lads," he shouted. At this all the patrons stood and cheered.

"Thank you, Mr Cavendish sir," they said in chorus. The inference was clear, he was in Cavendish's lair and he had better be careful and have the right answers.

"Now to business," Cavendish continued in a cold voice. "Kindly answer me, so that we can form a plan."

Terrance wondered how much of the latest news from Aserol Cavendish was privy to, he had only just learnt it from Mrs Grantham, but on reflection a man such as Cavendish would have an extensive network of informers. And he was beginning to doubt her honesty and efficiency.

"Well, I can't explain it," was his worried reply. "I thought that the plan was working well, my agent Mrs Grantham had manoeuvred everyone down the mine, but when they were ready to set the charge and seal the space, her men found that Obley and Strongman had returned to the surface. She tells me that she managed to track Obley down, and a secretary who had got involved. She took them both back underground." He paused as the potman served them. Taking a gulp of his ale he was about to resume his tale when Cavendish intervened.

"And she let Strongman go?" his voice incredulous.

"She told me that when she went to get char he had vanished and she said that there was no sign of him. As time was pressing she decided to make the explosion and attend to Strongman later. After all, she knew he would be at the hotel, apparently he had become involved with one of the women there."

Terrance had the feeling that Grantham was trying to save her own skin and that Cavendish had different information to him.

Cavendish waved his hand. "I don't need details of his every breath, just to know that he will cause us no more trouble."

Terrance continued, "So the explosion was made, trapping everyone inside. Grantham sent my men to the hotel to tidy up, but Strongman escaped."

"How in Bal's name did he manage that?" exclaimed Cavendish. "I thought that you had sent the man to Aserol because he was small and a fool."

"I thought him so, and in my employ that has been the case." Terrance had the tone of one whose world is slowly falling apart, where nothing was as it had seemed. "Grantham had not heard from the two, so she went to the hotel herself and found them bound and gagged. They reported that Strongman had help, this woman I mentioned and another man; by the time she had freed them the trail had gone cold."

"This is not helpful," said Cavendish. "If this man has help, he may begin to deduce the truth of events."

"He cannot leave Aserol," confidently replied Terrance. "My men have all the routes covered; his likeness is on the front of the news-sheets and they have enlisted the local Watch, using the papers I provided as proof of their mission. He has nowhere to turn for help. My men know that they must not fail a second time."

Cavendish gave a chilling look straight into Terrance's eyes. "Let us hope that you are correct then. And what of the miners and their families?"

"As far as they are concerned, we are trying to save them; we will give it a few more days and then announce that we were unsuccessful. They will all be suffocated by the time we reach them."

"You must make sure that they are compensated, and that they never see the bodies, the fuss will die down." Cavendish took a sip of his drink, Best Malt noted Terrance, just like in the Club.

Terrance nodded, again he wondered at a man who would willingly sacrifice so many for his grasp on power, little realising that by association he had become as bad. Glumly he supped his ale.

His next remark concerned something that had been bothering Terrance, the whereabouts of the consignment of rocks bound for Northcastle.

"And the rocks that you sent to Northcastle, when might they arrive?"

"The vessel will be on its way soon," Terrance replied. "I have booked space in a normal ship to avoid suspicion. It left Ventis for Aserol yesterday. It will be in Northcastle within the month I hope."

Cavendish regarded him with contempt, he was not the man his father, Bal rest him, had been. He had no grasp on politics or the keeping of power. His usefulness would come to an end and then he would be surplus to requirements. The thought filled him with pleasure, for he enjoyed the sight of men pleading for their lives. The trick was to keep the pretence of forgiveness as a dangling carrot for as long as possible.

"Get back to your desk then," he said and watched as Terrance paled. "Get matters properly arranged and when you have, contact me again."

Relieved to have been excused, Terrance drained his glass and left the ale house.

Chapter 22, the *Swiftsure*

Horis slept a troubled sleep, he dreamt of floating rocks and collapsed mines and being chased by masked men. In the end he awoke, and finding himself strapped into the bunk, was gripped by panic. As he awoke fully, he remembered strapping himself in to arrest his motion in the rolling ship. Relieved, he set about making himself ready to face the day. Maloney was nowhere to be seen; he must have arisen earlier and set off on some purpose. Horis washed, but was unable to shave; he had left his razor at the hotel in the haste of their departure.

As Horis was tightening his necktie, the door opened and Grace entered, she had a mug of char and a sandwich in a tin bowl, from which the smell of fried porker rose. Horis realised that the ship's motion had almost stopped, or perhaps he was just used to it, and the smell of food made him realise that he was famished. "Here," said Grace, "I've brought you some fast-breaker; you look much better this morn." She kissed him on the cheek, and frowned at the stubble there. "I will find you a razor," she said.

"Thank you," replied Horis, picking up the sandwich and taking a huge bite. As he chewed he mumbled, "I had considered a beard as a disguise. Where are we?"

"Halfway to the Cape, and the weather has improved, the seas are from our rear now and the motion is easier. Maloney is about and gathering intelligence." She gave him a look. "You will not be growing a beard, not if you want my continued company."

Just then, Maloney entered the cabin, his mouth was surrounded with the suspicion of porker-grease and there were egg stains on his shirtfront. "Good morn, Horis," he called in a cheerful voice. "So you have chosen to wake, time's a wasting, come with me."

Horis hurriedly crammed the rest of his sandwich into his mouth, and washed it down with a draught of char. He was puzzled by Maloney's haste, but when he stepped out onto the deck, he felt struck by the beauty of the scene. He realised that on a day like this, being inside was a waste of time.

It was a beautiful day, the sun shone in a clear sky of the softest blue. The light reflected on the waters, sparkling in their foamed wake, while the seas were heaped in a gentle swell from which the occasional white equine broke. Gulls circled and called, and in the distance they could see the land, low hills and treetops. It was not hot, but pleasingly warm. Grace's curls rippled and bounced in the wind as she walked with Horis towards the wheel-space.

Many other vessels could be seen in the vicinity, sailers and steamers, whilst inshore fisher-boats worked.

Maloney stood by the door to the wheel-space. "May we enter?" he called.

Hector was inside, talking with the navigator. "Please do, good morn all, I trust that you have eaten?"

"Thank you, Captain," Horis answered. "We have. May I presume to ask our itinerary?" The navigator excused himself and returned to his duties, sweeping the seas with binoculars and noting the ship's progress on a large map. Horis watched him for a moment and was fascinated by the equipment he was using, it all looked so strange to him. He was imagining the uses of some of the things when Hector's words brought him back to the moment.

"Well, gentlemen and ladies, we shall round the Cape a little after lunch, and arrive in Ventis tomorrow morning, until then, there is not much for you to do but enjoy the journey. Please feel free to venture where you will on my vessel, but please do not enter the machinery space." He paused, then remembered, "Ah yes, Mr Strongman, you were going to show me this marvel of yours, perhaps you would come to my cabin shortly."

"Gladly sir, it's the least I can do, after your kindness."

Maloney and Grace were talking to the navigator, and Horis dearly wanted to ask him several things, however, seeing Nabbaro leaving, he felt bound to go with him. No matter, he thought, I can quiz him later.

Nabbaro left the wheel-space by the internal door, with Horis following. They descended the stairs and entered the Captain's cabin. It was a calm space, with wide windows giving a view over the fore part of the vessel. Potted plants grew in the window frames, and everywhere was shiny brass and oiled hardwood. A small display contained clockworks, Horis bent to look at them more closely. Hector saw his interest. "They repeat the readings of the compass and speed calculator," he said. "It means I can see the progress without going topside, and this one," he pointed to a dial with a ship's model in the centre, "it shows the winds direction and force. Now please sit, and make yourself at home. Char? Or would you prefer coffee?" He pressed a small lever on his desk.

A steward appeared at the door. "Char please," said Hector, and glanced questioningly at Horis.

"That will be excellent, char for me, thank you," he said. The steward nodded and left, returning in a couple of minutes with a silver tray, containing charpot, hot water and all the makings, with a plate of biscuits. He made to pour, but Nabbaro stopped him.

"That's fine, Seymour, I can manage thank you." The steward left again.

Hector poured the char and offered Horis milk and honey. After they were set he leant back in his chair, munching on a biscuit. "So to business, do not keep me in suspense a moment longer."

"Very well," said Horis, and opened his pocket. Taking out the muddied kerchief he threw it to Nabbaro. "Here, catch!" He wanted to see the other's reaction.

Just as Horis had done in Obley's office, Nabbaro moved as if the kerchief would fall towards him. When it rose, his look was priceless and Horis had to stop from laughing out loud. The kerchief hit the ceiling, where it rolled slowly from side to side with the vessel's motion.

Hector furrowed his brow. "I thought in all my years sailing the oceans that I had seen most things, but you, sir, have amazed me."

He stood and retrieved the bundle from the ceiling and felt it in his hand. Removing the wrapping he rubbed the rock against his sleeve, dislodging some of the mud. The rock was a dull grey colour underneath. Hector peered at it, sniffed it and licked the exposed surface.

"It seems soft. May I try and cut a small piece off?" he asked.

"You may try," said Horis, and he watched as Nabbaro produced a knife and tried to cut the rock, it kept escaping and floating up, the bizarre sight of Nabbaro flailing to catch it made them both laugh. After several attempts to cut the rock, Nabbaro gave up and surveyed his handiwork.

"Well, it's metallic in nature," he observed. "When you can keep hold of it, look!" He passed the rock back to Horis, who could see bold scratches from the blade, revealing a shiny surface, flecked with small crystals. It pulled against his grip. Shorn of its muddy coat, it seemed more able to rise.

Horis wrapped the rock back in his kerchief and returned it to his pocket. "I would be grateful, sir, if you kept this to yourself. I am in enough trouble as it is, and I would hate for you to get involved in any unpleasantness."

"I understand," replied Hector. "And you can rely on my discretion, but I must warn you," and his face became stern, "Grace is my family, and although I am not the closest of her kin I feel responsible for her. She spends time with me here and I don't like the thought of her at risk." His meaning was clear, but to ensure complete understanding, he put his face close to Horis; indeed his beard was touching him as he spoke. "If I find that you have led her to danger, or if you let harm befall her, you will have to answer to me."

Horis gulped. "You have my word." He tried to sound solemn, but thought that he must be sure not to add another to the list of those after him. And he was not sure if he should be more afraid of Nabbaro than of Terrance if it came to it. After all, the Captain held the power of Bal on his vessel. Maybe he should mention his feelings for her, or maybe not.

He was debating the point, when Nabbaro, who had paused to drink deeply from his mug of char, looked up at him and smiled. "Don't fret," he laughed. "I know that Grace is wilful and more than able to look out for herself. She has told me a little of your dilemma, perhaps you can elaborate."

Horis drank some char and started at the beginning, from the call to the Ministry that had set things in motion. Every so often Hector would ask a question, and Horis was surprised at the perception he showed. He had a cynical view of the workings of government, but one which Horis had to admit, fitted the facts. He laughed when Horis told of his night in The Drogan, with Grace and Divid. "Ah Divid, he is a man after my own heart, the best to have around you in a tight spot, and The Drogan, well, there is a place to behold." He confirmed Horis's opinions in a sentence. "Tell me, does Marie still ride the clockwork beast?" There was a twinkle in his eye at that and they laughed together again.

At the end of the telling, Hector sat back in his chair and stroked his beard. He remained deep in thought for a moment, and then reached a decision.

"You are doing the right thing," he opined. "The system, despite its outward appearance is rotten. Power is vested in too few men, and any dissent is ruthlessly squashed. I'm sure that Maloney has the makings of a good plan. If you hold true, you can upset the whole cart."

"But I feel responsible for all those trapped underground," explained Horis. "I worry that my actions led to the tragedy."

Nabbaro tried to reassure him. "Nonsense, your arrival or not would have changed nothing, as I said, these men are ruthless and will stop at nothing to keep their grip on the levers of power. You must not blame yourself for the actions of others."

"You are right I suppose," Horis replied hopefully. "I tell myself that, and think that if we are quick we may save some of them."

Hector shook his head. "A noble thought, but I fear it is misguided, they will not see daylight again, all you can do is make their loss a rod to beat those who caused it." He changed the subject. "Now to lighter matters, Grace tells me that you have an interest in the mechanics of the age?"

"I do, sir, but more in the field of statics than in engines, although I realise that one cannot have the statics without the engine, I feel that they are separate things."

"Perhaps you should speak with my statics artificer, Mr Hamman; he would enjoy showing you our equipment, but first," he consulted his timepiece, "it must be time for luncheon."

Chapter 23

When Horis and Hector entered the dining room, Maloney and Grace were already there, both drinking soup from large mugs. It smelt delicious, and looking at the timepiece on the wall, or bulkhead as Maloney called it, Horis saw that he had been talking with Nabbaro for three hours. Unbidden the steward brought him a mug of the soup, with a large piece of bread. Tasting the soup, Horis found that it was a mash of roots and shredded anatine meat, with a fiery kick, and quite delicious. He found that the two had spent the morning discussing plans for Metropol City, and felt somewhat annoyed that he had not been included. He resolved to tackle Maloney later.

After an excellent meal, and on getting directions from the steward, Horis found Hamman in his workshop, surrounded by the wires and fittings of his trade. The room smelt of burning and Horis could feel a tingling sensation in the tips of his fingers as he touched the arms of the chair in which he was bade sit.

Hamman was old and dressed in worn overalls, with singed holes on the chest and thigh, but his eyes were bright and his beard bushy. "Glad to meet a fellow enthusiast," he greeted Horis. "Sit a while and we shall talk; the crew regard me as a sorcerer and avoid me. The Captain doesn't understand me, so conversation is limited." He rummaged in the corner of his workshop and presently produced two mugs which he filled with char, made in a small cylindrical object that he called a brewer.

"It uses statics to heat the water without a stove," explained Hamman. "Then you add the leaves and brew the char. It is just one use of many that has been devised for the statics power."

Horis was well aware of the stir that the first demonstrations of statics had caused, and had taken the trouble to understand the method and principles of the science, so he was able to understand much of what Hamman said. He found to his surprise that an hour had passed and there was still much to talk about. Hamman was explaining the function of the dynamic in creating the statics charge, and the theory of transmission of power along wires when Horis noticed that the ship was turning. His view through the porthole behind Hamman was changing rapidly and the motion of the ship altered. "We must be rounding the Cape," he said, but Hamman was in full flow and never stopped his discourse.

After another hour, Horis found his ability to be entertained was starting to wane. Hamman had just started on his ideas for the future, when all gas lighting would be redundant and whole cities lit by statics, when Grace came to his rescue.

"Horis, there you are, come quick, you must see this," she was excited and Horis, relieved to have been rescued, made his excuses to Hamman.

"Ah, no matter," Hamman exclaimed. "I have enjoyed our conversation but now I must get below and tend to my dynamic, perhaps we can resume our discourse on the morrow."

Horis left with Grace. "You are my saviour," he said, "but what is so exciting?"

Grace led him to the ship's bow, leaning over to view the water. Horis did the same, and following her pointing hand saw a giant green Ichthus chasing small fishes in the bow wave. The aquatic breed of Drogan, it was a similar beast but without the large wings. Its long neck sat atop a body shaped like a barrel, with two sets of fins for propulsion. There was a tail, with a paddle-shaped fin at the end, while the large head was birdlike, with rows of fearsome teeth. The head wove about, following the fishes' attempts to escape, and they fancied that they could hear the jaws click together each time they closed over another victim.

Grace stood up, her eyes bright. "They are so rare these days," she explained, "and reputed to be bringers of good fortune, perhaps it's a sign that our quest will be successful."

Maloney joined them; he had come from the inside of the bow somewhere, and carried a small bag. "The crew on this ship have some useful bits and pieces," he remarked. "And they have loaned me a few." He did not say more, but the bag jingled as he walked, and he seemed pleased with the contents.

They returned to the accommodation deck and after Maloney had stowed his mysterious bag, they took advantage of the washrooms and cleaned themselves for dinner. There were no baths, one merely stood under a spray of warm water to wash. Horis found it refreshing and different. At table Hector regaled them with tales of his times at sea, but never mentioned the rock, which relieved Horis; the man seemed to be true to his word. Again the food was excellent, this time they ate shelled-fishes and flavoured breads.

After dinner Horis and Grace strolled on the deck. Watching the sun set, stars became visible and the water was laced with glowing streams of sea creatures, pulsing in reds and greens. They held each other close, talked and laughed together.

Seeing them so, Maloney was cheered by the developing romance. That reminds me of Shirl and me, he thought, all those years ago, good luck to them both.

Night fell quickly, the temperature dropped under a clear sky, and having nothing much else to do, the three repaired for an early night. In truth, the sea air had tired them all, that and the relief from the stress of the last few days, and they were all asleep in a matter of moments.

Next morn, they were woken by bells ringing, and the *Swiftsure* slowing down. "Come on you two," called Grace from outside their door. "We are arriving." Horis and Maloney rose and dressed quickly. Coming on deck in the early morning sunshine they stood and watched the *Swiftsure's* arrival in Ventis from the deck above the wheel-space.

As the town approached, Horis, even with his untrained eye, could see that they would not enter the harbour. The gap between the walls was very narrow, and inside there looked to be little space.

Grace was standing beside him at the rail; pressed against his side he could feel the heat from her.

"I missed you last night," she whispered, and as Horis turned towards her she kissed him. "I've never felt like this about anyone," she said, as their lips parted. "Not ever and so quickly and surely."

In truth Horis felt the same, but had not wanted to spoil the moment. Now he let his feelings out, and grabbed her round the waist, pulling her to him. "Oh Grace, I have waited forever for one such as you, I'm so glad you feel the same." They held each other, for a moment blissfully unaware of the world around them.

Maloney broke the spell with a cough. "Sorry to disturb you," he said, with a tone both mocking and jealous. "But as you can see, we will not be entering the port. Captain Nabbaro tells me we will drop anchor and goods will be transferred by steam tug and barge." He paused for a moment and then continued.

"We are to anchor near the Port Officer's boat, see it is over there." He pointed to a small craft, bobbing in the low swell half a mile away. "However, we may venture ashore if we wish, once the officials have finished, by hailing a water taxi."

As they watched, the *Swiftsure* closed on the boat, slowing all the time. The beat of the engine changed, suddenly becoming more violent as it was reversed, and the bow swung while white water boiled around the propeller. With a rattle and cloud of dust, the anchor was let go and the engine stopped. As the vessel settled down with her head to the tide, a stream of small boats came round the end of the harbour wall and made for her.

Chapter 24, Ventis

As they came close, the three could see that they were brightly coloured and rowed by energetic crews, all vying to be first alongside. Some were filled with fruits and produce, others with trinkets and clothing, and yet more with women, all shouting and offering items for sale.

The gangway was lowered for the Port officials, who had come in close, and they boarded, all golden braids on imposing uniforms. They carried rolled-up canvas bags, and made straight for the Captain's rooms. Behind them the traders swarmed, kept from boarding by a guard left at the bottom of the gangway. They shouted all the while, sounding like a flock of angry birds. In the distance, a steam tug, puffing black dots of smoke and towing barges, came slowly towards them. The ship's crew swarmed around the deck, derricks were topped and hatches opened, ready to work cargo, the clank of winches and hiss of steam adding to the noise.

After an hour, the officials left, with the canvas bags now bulging, and returned to their boat. At that the locals came aboard, setting up stalls on the deck for their wares.

"Come along then," said Maloney. "And if I may be so bold, kindly leave the talking to me, I know the tricks of these scoundrels. Well, they will not fleece us today." They had changed into clothes more appropriate for a provincial town, Horis was wearing a woollen hat pulled down over his ears, in an attempt to alter his appearance, and ship's overalls, making him look quite different to the likeness on the news-sheet in Aserol. Grace wore breeches, with long leather boots and a tight jacket also of leather, whilst Maloney had reverted to his one-arm disguise.

The three made their way through this throng, and found a man lounging beside a sign advertising a water taxi service. Maloney negotiated with him for passage to the town, and they soon found themselves sitting in a small craft that bobbed alarmingly as it was sculled to shore. They passed through the gap in the breakwaters, and found themselves in a small harbour, filled with fishers and a few fine sailing craft. The boat stopped by a sloping road that entered the water, where the waves lapped softly, and they alighted, after paying the boatman.

Ventis was a small town, very unlike Aserol. There was little smoke in the air and Maloney, who seemed to know every place, explained that there was reluctance on the part of the town to have steam generators. In fact they shunned any sort of mechanical device, preferring equines for transport and motive power, although they did have methane gas lighting on the streets and in the houses.

Horis anxiously looked for evidence of the presence of Watchmen on the wharf, but there were none, and desiring to obtain a news-sheet, they ventured into the town. The boatman had advised that they should go to a tavern called the "Dun Cervine" when they wished to return.

Horis need not have worried, their dress fitted in with that of the locals, and so they were paid little attention, the local news-sheet had nothing about him, or his supposed crime, indeed most of the news seemed to concern bovines or porkers.

Ventis had no Drogan nets that Horis could see, nor were there any watchtowers come to that. Perhaps the beasts didn't venture here, although Horis doubted that.

"Do they not have Drogans here?" he asked Maloney, assuming him to know, he seemed to know just about everything else.

Maloney laughed. "Oh yes they do, but they see the beasts as a part of Bal's plan and so ignore them."

"And do they not get eaten?"

"That's the strange thing," he replied. "By each leaving the other be they live together in harmony most of the time."

"It's a good idea," said Grace wistfully, "let all be and live in harmony."

Horis agreed but unfortunately his experience in the city rather destroyed the idyll, there it was each for himself and damn the rest.

There was a market, with stalls selling fine looking fruits and vegetables, there was a butcher with a line of tethered beasts and a bloodied block and many others. They spied the ship's cook, in his greasy apron negotiating for stores. He waved cheerfully as they passed.

Maloney went into the speaker office, and made a call to his wife. "I told her I'm away for a while, with some old mates from the regiment," he told the others. "She will not worry now, and she knows I am safe." His face darkened. "They are saying that many were killed in the cave-in, and there are many sorrowing wives and sweethearts." He pointed at Horis. "The word around is that you tricked as many miners as you could into going below and set the explosion."

"But you know the truth," cried Horis in an anguished tone. "I'm so sorry for the loss of lives. Please tell me that you know the truth."

"That I do," said Maloney, "and I explained, but told my Shirl that it was a secret. She said that Mrs Grantham had told the news-sheet that only she escaped your clutches to tell the tale. There was quite a piece in the sheet, you were made to sound like the worst kind of demon. The lies in the news have made me even more determined to help you get to the bottom of this."

Horis's mood deepened, he could see no way out of his troubles, except for Maloney and Grace, no-one else would believe him. Even though the population was hardened to death from accident and war, it was still a hard price to pay.

Having exhausted their curiosity and feeling deflated by the terrible news from Aserol, they were returning to the tavern, when Horis was accosted by a beggar man dressed in dirty overalls and wearing a leather cap. Thinking a few coins would placate him Horis was about to reach into his pocket, when the man whispered, "You know me." Horis was about to deny it, when he recognised the other under the grime and dirty cap. "You're Grieve," he said, amazed. "What in Bal's name are you doing here?"

"I got out of there by the skin on my teeth," replied Grieve. "When we were setting up the lines to light the cave, as you instructed me, I saw men coming with blasting sticks. Obley was with them, but not of his choosing, I could tell. That old witch Grantham was in charge, she got everyone into the cave and they set up the blasting sticks outside. I hid in a side tunnel and cut across to the other shaft. I mingled with the miners there. They all know me and didn't let on a word."

Horis was amazed that of all the chances, they would find each other here. "You must come with us," he said. "We have a berth on a ship, and we are off to the capital to get an explanation."

But Grieve was having none of it. "Not me, I'm just trying to survive. When I got topside I hid round the back of the boiler sheds, and I saw the men and Grantham come out laughing, and then there was an explosion. I don't want to be found, I'm dead as far as they know and I'd rather keep it that way."

Grace spoke up, "You're a fine example of a man. Sir, do you not want justice for your kin, and your mates? Horis here is on the run as the cause of the deaths, but he's ready to go to Metropol City and fight to clear his name. How will your hiding out here help right this wrong?"

Grieve hung his head and Maloney spoke, "Grieve, you know me, and my family. I mean to get justice and help unravel this thing, now if you don't want to help that's fine, but once I have spread the word about you, you will never be able to go home."

Grieve had not seen Maloney, and his face was a picture, his tone changed immediately. "Well Mr Maloney, if you're here that alters things in our favour. I know this man was not with Grantham at the end of it all. Very well then, I'm coming with you." Horis noted how the sight of Maloney had changed his attitude. It had quickly changed from "I'm just trying to survive" to "things in our favour".

As they walked on, Maloney came up close to Horis and whispered in his ear, "He turns faster than a vulpine hunting rabbits; I will try and gauge his intentions, until then, trust him not."

Chapter 25

The *Swiftsure* lay off Ventis till late in the afternoon, and Horis fretted about the delay in getting to the city. Maloney and Grieve were in the cabin, no doubt talking over their meeting whilst Horis and Grace spent the time at the ship's side, gazing at the shore and making plans for a future together.

Finally, cargo work was completed and all the locals departed. The holds were shut and the derricks housed. Maloney and Grieve showed up together at dinner, and the atmosphere between them had changed.

While they were eating, Horis felt the beat of the engine as the *Swiftsure* hove up her anchor and got under way for the city.

"I'm sorry," said Grieve to the group. "I was in a panic after the events at the mine and I must admit I ran. I saw my mates trapped and was powerless to help them. I lost my nerve. But Mr Maloney has reminded me of my backbone, and I am ready to assist."

"And there is more, isn't there?" prompted Maloney. "More than the rocks have been hidden in the mine."

"Oh yes," replied Grieve. "Not only the rocks, but a strange liquid has been found in the lower levels, far below the cavern you saw. This substance is noxious and burns, it seeps from cracks in the strata and has curtailed operations by its presence."

All these things increased their feeling that events had a larger purpose. Nabbaro was absent from the meal, overseeing their departure, so did not add his thoughts to the conversation. The next morning Horis sought him out.

The Captain was standing on the platform at the side of the wheel-space, puffing on a large clay pipe of nicoweed.

"Good morn, Horis," he boomed, lodging the pipe in the corner of his mouth as he spoke. "I see you have attracted another to your cause." He sucked on the pipe as he waited for an answer. It gurgled and smoked and the weed inside set off an aroma that was quite pleasant. Although Horis had never tried it, he liked the smell it produced. There were those who said it was bad for your health yet many still puffed, apparently it was addictive. Horis could sense the relaxing nature of the habit, particularly as practised by Nabbaro.

"Indeed sir," replied Horis. "He was present for the deed which I stand accused of, and knows my innocence. He is afeared for his safety."

"Well," replied Hector, "he will be safe enough with you three I expect. What is his story?"

Horis told him of Grieve's escape and of the things he had said about the mine. Hector's pipe waggled as he puffed and his brow furrowed. "Hmm," he muttered at length, "a liquid that burns, you know I have oft thought that if coal could be made a liquid it would be easier to handle and combust. We would not need stokers on the ship for instance. Indeed, I fancy that there would be a tidy profit for a man who could control the supply of such a liquid coal." Horis had not even considered any use for the thing described by Grieve. He reflected that he was indeed an innocent in these matters.

They were due to arrive at the city late in the next day but they could hear and see the capital long before they reached it. A plume of thick black smoke from a hundred or more steam Locals drifted downwind, staining the sky black and leaving a sheen on the water where it fell. There were bright lights in the daylight too, from the furnaces of the steelworks and other factories, and strings of gas lanterns stretching up and down the hills, following the line of streets of identical houses, dwellings for the toiling masses.

Off to one side were the more genteel avenues where the wealthy lived, with large gardens and tree lined verges, many with personal steam-mobiles parked outside.

In the midst of this was the port, and it was full of ships of all descriptions, there were the once mighty sailing barks, now reduced to the coastal trades, forced out of the deep oceans by the steel steamers. There were Norlandic ships freshly returned from the Western Isles, and some vessels from the Southern Alliance and further than that, even from the far reaches of the oceans, the rich lands of the fabled Spicer's Guild.

The air was thick with the scents of foreign places and things, and the *Swiftsure* had to squeeze into a berth a long way from the centre of the city. By the time they were secure alongside, night had fallen and so Horis and his companions decided to rest and start their operations on the morrow.

The next day dawned bright but cold, with a brisk wind that sang in the ship's rigging, and blew the ever present smoke horizontally away from the chimneys. The spotter balloons bobbed overhead, their mooring ropes singing as they fought to ride the wind. Cargo work had started at six and by seven the four were ready to take their leave. Grace sought out her uncle for a goodbye. "Thank you." She hugged him, with a moist eye. "You have helped us greatly; I hope to see you again soon."

"Hush child," Hector replied. "We will be here until tomorrow evening if you have completed your business, or else we return in about three weeks, we always secure at this wharf."

To Maloney he said, "Good luck, sir, the military service's loss is Mr Strongman's gain. Remember what I told you, if you need help, any captain here knows me, and will pass a message or assist in my name."

Grieve was next, he shook Hector's hand and thanked him for his hospitality. "I scarce know you," he replied. "You should help this man to clear his name and then you can go back to your family." Grieve nodded, he had been silent in Nabbaro's company for the voyage from Ventis and Horis suspected it was embarrassment as much as anything else. In private, Grieve had regained the confidence that Horis had seen in the mine. The thought that he would never see his family again had been banished from his mind and with its passing had come determination to see the job done.

Hector turned to Horis, putting a broad hand on his shoulder. "And you, I see you with Grace and it gladdens my old heart, look out for each other and you will be fine."

Hector shook all their hands again and wished them luck; they departed to put their plans into action.

Chapter 26, Metropol City

On the voyage from Ventis, the four had discussed the events in Aserol and the best way to determine who was responsible for them. It had been decided that Grace would pose as a relative from one of the miners' families, offering information at the Ministry, and would try to obtain an interview with Terrance to this end.

"What if he won't see me?" asked Grace. "That would stop us in our tracks."

"I don't think that will be a problem," was Maloney's opinion. "He will want to find out what you know, and who shares the information with you."

"I shall pretend to be a relative of a miner," she said, "unable to get news of my family. It may get us some information."

"Or provoke a response," was Maloney's hopeful reply.

Grieve would then watch out for Grace as she left the building, to see if she was followed, and protect her if he must.

Meanwhile, Maloney planned to take Horis to lodge in safety with his old regiment, and then he would wait at the address given by Grace with some of his mates. The plan was to capture anyone who came to the bait and extract information from them. At the time it had seemed like a good plan, now they would see if it was a practical one.

Grace had heard tell of the Grosvenor apartments, near the great park of Brunswick in the city centre. They featured as the site of intrigue and adventure in many of the books and plays in popular culture and she thought it fitting that she should stay there. Accompanied by Grieve and using an assumed name, she was able to obtain a short lease on a fine suite. She paid with money which she had borrowed from her uncle. Following Maloney's instructions, she also purchased a distinctive gown for her meeting, to make sure that she was easy to follow.

Horis and Maloney journeyed to the barracks at Herbert's Fort, near the river crossing at Greenway, where he found some of his old colleagues. Horis was found a billet and settled down to wait in safety until his enemy's intentions were better known. Maloney said that he would have no trouble persuading several of his old messmates to help him; they were all bored with the inactivity of their current situation and jumped at the chance.

Horis met the man called Sapper, whom Maloney had referred to on the *Swiftsure*. A man of medium height and muscular build, he had a twinkle in his eye and became quite emotional when he saw Maloney.

"Well met, Maloney," he said, his voice choked with emotion. "It's good to see you again. And how is the arm?"

Maloney waved his false arm around. "All the better for seeing you," he laughed and the men laughed with him. Horis was quite jealous of their camaraderie, he had few real friendships and none forged in the harshness of battle like these men.

Maloney introduced Horis as a man who needed help in a personal matter and they asked for no other explanation. He was a friend of Maloney and that was sufficient for them. They clamoured to assist in the enterprise, before any details were known to them.

Selecting the number that he required to watch at the apartments was difficult for Maloney, as they were all willing to help. In the end he narrowed it down, with the promise that others could join in if needed. They were split into groups so as to listen at all times for anyone enquiring for Grace. The first group set off for the apartments, where they installed themselves in the lobby, drinking ale and playing cards within earshot of the desk. Maloney went with them and explained the situation to Grace and Grieve, it was arranged that Grace would contact the Ministry on the morrow. A fresh group would take over the watch in the morn. Satisfied that all was ready, Maloney returned to the barracks.

The next morning after a good fast-breaker, Grace called the

Ministry by speaker, and obtained an interview with Terrance for later that afternoon. Maloney had been right. As soon as she mentioned the mine, Terrance could not hide his eagerness to see her. Grace passed the details of the meeting to the soldiers in the lobby; when they changed over Maloney would learn of it.

Grace and Grieve took the steam tram to the Ministry. They sat apart and kept to themselves. She left Grieve in the park opposite, sitting on a bench reading the news-sheet. Grace felt comforted to know of his presence. She made herself known at the desk and was sent to wait in an ante-chamber, where she was served char.

After a very short wait, barely long enough to drink her char, she was ushered into the office of Mr Terrance, Horis's superior. He was dressed in the latest fashion, and as he rose to greet her, she caught the smell of expensive shaving balm. After greeting her, and seating her in the armchair opposite his desk, he returned to its twin and sat. Grace looked at his desk, which was clean and devoid of any paperwork, fitted only with a clockwork writer and a speaker handset. He did not appear to be overburdened with tasks.

"Now then, madam," he leant back in his chair and gazed at her. "You said you had urgent business regarding Waster Mine in Aserol; can you tell me more please."

"Of course," she replied. "My brother is a miner at the Waster, and I received a strange message from his wife about five days ago." Grace was giving her voice a hesitant air, playing the part of a concerned relative.

"Go on," said Terrance gently.

"Well, she said that they had found something remarkable at the mine, and now I hear that there has been an accident. I cannot help but wonder if my brother is alright, I cannot contact his wife, they say that the speakers are not working and I am worried for him."

Terrance kept his face emotionless. "There is a fault with the speakers to Aserol, I believe, but it is not because of any mine accident. There are brigands abroad in the countryside and they love to disrupt civilisation. I daresay they have stolen the copper wires." His voice became sad and doom laden. "However, it is true that there has been an incident at the mine. A terrorist, acting on some crusade has exploded a charge in one of the shafts. Many miners have been trapped underground, and we are trying to reach them. This terrorist has escaped and we hunt him still. That is the truth of it."

He sounded sincere, and Grace was tempted to shout, "It's a lie, you are hiding something, the man I love is innocent" but she kept up her act, starting to shake and sob.

"Then my brother may be trapped in the mine, or worse." Grace burst into tears, and Terrance came to offer his handkerchief; it was of the finest silk and had the same perfumed aroma as he did, only more cloying.

"There my dear, we are working to rescue your brother and the rest. When the speakers are mended you will talk to his wife and hopefully find that all is well. Did the message say what had been found?" He asked the last innocently, but Grace heard the tone of his voice change.

"It made no sense to me, but I am only a simple woman, she said that a rock had been found that did not fall to the ground when cut from the earth."

Terrance laughed. "Rocks that do not fall, madam? Your sister is playing jests with you, what a notion. Take it from me, there are no such things, and as soon the situation with the speakers is resolved, you must tell your sister-in-law that you are not such a fool as to believe that."

"Please say that you will rescue my brother, sir." Grace looked at him and tried to gauge his mood. By his face, he was attracted to her but she could see evasion in his eye.

"We will do all we can." Terrance was still chuckling to himself. "Floating rocks indeed. Madam, if there is nothing else, I am a busy man, please excuse me." He rose and crossed to his desk, pressing a switch on the handset of his speaker. After a minute the door opened. "Mr Dandier will show you out, good day."

As he walked her to the front door, Dandier tried to comfort Grace, who was still sobbing. "There my dear," he said. "Pray tell me of your location in the city, that I might send you any news."

"Of course sir, and thank you." She sobbed a little more. "I am at the Grosvenor apartments, under the name of Nelson."

After Grace had left the building, Dandier returned to Terrance's office. He was on the speaker, and motioned Dandier to wait outside. He listened, nodding and saying "Yes" several times. Replacing the handset in its cradle he called Dandier into the room. "Have you found out where she is staying?" When Dandier nodded, Terrance continued, "Well done, she knows more than she should. Get your boys to visit her."

"Do you want her silenced, sir?"

"Yes, we had the situation nicely under control, or so I thought. Now she shows up and knows of the rocks, but before you kill her, try to find out how much else she knows, I don't believe her story."

Chapter 27

As Grace left the Ministry, she ignored Grieve and following the plan, walked to a coffee house near the tram stop, here she sat at a table in the street and ordered a cup. As she sipped she saw Grieve, he was watching the street in both directions, his gaze sweeping over her. He nodded and smiled and she felt reassured.

Meanwhile, Dandier had returned to his office. Through the window he could see Grace sat outside the coffee house. He used his private speaker to make two calls. The second was to his contact in the local criminal underworld. The man, called Eavis, was a shaven headed ex coal-heaver, heavily muscled and of low intelligence. He was however cunning, fiercely loyal to Dandier, or at least his money, and held sway over several other like-minded fellows. Eavis received his instructions and after making a call of his own, was on the scene in time to see Grace finish her coffee and rise.

She wandered off towards the tram halt, pausing every now and again to gaze in the shop windows and Eavis followed. In truth, there were things for sale here that Grace had never seen, and it was not difficult for her to dawdle and browse. She did not look to see if she was followed, trusting Grieve to keep her from harm. Eavis was twenty yards behind her and also pretending to window shop, although he looked less inconspicuous as most of the shops contained ladies clothing.

Grieve had spotted the arrival of Eavis, he stood out among the well-dressed pedestrians in his workman's clothes and dusty cap. Not only that, he was hardly the picture of subtlety in his attempts to spot Grace. Folding his news-sheet neatly, Grieve rose from his seat and joined the procession. Grace was walking slowly, ensuring that she was easy to follow. In the end they all stood at the tram halt together and caught the same tram back to the apartments.

As they crossed the busy street to the apartment's entrance, Grieve saw a steam-mobile arrive at the side of the building, out stepped three large men, similar in appearance to Eavis. There were shouted greetings and they entered the building as a group. Grace walked across the lobby, and disappeared into the lift whilst Eavis and his party went to the desk and demanded the whereabouts of Miss Nelson's rooms. Grieve had spotted Maloney at a table with several people, different from the ones that had been there when they had left. He joined them, sitting at a chair which one of the group pulled up from an adjoining table. A flagon was passed to him and he drank.

"Grieve," said Maloney, "these are Wilson, Daniel, Michal, Keen and Harris." He nodded to each and they all said good day. Maloney turned to the last. "And this is my mate Sapper, of whom I have spoken."

"Honoured to meet you all, gents," said Grieve. "I'm Grieve, a foreman from the mine and I hope, a friend of Horis's. Do you see the opposition?"

"Oh yes," replied one of the party who had been introduced as Sapper. "There's only four of them, this should be fun, eh lads." There was a murmur of agreement.

Eavis and his mates passed them, intent on the lift; they all squeezed into one car which ascended.

Maloney spoke, "We don't want killing, lads. Just get them out of the game quietly and we'll ask them a few questions, these are just the hired hands, we want the brains behind the operation." Maloney was clearly in charge, and all the others deferred to him easily, as he gave some more orders. "Wilson, follow us up the front stairs. Daniel, take one of the lifts, and Harris, you watch the back stairs. That's all the exits covered. Sapper, you and Keen come with me in the other lift."

"What's my part in this?" asked Grieve.

"You stay here with Michal," he was told. "And keep an eye for anyone who gets past us."

The group split up and headed for the lifts and stairs, there was nowhere for the four to escape so they did not hurry. They had the relaxed air of professionals who were in total control of the situation. The plan meant that there was no way for Eavis and his men to escape. Maloney and the two walked down the corridor towards Grace's door about fifteen yards behind the four thugs. The stairs and lift behind them were covered and as they rounded a corner in the passageway, they could see Harris come through the door from the back stairs and take up position. Thus far the four were unaware that they were already surrounded and at a disadvantage.

Eavis was rattling the door to Grace's suite, fixed on his purpose he failed to notice the soldiers approach until they were close.

"Can I help you, gentlemen?" This came from Maloney, spoken in a quiet voice to the four. They stopped their rattling and turned, Eavis spoke. "You'd best be off, mate. This ain't to do wiv you."

"Perhaps it is, my friends and I are concerned for the safety of the young lady in this apartment, there seem to be more than enough of you for a social visit."

Eavis looked at his partners and they grinned. "We might just have to teach you a lesson," one snarled, and they charged at the three soldiers.

They may have been large and strong, but they were obviously more used to intimidation and dealing with untrained fighters. The soldiers were all expert in unarmed combat, and seasoned by hand to hand fighting in the jungle wars of the Western Isles. The confines of the corridor meant nothing to them but hampered the thugs who were bunched together and easy to deal with. One turned and tried to run, only to face Harris who stood aside. Harris casually flicked out his arm as he passed; the thug grabbed his throat and fell to the floor. "One," he shouted. Meanwhile the others had surrounded the remainder, who were penned in and unable to manoeuvre. Wilson and Daniel were grappling with a thug apiece. Maloney approached Eavis who was shouting encouragement to his mates. "You're mine," said Maloney. At this Eavis grinned and brandished a wicked looking knife. If its appearance was intended to intimidate Maloney it had not worked.

"I hope you know how to use that," said Maloney, who advanced. Eavis lunged and the knife sunk into Maloney's arm and stuck there.

"Hah," exclaimed Eavis but Maloney never flinched.

"Is that your best?" he asked as a whirring was heard from the limb. "You had better not have damaged the clockworks." Behind him he heard Wilson and Daniel call "Two" and "Three" and smiled. "So it's just you now then," he said. Without his knife, which hung from the limb, Eavis resorted to a savage kick, aimed at Maloney's knee. He sidestepped neatly; Eavis was off balance from the lack of resistance to his kick and his head came into range. Maloney swung his good arm, it connected with a satisfying noise and Eavis went limp and fell.

The four were searched and relieved of their weapons, several knives and a cosh of wood and leather, weighted with metal balls at one end. Maloney knocked on the apartment door and it was opened by a soldier. Grace had been quite safe; he had been in the rooms with her all the time.

The soldiers bound and gagged the three thugs, and dragged them into one of the bedrooms. One of them produced a small canister, the contents of which were sprayed in the face of each of the three in turn. The effect was to render them unconscious, they were left in a huddle in the room and the door was jammed shut from the outside. Now they could not escape, should they be able to remove their bonds.

Sapper and Keen took hold of Maloney's false arm and held it still, Wilson gently eased the blade from the workings and Maloney flexed his elbow and fingers. "That seems to be working correctly," he said. "Every bit is doing as its bid."

Wilson turned the blade over in his hands; it was long and curved, with a barb on the end of the blade. "This belongs to a fellow called Eavis," he announced.

The blade's shape marks him out as a coal-heaver," said Keen, "the barb is used to split the bindings on coal sacks."

Maloney sat Eavis down in a chair and bound his arms and legs to it. Sapper had filled the chamber pot with water and now he splashed it in Eavis's face. Spluttering, he awoke and resumed his bluster. Breathing heavily he faced the soldiers. "You fools," he gasped. "When you find out who we are working for you'll change your tune."

Maloney surprised him with his reply, his voice calm. "Oh, you mean the man at the Ministry do you? Well he will be next on our list." At this Eavis's face fell.

"So, Mr Eavis," Maloney questioned him, holding the knife loosely, "you can tell me, on whose orders are you attacking this lady?"

"I'm saying nothing to you lot, and you won't make me," came the reply. "You might as well gas me now." He had seen the cylinder and guessed what had happened to his mates.

"Well I'm sure you are brave," replied Maloney, "but we have faced the hill tribes of the Western Isles, and you are not them. Sapper, have you your implements?"

"Here sir, would you like me to start?" The man opened a bag and rummaged around, metallic clanking could be heard and Eavis paled.

"Now then, this is your last chance to tell us who you are working for and what your instructions today were. Sapper is well versed in obtaining this information, but you may not enjoy his methods."

Eavis was sweating and he swallowed nervously. "If I tell you I'm a dead man."

"I think that goes without saying either way, but Sapper can keep you alive longer than you would wish, once he gets started."

"Very well, but you must protect me from him," he pleaded, not so brave now.

"I will make no promise until I have heard your story and considered its worth."

"There is a man at the Ministry, he gives me work and since I was sacked from the coal-heaving times have been hard."

"What sort of work?"

"He has me explain things to people, collect payments and tidy up."

Grace shuddered at the cold dispassionate way he said it, but recognised the bag that Sapper was rummaging in, it was from the *Swiftsure*, she remembered its clanking and wondered at its contents.

Maloney persisted, "And this man's name?"

Eavis looked terrified, he swallowed nervously before replying. "He is called Dandier, I believe he answers to someone called Terrance, but I have never seen him, come to that all my recent dealings have been by speaker. He pays me in cash, pushed through my posthole."

"I saw this Dandier today," gasped Grace. "He tried to put his arm round me and called me 'dear'." She shuddered.

Maloney's face wore a mask of pure disgust. He continued to Eavis, "And what were your instructions today?"

"I was to take the lady to him, after I had dealt with any who might be helping her." Eavis had neglected to mention that he was ordered to kill her. He reckoned that fact could be ignored for the moment. "She's been asking too many questions. That's all I know, I brought the lads to turn her rooms over, make it look like a robbery."

"You will call this Dandier now," demanded Maloney, "and get him here, so that I can have words."

Just then Sapper pulled a pair of rusty pliers from the bag, snapped them together and advanced on Eavis. His face wore a wild grin.

Eavis was in a panic; he shook his head and tried to free his arms. "He won't come, and that's the truth. I know nothing else."

"Are you sure?" enquired Maloney, in the same soft voice. "It appears that Sapper has found his pliers; he doesn't like to put them away unused."

Eavis had gone grey and was gasping for breath. It almost looked like his heart was giving out. "No sir, he don't get too close to the action. If he don't hear from me, he will come looking for me at my place."

"Very well, then tell us where it is and we will wait for him." After supplying the address, Eavis was gagged and gassed. Gathering all evidence of Grace's presence in the apartment the group left, collecting Grieve and Michal from the lobby. The rooms had been rented for a week, so the captives would not be found immediately. The gas would keep them quiet for a day or so. They split up. Grace and Grieve went in search of secure lodgings, accompanied by Michal whilst the rest returned to the barracks.

Chapter 28

Horis meanwhile had spent a very entertaining day at the barracks, he found that the soldiers there were a friendly bunch and once they knew of his relationship with Maloney, they warmed to him. Maloney was held in high regard by the troops, having been a leading figure in the regiment before his injury.

Horis had learnt that he had decided to resign, despite being offered a post as an instructor. Although he was unable to perform physical duties, his knowledge was extensive and valuable. The regiment did not want to let him leave, but as he had completed his fifteen years' agreed service, they were powerless to keep him.

Horis was careful to tell them little about the reasons for his stay, he merely said that Maloney was helping him and he needed a place to be secure whilst enquiries were ongoing. They accepted this, as if it were the kind of thing that was always happening. They played cards, talked and did what waiting soldiers everywhere did, they drank an incredible amount of char. Horis found that the time passed quickly.

Maloney and the others arrived at the barracks in the late evening. They updated Horis on the events of the day, and of the plans to snatch Dandier. Horis was surprised to hear of the depths that Terrance would go to keep the rocks a secret, he realised that although Maloney was capable Grace was in danger. He thought of Nabbaro's words and wanted to be with her, but they did not know of her whereabouts.

"That's an advantage, sir," Sapper explained. "If we don't know then the opposition cannot. Mr Grieve is with her, and Michal is a good man." This knowledge comforted Horis, he was not used to this world and realised that he was in the company of experts. He marvelled at Maloney's planning, even down to the bag of rusty tools he had borrowed. In answer to Sapper's request he described Dandier. "He is tall and thin, I like him not. He wears smart suiting with a regimental necktie." At that Maloney's ears pricked up.

"Which regiment?" he asked.

"The twenty-fifth," Horis answered.

"Ahh," said Maloney and the others grinned.

Horis was confused. "What do you mean 'Ahh'?" he enquired.

"Well Horis, let's just say that the twenty-fifth never saw much action."

Horis had heard Dandier's tales of the wars and been envious of the way it gained him respect, especially with pretty ladies. By the reactions here it appeared that Dandier may have been over-egging his deeds. Horis was not surprised as in all honesty he had never liked the man's arrogant attitude. But as a man who had only been a messenger for the Drogan Watch he had not felt able to question the words of an officer.

During their discussions, Horis had mentioned the name Terrance to several of the troops and whilst the name meant little to some of them, others recognised it as the name behind one of the largest manufacturing families in the country. As well as owning the Waster Mine, they controlled factories which made boilers, pipes and the like. Their equipment was used in factories and Locals, and they made parts for all manner of omnibuses and steam-mobiles. It would seem to Horis that they had an interest in keeping the system as it was, any new discovery, such as improved statics, might seriously harm their business by reducing the need for their products. Certainly if Hamman's vision came to pass, and cities were supplied with power from statics, the need for boilers on every street corner would be removed, cutting their influence and profits. Perhaps the rocks were a sideshow, an extra piece in a larger puzzle.

With nothing else to do but wait for developments, Horis slept an uneasy sleep in his bunk at the barracks. He knew not where Grace was but was comforted to know that she was not alone.

Chapter 29

The next day, after a late fast-breaker Horis was told to wait at the barracks for news. Maloney and Sapper had already left to find Dandier. They were armed with the description that Horis had given and had found his home address from the speaker directory. They first went to his home where they learnt from his man that he had left for the Ministry as usual. They then took the omnibus to the Ministry and settled down in the park, on the same bench that Grieve had used to keep watch. They assumed that Dandier was inside, as he had no reason to think anything was amiss it seemed reasonable.

"Perhaps we should check," suggested Sapper. "It would be a bit pointless waiting here all day if he was not here."

"Horis says he lunches at the same place every day," said Maloney, in a relaxed tone. "We will see if he does. Now, Sapper, there is a stand selling char over there." He waved his good hand across the park. "Get us both a brew." And he sat back with a contented look.

Sapper had to leave it at that.

Sure enough, Dandier left his office for luncheon and was spotted by the pair. They were about to move off and follow him when they saw him meet a tall, distinguished gentleman outside the eatery. An animated discussion ensued whilst they kept their distance. Sapper walked casually past in an effort to get the gist of their words but they stopped talking as he passed. The meeting ended with raised voices and Dandier, instead of eating, returned to the Ministry.

"Who was that with him?" Sapper asked Maloney. "And what was so important?"

"It must be to do with Horis," Maloney decided. "It was obviously unexpected. We will just have to see where he goes tonight then."

By the late afternoon, Dandier was becoming concerned that he had not had word from Eavis. Whilst not unheard of it was unusual, after all the man would want his payment. Dandier knew that in the past, Eavis had turned to drink after his more messy jobs, so perhaps that was the reason. He decided to look round Eavis's haunts on his way home from work and see if he could find him. He took the money that he had agreed to pay, intending to deliver it at his dwelling if he could not find him.

As he left the Ministry in the dusk, he was followed by Maloney and Sapper, who after a day on the bench were full of char and ready for some exercise. They expected Dandier to head straight for Eavis's dwelling and were surprised when he instead went to a rough looking ale house. Sapper stayed outside whilst Maloney went in. After half an hour or so Maloney came out, his breath smelt of ale and his clothes of nicoweed. He licked his lips and smiled. "A lovely drop in there, Sapper," he said.

"May I go in and try some then?" Sapper asked but Maloney stopped him.

"Our boy's on his way out," he said. "He asked around for Eavis and had to buy ale in exchange for the information that no-one has seen him."

Sapper looked peeved. "Of course not, we know where he is."

Just then Dandier came out of the building and passed close by them, his face bore a worried expression and he hurried down the gas lit road without a glance at the two comrades talking.

"He must be going home now, then," said Maloney, but instead he entered another ale house, this one near a Local, full of off duty coal-heavers. Wild singing could be heard through the open windows.

"I'll go," volunteered Sapper and before Maloney could say a word it seemed that Sapper was inside. Maloney loitered by the window and could see him with a tankard in his hand, near to Dandier in the press. Maloney smiled. Poor old Sapper, he thought, he does get excited, he could do with relaxing a little.

Sapper finished his tankard and debated another. He could

hear Dandier quizzing the barkeep; he seemed to be getting no information. Dandier had a glass of Malt, the ordering of which had raised eyebrows among the patrons, clearly he was out of place in the establishment. As Sapper watched, Dandier was approached by a brutish looking man, Eavis's twin in build.

"You the law?" he asked in a thick, beer stained accent. He grasped Dandier's lapels and pulled him close. "Asking questions, why d'yer wants ter know 'bout Eavis? Keep yer nose out." Suddenly all the noise stopped and every head turned as if on strings towards the pair.

Dandier tried to pull away but the man's grip was firm. "Of course not, now unhand me, sir," he said in a cultured drawl. This only raised laughter from the ruffian. "Ohhh, unhand me, sir," his assailant mimicked. "Well, Mr Questioner, seeing as you're not the law, perhaps you can make me."

The atmosphere in the room was charged, everyone waiting to see what the cultured fool would do and Sapper feared that Dandier might be harmed. If he were beaten and disabled or worse, then he would not be of use to their plans. Looking out of the window he spied Maloney, who had noticed the lack of noise and was taking an interest. He jerked his head towards Dandier, Maloney nodded.

Sapper approached the man. "Alright mate," he said, adopting the rough tones of the coal-heaver, his shoulders slumped and he fitted the part.

"Who're you then, and what's your business. He your fancy man?" The man made an obscene gesture, releasing his hold of Dandier, who scuttled behind Sapper.

"Now then," said Sapper, "he was just havin' a drink and lookin' for a mate, no need for rough stuff." There was a growl from the room, as if Sapper had poked a wasps' nest. Clearly the bully was among friends, Sapper was an outsider, surrounded by adversaries.

"Seems to me," replied the man, "you're one and we're several." He walked towards Sapper confidently.

"There are more of us," said Maloney, who had come through the press and now stood by Sapper's side. "We are regimental colleagues of this man; we spied his necktie. He has fought for the likes of you, show him some respect."

The crowd murmured, like surf on shingle. Maloney was relying on the patriotic fervour of the common man, spurred on by propaganda of the heroism of the army. There was a pause as the two factions faced each other.

Dandier was confused and scared. This was the second of Eavis's favourite ale houses he had asked in. There had been no sign of him or his cronies in either of them. Worse than that, he had been forced to buy drinks in exchange for information, and because in his nervousness he had drunk quickly, he was now more than a little drunk. The suppressed violence in the coal-heaver had rattled him. And now he had been rescued by two men of lower class who had spotted his necktie. Dandier was aware that his army stories, although impressive to ladies and juniors, would not stand up to scrutiny by real fighting men. Whilst the attention of the crowd was focused on Maloney and Sapper he took the opportunity to creep out of the ale house. He would go to Eavis's home, he decided and set off.

Maloney and Sapper faced the mob. "He's gone," yelled a voice from the back of the crowd as Dandier's absence was finally noticed. "Where's your mate now then?" asked the ringleader and there was pandemonium in the room as the coal-heavers charged at Maloney and Sapper.

It was nearly midnight by the time Dandier got to Eavis's small house, he had sobered up a little on the walk and had taken longer than he expected. In his haste to get away he had taken a wrong turning and then lost his way. Surely, he thought, the man must be here. The entrance was down a dark alley, away from the gas lighting. There were no lights on in the rooms as he walked up the rubbish-strewn path to the man's front door.

As he knocked, he felt a sharp object pressed into his back by a man who had closed on him silently. A voice hissed in his ear, "Quietly now, sir. The one you're after is not home, perhaps you would come with me." Dandier was not thinking clearly, the drink and his agitation had slowed him but he thought he recognised the voice.

"Weren't you the man from the ale house?" he croaked.

"That's right, sir," replied Sapper. "I couldn't see an old mess-mate in danger, eh. Funny thing though, when the fight started you were nowhere to be seen."

Dandier was stuck, he couldn't admit to running away but neither could he trade army tales. He panicked and turned to run again, but in the confined space only succeeded in running straight onto the knife. The wickedly sharp blade did its work and Dandier cried out as he fell to the ground. Maloney came forward out of the shadows. "What happened?" he asked.

"Sorry, sir," said Sapper. "He ran onto it before I could move."

There was the sound of a window opening somewhere in the darkness. "Who's there?" a woman's voice called. "I'm rousing the Watch."

Bending over the prone body, Maloney felt for a pulse, finding none he straightened. "Well, that's not helped our cause, but no matter, we will have to go after Terrance instead. Leave the body here for the Watchmen, and the knife. They will connect it to our man, and give him some questions to answer."

"Looks like our efforts in the ale house were in vain then," said Sapper, rubbing his knuckles.

"I do enjoy a good fight though, even with one arm I seem to manage quite well." Maloney laughed as they hurried away.

At around the same time in the apartment, the four thugs had all awoken and were trying to undo their bonds, with little success. However, their efforts had made a commotion, which resulted in the floor manager entering the room. Finding no trace of his tenant, only four known criminals tied and gagged, he called the Watchmen immediately. The four were taken into custody, watched by Maloney's man Daniel, who was loitering in the lobby.

Chapter 30

Next morning, Terrance arrived for work at the Ministry as usual, and after a cup of char, settled down to read the news-sheet. With his feet up on the desk, he unfolded the sheet and smoothed it out. The next second he almost fell off his chair, and bile rose into his mouth as he saw the banner headline: "Ministry worker found slain". There was an image of Dandier's corpse. Feeling sick he read on:

"The body of Mr Rydel Dandier, a Ministry of Coal employee was found outside the home of a known criminal in central Metropol City last night. The fellow had been stabbed, and left in the alley to bleed to death. The murder weapon has been linked to four men who have been detained by the city Watchmen".

Terrance knew that Dandier had contacts in the underworld, he was not so stupid not to realise that that was how he was able to fix things on his behalf. However, to see that table turned on him in this way brought the results of his actions closer to him than he would have liked. But in a way he felt relief, for the trail stopped with Dandier.

Lucy, his secretary, opened his office door. "Sorry to disturb you, sir, but the Watchmen are here, a Captain Wandell, may I show him in?"

"Yes please, Lucy, and bring some fresh char, there's a love." He realised that she could not have seen the news of Dandier's demise. In a way that was good; she was the reason for him getting home late to his wife on a Wednesday and he had found her to get emotional over quite trivial things. He could not imagine her reaction to this news.

Wandell was a large, capable looking gentleman, imposing in

full black uniform, his leather gleaming. He strode in, looking disdainfully at the surroundings, and sat without speaking, in the chair opposite Terrance. He removed his cap, which he set on the desk, together with his staff of office. Looking straight at Terrance, he spoke:

"Mr Terrance, I believe that Mr Dandier was your assistant."

Terrance tried to answer but his voice did not seem to be working. He had a fear of the Watch, instilled in him from childhood. Although he knew the truth of things, that the Watch were not all-powerful and as fearsome as children and the lower orders thought, his reaction was instinctive.

He squeaked, "Yes, I'm sorry, Captain. I have just seen the news-sheet and I am lost for words. He was indeed my assistant, but he also worked for several of the second ministers in this building, he was our communal junior."

"I see, and did you give him any orders yesterday, sir, that might have sent him to the address of a known criminal." The man was being polite, thought Terrance, I wonder if he is on Cavendish's payroll. He decided not to try and find out, just in case Wandell was one of the honest ones.

Gaining in confidence, Terrance gave him a plausible story. "I gave him some work concerning the anarchist's bombing at Waster Mine and he told me he would be following up his enquiries. It may be that they led him to this part of town. Tell me, was he robbed?"

"No sir, his timepiece and a large amount of money was on his person when we arrived at the scene. You say that he was engaged on work concerning the Waster incident?"

"Yes." Terrance had decided to implicate Grace. "We had a visit from a lady, with some fanciful tale about the mine, and Mr Dandier was checking her story."

"And her name?" at this Terrance realised that he did not know it. He made time to think by opening a drawer in his desk as if looking for papers, and then by calling Lucy. "What was that lady's name yesterday afternoon, Lucy?" he asked, but she did not know.

Wandell was clearly suspicious of the situation, but had little to go on. "When you find it, let me know, and if you remember anything else that may be helpful, here is my card." He passed it to Terrance.

"By coincidence, whilst investigating another matter, we have suspects in custody, we will interrogate them presently." Rising, he shook Terrance's hand. Terrance hoped that he thought it was damp and shaking because of the news concerning Dandier.

Chapter 31

At the barracks, Maloney and his men had slept soundly. Horis had been shocked to hear of the turn of events on Maloney's return, although he had never trusted Dandier, and had tried to avoid him where possible. He was sorry for his death but to have it confirmed that he was involved in a plot to harm Grace had kept him from slumber.

Over porker and eggs, they discussed the plans for the day. They were waiting to hear from Michal, who had gone with Grace and Grieve to find a new hiding place, and until then, they could not form a strategy.

On the advice of Maloney, he had not told any of the soldiers about the discovery at the mine. As far as they were concerned, they were merely repaying a favour.

"So what will we do?" asked Horis. "Dandier was the link, Terrance can now deny all knowledge of the attack and of the men at the apartments."

"We will just have to go up the chain, instead of down," replied Maloney. "And see where that leads us. I think another visit to Terrance is in order, this time he cannot set his thugs on us, he will have to go to his master, whoever that may be, for instructions."

"Of course," said Sapper, who had been listening carefully, "it may be that this Terrance is the master, in which case he will show us his hand, so to speak."

"You're right, Sapper, and in so doing he will sow the seeds of his undoing. But I think it will be better if Grace does not approach him this time, I have better plans."

Horis was intrigued, Maloney was becoming a revelation. "What might they be then?" he queried.

"Let's send Grieve in, if he says he was a surviving foreman, it must provoke a reaction." There were nodding heads around the room.

"Perhaps if some of us took Grieve in, and say we found him wandering the streets, it will be enough to get a response," said Sapper, "and our numbers would keep him safer than if he went in alone."

"That is very true," Horis agreed. "We have seen the lengths they will go to, we need to keep Grieve safe. He is the only one who can vouch for my innocence."

Maloney nodded. "Terrance will certainly want to meet him, and he can give enough details to prove his story. Perhaps he can say he knows where to find you, Horis. After all, if the Watchmen hear Grieve's story, they will not consider you the guilty party. And Terrance cannot own the Watchmen; we all know they are incorruptible."

Horis was pensive. "But I still want to know the reason for it all, it cannot be just the rocks, there has to be more to all this."

"What rocks are these?" asked Sapper.

"I wasn't intending to show you," said Horis, "but you have done so much to help me, that it's only right that you should see what all this is about. And I'm sure that you can all be trusted." With a flourish he produced the rock from his pocket, bobbing on its string.

"Well I never," said Sapper. "Wars have been started for less than this. You take my word for it. If knowledge of these becomes public, and the Ministry controls the supply, there's nothing in it for this Terrance, all the power and money go to the Ministry. But if he alone knows where they are, and gives them out grudgingly, then the money and influence he could wield would be enough for him to do, well, just about anything."

The rest of the group crowded round, eager to examine the rock, still encased in Horis's kerchief and tied to his buttonhole with a bootlace. They were all talking at once, and Horis made out snatches of the ideas they came up with: Flying machines, statics generators, fighting machines and elevators were just some of them. For what Horis had assumed to be a bunch of soldiers, they were remarkably educated men, and the more he thought about it, the more he could see that the discovery had a potential great enough to kill for.

Chapter 32

Eavis and his men were shut in a cell at the Watch station, after their arrest at Grace's apartment. True to form, they had said nothing, as in the past Dandier had always come to bail them out. They waited confidently, every now and then one would shout for char, but their calls were ignored by the Custodyman. The gas had left little effect on them, merely given them a deep sleep, and they were not aware that an extra day had passed since the fight in Grace's apartment.

When they had been there a while, they began to get worried. Eavis, although not particularly clever, was smart enough to realise that he was up against a more organised adversary this time, and the fact that he had given Dandier's name away was a worry to him. At least his three comrades were not aware of his confession.

But they were all aware of the trouble they were in, all of them had had dealings with the Watch and, dependant on the magistrate, could be in line for prison or worse this time. And they were out of pocket; Eavis had promised them payment for the job at the apartment and they argued long and hard. Eavis insisted that he had not received any money yet and the others, who did not believe him, demanded assurances. Shouts and then blows were exchanged; the Custodymen ignored the noise and let them get on with it.

Later, the cell door opened, and a Watchman entered, along with a man that Eavis did not recognise. "On your feet, you rabble!" shouted the Watchman. "This good gentleman has arranged your release, so look lively and off you go."

The group emerged onto the street. "Thank you, sir," Eavis whined like a grateful dog. "Are you Dandier's assistant?"

The man laughed. "Only in a manner of speaking," he replied. "You will not know but Dandier is dead, slain outside your dwelling by a knife that bears your name. Fortunately I have managed to smooth this over with the Watch, and that alone puts you in my debt."

Eavis was shocked and his face fell, visions of the money he had lost flashed before his eyes, and no doubt it flashed before those of his three mates as well. Delicately he broached the subject. "Will you be settling Mr Dandier's accounts then, Bal rest him?"

The other's voice was cold and harsh. "I just saved you from the noose; I would think that squares things nicely." Glumly Eavis nodded.

"But," continued the stranger, "if you want to make up for your previous failures, you could do worse than to go to the Ministry and seek out a Mr Terrance."

And with a few whispered words the stranger departed.

Chapter 33

Terrance was sat at his desk, since Captain Wandell's departure he was finding it hard to accept the turn of events. Dandier had been his right-hand, and had always known of a way to solve problems, and Terrance had been smart enough not to enquire too deeply into his methods. He realised that his strategy was unfolding, and was contemplating his next move when his speaker rang, its shrill note disturbing his thoughts. He picked up the handset and Lucy's voice, cheerful as ever told him that he had a personal call. The caller had not identified himself but was insistent. "Thank you, Lucy," replied Terrance, "but I am not receiving calls from anonymous persons, pray tell them to call back when they are ready to identify themselves."

Terrance got up and left his office by the back door, away from Lucy's gaze. He knew that the call meant that Cavendish wanted to see him, and he knew where. He did not want to see Cavendish, but with a sinking feeling knew that he must. He was desperately trying to think of a way out as he walked to the park, sitting at the same bench from where Grieve had kept watch.

A shadow fell across his face and he looked up as Cavendish sat beside him. About twenty yards away, he could see two large gentlemen eyeing him, as a shark looks at dinner; his stomach lurched. Cavendish was abrupt. "So you have failed again?" he said. "And now my cousin is dead."

Terrance could not have felt worse if the blade had entered his heart instead of Dandier's. He felt bad enough but this extra news made matters worse. He started to mumble but Cavendish cut him off.

"Don't give me any of your excuses," Cavendish continued. "I thought that you could be trusted to sort this out, yet it seems that I must do everything. I have just managed to bail your thugs out. Do you even know where Strongman and his rabble are?"

"I have had no time to sort anything out, I have been questioned by the Watch," began Terrance but Cavendish cut him off again.

"Fool, Wandell will do as he is bid, I told you, no excuses, this will be your last chance to make amends. My spies, who seem to be a lot better than yours, have found the hiding place of the woman who saw you previously. She will be there with only a single minder all day. Her companion, who incidentally is a foreman from the Waster," he paused, "and who appears to have escaped the mine and who you neglected to mention, will in all likelihood be coming here to see you. This gives you an opportunity to arrange her capture."

Terrance was about to ask how Cavendish had information about the escaped foreman, he knew nothing of it, but thought better of it and merely nodded agreement. "I will kill her myself if I have to," he announced. Beside him Cavendish shook his head, in a way that suggested he was in the company of idiots.

"No you won't, I had to stop Eavis once, after my cousin told me of your initial plan." Terrance looked shocked. "How…" he started.

"What!" exclaimed Cavendish. "Did you not think he would tell me? You will capture the woman and send the man back with a message."

"I did not know he was your cousin," gasped a shocked Terrance, he realised then how Cavendish seemed to know so much.

"I have been following this as well as you have," Cavendish continued. "For a time there was the woman, your thug, the foreman and my man all in a line and all following each other. This junior of yours, he has found some useful allies, men of ability and I hate to admit it, but they are doing a good job. However, they think that they are at a dead end now, with Rydel's death. My man followed the woman to a house by the docks. If you can get the woman, and send the man back, it will draw Strongman out in a rescue attempt. You can round up the whole crew and get them to Northcastle.

We can then deal with them at our leisure." Cavendish rose and handed Terrance a piece of parchment. "Here is the address, don't fail again, or I will lose interest in your continued existence and take all your work so far for my own."

Visibly shaken by the threat, and the realisation that he was in very deep water, Terrance returned to his office. Without Dandier he had no idea where to start, who to call or how to arrange a kidnap. In desperation he called Lucy into his office. She would have to be told.

"Now my dear," he played the role of a bearer of bad news, "Mr Dandier has been cruelly murdered." She started to cry and looked as if she would faint; Terrance put his arms around her and held her tight as she sobbed. He gave her a few moments, then asked her if she could bring him Dandier's speaker index book. Nodding through her sobs, she went in search of the document.

Moments later she returned, with Eavis and his henchmen in tow. Eavis touched his forelock and waited, whilst she was dismissed. After she had left, Eavis spoke.

"Good day, sir. I am Eavis, me and my boys here used to work for Dandier. I'm guessing that it was your orders that we carried out. Your friend got us free from the Watch and we've come here for our reward."

This was good news to Terrance, and he realised that fortune was smiling on him. "Of course," he replied, "but how about another little job first and double money after?"

Eavis grinned and his associates smirked. "I believe we have a deal."

"Right then, listen carefully."

Chapter 34

Later that day, Michal returned to the barracks, he reported that Grace and Grieve were safe in a house near to the docks, in a part of the city where few ventured. "My kin are from there," explained Michal, "and my aunt Vi was more than willing to lend her house for a few days. She's gone off visiting till she gets a message that we've done."

"Good work, lad," said Maloney, "that solves one problem."

Horis of course, wished to hear news of Grace, they had only been parted for a short while, but to Horis, it felt like an eternity. Michal told him that she was in good spirits, and longing for all this to end, that they may be reunited. "Not long now," was Maloney's reassuring opinion. "We can get Terrance on his own tomorrow, after some of Sapper's persuasion he will solve our problems. Then we can go to the Watch, or at least the honest ones, and get all this out in the open."

He turned to Michal. "Now then, you must return to the house, tell Grieve that he should come to the Ministry tomorrow. Someone will come and take over the watch on Grace before he goes. We will meet him in the park and go to see Terrance in numbers." Michal nodded several times, and then repeated his orders back to Maloney. He left to cries of "Good Luck" from the other soldiers. "Send her my love," was Horis's cry as he departed, Michal waved his arm in acknowledgement.

"That's that then," said Maloney, with a relieved air. "We are set, Horis. Tomorrow will be a busy day, best get a good meal inside us and have an early night."

It was a long journey back from the barracks to the house and darkness had fallen as Michal approached. The curtains were drawn, and the flickering gas light from within cast shadows as Grace and Grieve moved in the room.

Michal knocked, bent to the posthole and whispered, "Aserol." The door was opened by Grieve, in his other hand he held a wooden stave, he relaxed when he saw Michal.

"Come in," he urged, shutting and bolting the door.

Michal's aunt Vi had a well-stocked larder, and Grace had made them a meal of braised ovine with fresh vegetables and gravy. The three ate it, talking of the events of the day and of the plans for the morrow. Grace was heartened to hear of Horis's concerns and expression of love.

Michal pushed his chair back. "I'm just going out for a turn around the area, make sure we are all alone," he announced. Grieve nodded, he was sat in a comfortable chair, the meal had made him sleepy and he dozed. Grace retired to the bedroom and fell asleep.

Michal moved cautiously round the streets, keeping to the shadows. His senses were tuned to the small sounds of the night, dogs barking and muted music from an ale house, when he heard a moan of pain from the side of the road. There was a body lying in the gutter, and he stepped closer to see if it was a lady in distress.

He bent towards the body, his attention was distracted from the man who came up behind him, pinning his arms to his sides. As he struggled, the body rose and was revealed in the moonlight to be a man. He clamped a hand over Michal's mouth and between the two of them they dragged the struggling soldier to an alley.

Chapter 35

Next morn, Grace awoke as the sun shone through the thin curtains. Rising, she pulled them back and looked out.

The day had dawned warm and clear for so late in the summer, and already the cranes in the docks were swinging and whistling, there was a stream of people passing the door as more workers set off to their toil. The road was filled with steam-lorries and equine carts, moving goods of all descriptions to and fro.

She left the room, used the bathroom to wash and dress herself, and then descended the stairs, finding Grieve asleep in the chair, where she had left him. She went to the kitchen and stirred the fire into life, then put the kettle on the gas hob for char. The noise had awoken Grieve, who came to the doorway, bleary eyed and rubbing his stiff legs.

"Morn," he mumbled, "is there char on the boil?"

"Morn to you," Grace replied cheerily, setting the cups and pot ready. Despite the less than perfect surroundings, and the lumpy mattress, Grace had slept well, at least better than Grieve.

"Where is Michal?" she asked, his absence was obvious, as these were the only rooms in the dwelling.

"I know not," replied Grieve. "I was sound asleep; he must be out and about somewhere."

They were drinking their char and deciding what to eat before starting for the Ministry, when there was a knock on the door.

"Stay there, I'll get it," advised Grieve, thinking that it would be Michal, or his relief; he was relaxed as he moved to the door. Remembering the code word, he called, "Who is there?" expecting to hear the reply "Aserol". When the knock was repeated, he put his finger to his lips, and motioned Grace into the corner of the room.

Carefully keeping in the shelter of the door, he opened it.

A large man burst in, he must have been observing them through the window as he made straight for Grace, who instead of cowering in the corner, uttered a piercing scream and lashed out with the nearest thing to hand, a table fork. The man was unprepared for her attack and yelled with pain as the tines of the fork stuck in his face and blood splashed.

Grieve dropped his shoulder and charged at the man, knocking him into the wall. He slumped to the ground and as Grieve moved towards him there was a sound from the doorway, not unlike that of a soda bottle opening. Grieve's torso jolted and he gazed down in surprise at the red stain spreading on his shirt-front. The weight of his body became too much for his legs and he fell to the ground, the puzzled expression fixed on his face as his life ebbed away.

The first man had regained his feet and advanced again towards Grace, the fork swinging from his cheek and blood dripping from the end of his chin as he pulled a gas pistol from his pocket. He pointed it at her as Eavis entered the room.

"Stop!" Eavis shouted. "We need her alive." A faint wisp of gas drifted from the barrel of his pistol as he also pointed it at Grace.

"But she's hurt me bad," protested the first. Reversing the pistol, he swung it into Grace's face; the butt cut her cheek and sent her sprawling. "Bitch," he spat at her, and made to hit her again.

"Fool," said Eavis. "We need her alive." He shot him in the knee, the pistol again making the quiet "phut". The projectile shattered the man's kneecap and he let out a high-pitched squeal. Clutching his ruined knee, blood welling between his fingers he hopped around the room, finally collapsing in the corner, where he continued to wail as he thrashed in pain.

"I'm under orders not to kill you," said Eavis to Grace. "But then I haven't killed him, have I?" The implication was clear, and meekly she raised her hands, but her gaze never left Grieve's motionless face as Eavis bound her wrists and marched her into the waiting steam-mobile. His two henchmen opened the luggage hold and bundled her in, after tying and gagging her.

Eavis returned to the room and stooped to help his crippled companion up. "Come on, Bert," he puffed, for the man was heavy.

"You getting me to a quack?" gasped Bert through gritted teeth, his pain had been dulled by shock and he was pale from loss of blood.

"You're too heavy to get you to a doctor," said Eavis. "I'm just making it look more like an unfortunate event, we was told to keep both alive, so as to have one to tell the tale." He dumped Bert's body by Grieve and took the pistol from Bert, placing it in Grieve's dead hand.

"What are you doing then, mate?" asked Bert.

"Looks like you shot each other don't it?" was Eavis's reply, and using his pistol, he shot Bert between the eyes. He then put the still smoking weapon into Bert's grip, setting the scene.

Leaving the room, he shut the door and walked to the steam-mobile without a care. Climbing into the front seat, he announced to the two men within, in a voice devoid of emotion, "Bert's not coming."

They could see the blood on his shirtfront and knew of his reputation. Catching his meaning, one shrugged and turned to the other. "Oh well, poor old Bert, more for us then." But they both resolved to keep their eye on Eavis, in case he had designs on their share too.

Chapter 36

Horis and Maloney, who were waiting in the park under a large oaken tree, were concerned at Grieve's non-arrival. Scattered around the area were several of the soldiers from the barracks, whom Horis now thought of as friends and fellow conspirators. They were all trying to ignore each other and remain alert to any trouble. They had a mobile situated in the street, ready if needed.

They were deciding how to proceed, when Horis spied Terrance leaving his building and walking towards them. Maloney sensed Horis stiffen and asked the reason.

"That's Terrance, the one who would have me dead," he said and shrank behind the tree.

"Hey there," said Maloney, as he approached. "Are you Mr Terrance?"

"I am," replied Terrance. "And am I to assume that you are connected with my junior and his ridiculous actions?" He stepped to the side and spied Horis. "Come, Horis," his tone soft and persuasive. "We can sort this out, come with me."

Horis was almost deceived by his words, but Maloney held him by the arm as he started to comply. "Don't be silly, Horis. We have what he needs, we should not give our advantage away." He waved his arm, and from around the park, the soldiers started to converge on them.

"Call off your rabble, sir," Terrance said. "For I have the lady now, so it is I who you should listen to."

"That is not possible," said Horis and Maloney, almost in unison. Terrance merely smiled.

"You mean I should not know of the rat-infested room where she was hiding, in the docklands. Where was it? Cookson's Row?"

"How?" said Horis and Terrance smiled again. "Do you really think you are as clever as I? My associates and I know your moves, but fear not, the lady is safe, and will not be harmed."

"No doubt there is some condition?" said Maloney, playing for time, his mind desperately trying to work an advantage.

"Oh yes, you are both to come with me, and she will be released. I must admit the presence of so many others complicates things, but without you they would not be listened to."

"I'm sorry," said Maloney. "But that will not be possible." He indicated the soldiers. "And I think that you would not be able to persuade us."

It was now Terrance's turn to make a signal. He lifted his hat and waved it. A steam-mobile came round the corner and pulled up beside them. Terrance opened the door and Eavis jumped out. The other two thugs appeared from the back seat.

Eavis glowered at Maloney, no doubt remembering the beating and threats he had received last time they had met. "Ah," he said. "You again, we have business to settle."

"Not now," Terrance spoke. "You can settle accounts later, I promise. Show them the woman."

Eavis went to the rear of the vehicle and opened the luggage hold. He lifted up a trussed figure, it was Grace, her eyes were blazing and she shed a tear when she saw Horis. Her fingers waggled in greeting and her head bobbed as she tried to express herself. A dirty rag was tied around her mouth and all she could do was grunt. Horis could see the cut on the side of her face and the blood on her neck glistened.

He moved towards her, but Maloney held him back. Eavis's two henchmen made a dash for Horis but Sapper and the other soldiers converged on them and held them. As they wrestled them to the ground, Eavis and Terrance jumped into the steam-mobile, doors slammed and the vehicle sped away. Horis and Maloney were powerless to stop them.

Horis was devastated, he stood by the road and wept, his shoulders shaking. Maloney, being a practical man, could think of nothing to say or do to comfort him. So he just stood in embarrassed silence.

Maloney made a decision. "Well then," he said. "We will just have to get her back. Fear not, Horis, me and the boys will sort this out."

Horis was flattered, but confused; his despair had mellowed into a lump in the base of his stomach. "And how can you do that, surely you have army duties to detain you?"

Sapper grinned. "You have it wrong, Horis. We are all at the end of our service; we have been using the barracks as a base until we have our futures sorted out. The army lets us stay until we have a place to go."

"And now we have a purpose, thanks to you," added Daniel. "And a bit of an adventure as well. We just need to find where they are bound."

"Let's ask these two then," suggested Horis. "Maybe they can say."

"First we must get them to a place where their screams will not be noticed," said Sapper. The two ruffians quailed.

Summoning their steam-mobile, they tied the arms of the two ruffians and threw them into the back. Horis, Maloney, Sapper and the driver, who was Daniel, set off for the rooms at Cookson's Row. The rest returned to the barracks.

On arrival at the house, they found the two dead men, and Keen, who had arrived to take over from Michal. "It looks like Grieve and this fellow shot each other," said Keen, but Maloney was not convinced.

"Grieve had no gas pistol," he said. "Both of these are Ministry issue. Look." He pulled a bayonet from Grieve's belt. "This was his only weapon and it has not been drawn. No, I think this was made to look like a robbery, in case the Watch arrived."

"No-one hereabouts will call the Watch," said Keen, "and they will not venture into these parts on a whim. And even if they did, there's no way of telling who was killed by which pistol."

Meanwhile, Sapper had introduced the two men to his collection of implements and was attempting to gain intelligence. They were both petrified, but more so of the wrath of Eavis than of Sapper and his rusty pliers.

"We don't know nuffin'," they both wailed. "We reckon that Eavis shot Bert and your man, he's crazy, and we're safer with you. All we know is that we was supposed to get the girl. The Ministry man wanted Horis Strongman as well, and the rest of you were expendable. Them was his words. He never said more."

"And where is our man Michal?" was the next question.

"He is down an alley, Bert slit his throat last night," they wailed in unison.

"Funny that," said Sapper, "how the conveniently dead can be blamed for all ills."

"It's truth," they repeated. "It was Bert."

"Are the walls thick here?" enquired Maloney. "For Grieve here was a friend of mine." His tone was so flat that all conversation in the room stopped. The two thugs looked at him, realisation dawning on them. "Sapper, give me those pliers."

But the two didn't know more, and eventually Sapper and Maloney gave up. The two were unconscious and blood stained the room. "We must clean up for Michal's aunt before she returns," said Maloney. "And dispose of these two somewhere."

"We can do that," said Daniel and Keen in unison. "If we dump them in the reeds past the port, the fishes will deal with the evidence."

Horis was shocked. "But they are still living," he protested. "Horis," said Maloney kindly, "these two would have killed you; they were at the hotel and are certainly responsible for much. No, the time for scruples is past. We are all hard men and these have killed our brothers. Now we understand you are not from our world but you're in it now. Let us do our work."

Horis could see the sense in his words; he must harden his heart to get Grace back safe.

Chapter 37

"Who's with us?" asked Maloney, of the assembled soldiers at evening meal that day, and was gratified, but not surprised, when they all indicated their willingness to help. Most had seen the rock, or had heard of it, and all knew the story of Grace's capture. Horis was more comfortable now in their company, he had come to trust them all.

"Well thank you, I'm humbled," said Horis. "In these matters I'm no expert, so I will leave it to Maloney to select as many of you as he feels fit our needs."

"But where will he go with her, do you think he will keep her in the city?" asked Daniel. This gave Horis a thought.

"I wonder," he mused. "Terrance must have left word of his whereabouts and plans at the Ministry, perhaps we can learn from there what he intends." He left the room for the speaker cubicle.

Lucy was eager to help Horis when he called by speaker. "Oh sir, it is good to hear from you, I was feared that you were in the cave-in, and then there was Mr Dandier's murder. It seemed to me as if Bal was displeased for some reason. I assume you would wish to speak to Mr Terrance?" Before Horis could reply, she continued. "He is not here. He has gone home to prepare for a trip to Northcastle, on Ministry business. Something urgent requires his presence. He will be departing on the morning Ryde. Shall I tell him of your whereabouts when he calls next?"

"There is no need, Lucy. I can call his house directly." Horis replaced the speaker with a smile and returned to where the others were sitting.

"She cannot stop talking that one. I didn't even have to ask her."

"Where are they bound?" asked Maloney.

"Northcastle," replied Horis. "The Government has a large facility there. I believe it is used for the testing and development of new technology. The Ministry has a factory there."

One of the soldiers broke in, "I've heard tell that there is a prison there also, for the worst undesirables and enemies of the state. They use them to labour as slaves on the things that go on."

"You seem to know about the place, Meek," said Maloney.

"Yessir," he replied. "I was there when they were building the place."

"How do we get in and out?"

"You don't," was the short reply. "There is a double fence with guard posts every mile or so. The gap between is patrolled by mobiles."

It sounded like a fortress to Horis and his heart sank, once Grace was inside surely he would never see her again.

"How about from the sea?" asked Sapper.

"I never saw but the word was that the navy looked after that end, how I can't say."

"Ah well," said Maloney, "it seems like we have a job on our hands then lads, but as we all know, there is always a way." Over the next few hours, they drank char and discussed the best way of getting Grace back.

When they retired for the night they had the makings of a plan. It was decided that they would watch the Ryde to Northcastle in the morn. If Grace was on it Harris would go with it and see where she was taken. The rest could then follow. Initially the troops were intending to camp but the advent of winter and the amount of gear that they would have to take had made them pause for thought. "It will be easier if we could find lodgings," Daniel had suggested and the others agreed. In reality each was relieved that another had said it first. "I will organise that then, as soon as I can," suggested Harris. "I'm all for a bit of comfort in my old age."

Horis fretted about the costs. "I cannot pay for your services," he protested, the soldiers would hear no such talk.

"We are glad for the distraction," Keen said. "And we all have our pay and war bonus."

The next morning, Harris and Meek left early to keep watch on the Rail-Ryde to Northcastle. On arrival at the terminus, they found a large number of Watchmen. All persons entering were stopped and had their papers checked. They were allowed through and Harris bought a ticket to Northcastle. If Grace was on the Ryde he was to follow her and gain such intelligence as he could, pending the arrival of the rest. He and Meek expected to see Grace, under the escort of the Watch, taken onto the Ryde for the trip north. In fact Terrance had used the offices of the Club to secure a special carriage, showing the livery of a private hospital which had been attached to the rear of the Ryde.

They loitered by the carriage and just before Harris had to board, he saw Terrance arrive in a mobile bearing the name of a hospital. They watched as a figure, sedated and on a stretcher, was taken on board.

They could see that the patient, who they assumed to be Grace, was attached to the stretcher by a steel chain around each wrist and was accompanied by two men dressed as Corpsemen. Terrance kept glancing around to see who was taking an interest in the operation, so it was fortunate that Maloney had prevailed on Horis to leave this part of the plan to those unknown to him. Harris made his farewells to Meek and caught the Ryde, leaving him to report back.

"Good," said Maloney when the news reached him. "Now we know we are on the right track."

Chapter 38, The *Rainbow*

Northcastle was the most out of the way city in Norlandia, nestling in a small triangular valley surrounded by craggy cliffs on two sides and the sea on a third. Apart from by sea, the only access was along the valley of the Gurden River, which with its twin the Gudrun wove its way through the mountains of the Northlands.

The Rail had only reached Northcastle in the last year, a major feat of construction had seen it stride over valleys and eventually bore a long tunnel through the mountains, it being too difficult to construct a line in the valley, as well as adding miles to the journey from the only suitable place to start.

The Rail was the logical way in, but after the news that the terminus was well watched, Horis and Maloney decided it would be better if the soldiers went that way, whilst they arrived by sea. There was a constant stream of ships of all sizes on the route from Metropol City. As most goods and passengers were still transported by sea they thought that they would have no difficulty in arranging passage. There was a list in the news-sheet giving the names of all the movements in the port and Horis scanned it to find the next available sailing. To his annoyance there was a delay of several days before the next passenger ship.

"Let's get the men on their way, Horis," said Maloney. "We can then go and see if Nabbaro's name can get us there any quicker."

Horis had forgotten Grace's uncle. Now with a jolt he remembered his promise to keep her safe. "Not on the *Swiftsure*," he pleaded. "I could not face Hector knowing I've failed him."

"The *Swiftsure* is not on the list, Horis," reassured Maloney. "We will find a way to deal with Hector when we have to."

They used the next two days to get the rest of the party to

Northcastle. To avoid arousing any local suspicion that the arrival of the soldiers might cause, and because they knew not the situation they would be arriving into, they planned to travel in two groups. They would arrive on consecutive days. They could meet up with Harris and put their plan into action.

Meek had been to Northcastle and made additions to a map which they had obtained locally which showed the features of the city. He added the Ministry buildings and the camp from his memory of the place.

Northcastle was on the northern side of a wide bay, where the Gurden River entered the sea. To the north, on the other side of some hills, was the point where the Gudrun River met the sea, all details were missing from the map regarding the hinterland, there was merely a blank space with the words "Prohibited Area" printed over the parchment.

Sapper was a reconnaissance expert. "I'll fill in the gaps for you," he offered. "It will pass the time and give me some practise whilst you lot," and he indicated the others, "drink char and rest up." There was a rush of banter and laughing.

Horis and Maloney watched the second group of soldiers depart and went to the port. They avoided the ferry terminus with its Watchmen and went to a small shipping agency instead. The name of Captain Nabbaro helped smooth their way; the Captain was well known and liked. Horis and Maloney had debated on the amount of information they should give the agent, as soon as it was suggested that Hector's niece was in danger, they found ship masters falling over themselves in eagerness to assist. The pair found passage on a steamer called the *Rainbow*. "The Captain's an old rogue," said the agent. "A bit like Hector in many ways, dependable and discreet, his name is Willem Faustus. I will take you on board tomorrow morn just before sailing." The *Rainbow* would take longer than a ferry service to arrive, stopping as it did along the way but it was the first to leave, so they agreed to return on the morrow.

Next day, Horis and Maloney returned to the agent's. They were taken aboard the *Rainbow* in the early morn. They carried scant gear;

they had little need of anything save a change of clothes and their toilet things. The soldiers had taken the rest of their possessions to Northcastle with them.

The wind was rising as they mounted the gangplank. Dark clouds were scudding across the sky, and it looked as if it would rain soon. Horis had been quite looking forward to another sea passage, particularly if the weather were to be calm; he viewed the weather with apprehension.

Captain Faustus welcomed them at the head of the gangway. "I'm looking for the port officials," he told them. "And for my clearance to depart. The ship is ready, as soon as the bureaucrats will let me, we are off. I will fetch a crewman to show you to your berths." And with that he gave a whistle and a small, wizened man appeared, as if awaiting the call.

"This is Mik," Faustus explained. "He is my steward. He will take you topside." Mik nodded and smiled, showing a lack of teeth, and scampered away. He stopped and turned, beckoning them towards him. "Best keep up," said Faustus, "he moves like the wind."

Mik led them up several decks, to the level of the wheel-space, and, in the same fashion as on the *Swiftsure*, they found themselves in a suite of cabins marked for passenger use. Unlike those on the *Swiftsure* however, these were all single berth cabins with a shared washroom. They put their bags down and turned to thank Mik, but he had gone.

As they were setting out their things they felt the ship's engine start. They heard steam whistles and venturing outside saw that they were being pulled away from the jetty by tugboats. As they watched, the *Rainbow* picked up speed, the towlines were cast off and the harbour pilot descended to a small craft, which rowed back towards the jetty.

As soon as the *Rainbow* passed between the breakwaters, it encountered the brisk swell, and began to roll and pitch. After an hour, it turned onto a northerly course. They were clear of the shelter of land now and the wind rose, heaping white foam on the waves. The *Rainbow* dug its bow into each oncoming wave and showers of spray blew over the whole length of the vessel.

Horis left his cabin, following Grace's advice he stood in the open air, holding onto the railings as the vessel bucked and twisted. Looking into the wheel-space he could see Captain Faustus, wedged into his chair, with an unconcerned expression, drawing on his pipe. His relaxed air gave Horis confidence, and he began to enjoy the sensation of motion. To his surprise, he realised that he did not feel ill. Perhaps he was becoming a sailor. The ship climbed up steep hills of grey bearded water, plunging down into deep troughs with explosions of spray. Horis went into the wheel-space and greeted Faustus, meaning to thank him for agreeing to carry them north.

"You're welcome, young man," said Faustus, "but please enlighten me; my agent says you are in rush to get to Northcastle but in need of discretion. Apparently Grace is involved yet she is not here. You are now safe on my ship and on your way."

At that point the vessel's motion changed, tilting over it slid sideways down a wave, meeting the trough with a booming rattle which shook dust and threw spray. Faustus chuckled, "You are safe, this is a light blow, where was I? Oh yes," he continued, "Hector is my dear friend, pardon me but I must ask, is Grace involved in some nefarious activity in the North? Escaping from justice perhaps?"

Horis, who was holding on to the railing on the bulkhead stared into the Captain's eyes, how much could he safely tell him? "I assure you sir, none of us are criminals, let us say we are on an errand of mercy," Horis hesitated, "and Grace's life is at stake. She is in Northcastle already, although not through choice. She is held captive."

Faustus shook his head. "That is bad. Yet she has no great influence on things, a lovely girl but not normally involved in matters of intrigue. So how are you all bound together? I can't see why she would be taken off to Northcastle."

"Well, sir," replied Horis, "I regret to say that it's my entire fault, I have stumbled upon a secret, and Grace is being used to persuade me in another direction. I need to remove her from danger."

"Hmm," mused Faustus, "and no doubt you do not wish to trust me with the secret?"

"I'm sorry, sir, but everyone that gets involved thus far seems to come to grief, it may be better the less you know. Although I do not wish it to be a problem between us, as you have helped greatly."

He failed to add, and at least two men are dead because of it, which weighs on my mind. So the thought that a lady who has come to mean a lot to me is in danger makes me more careful with whom I take into my confidence.

Faustus was silent for a moment, sucking on his pipe, which gurgled and spluttered, almost in time with his thoughts. "Yes I see," he finally said. "And of course, if anyone were to ask me what you were up to, I could not tell." Nodding, Faustus placed his pipe in a stand cut into the arm of his chair, and got to his feet. Seemingly unaware of the vessel's motion, he walked in a straight line to the compass. Gazing out at the onrushing seas, he adjusted the clockwork, and the *Rainbow* altered course slightly. In a short while the motion eased, and Faustus muttered, half to himself. "The wind's backing," he said. "This squall will soon blow itself out, and we can increase speed. Don't fret, I don't need to know all the details, but I will help, for Grace and for Hector."

Just then Maloney came through the door. "Ah, I have found you, Horis," he said cheerfully. "Luncheon is served, and by the look of the menu, it will be a feast."

Horis was about to complain that the motion and excitement had taken his appetite, but he was pleased to note that in fact it had not.

"Go," said Faustus. "I will have my luncheon here, for I am the watch-keeper till mid-afternoon, Mik will bring me something."

"I'm intrigued," said Maloney. "He has the look of a tribesman from the Western Isles, how did he come to be in your service?"

Faustus smiled. "They have a reputation, do they not, and from your bearing, I would say that you have fought them. Well, I saved Mik and his family from certain death and he agreed to serve me, in thanks."

"And does he understand you?"

"Why yes, they may not be civilised by our standards, but they are by no means stupid. Mik is clever and remembers everything."

Horis and Maloney left the Captain to his watch and went below. They dined well, and afterwards took a turn on the deck, as Faustus had predicted the weather had moderated. Looking over the ship's side, they caught a glimpse of pterosaurs frolicking around the bow, jumping up and sparkling in the sunshine as they chased flying fish.

There were other ships in the vicinity, steamers and sailers alike, plying the oceans between Metropol City and the rest of the world. On the breeze they caught smells of exotic spice and coffee as the vessels passed close by, and occasionally hailed for news.

There being little for them to do on the ship, they repaired to their cabins as night fell, they turned in early as the *Rainbow* had no statics.

Next morning, they were woken by Mik with char, and on dressing and coming outside, saw that they were alone on the ocean. To their right (Horis was not yet enough a seaman to say starboard) the sun was low in the sky, and to their left the cliffs of Norlandia were a few miles away, as a low grey line on the horizon. Captain Faustus was breaking his fast in the saloon, together with the rest of the off watch. He waved a fork laden with fried porker at them in greeting as they sat to eat.

Mik appeared at their side with plates of food, Maloney spoke to him in his own tongue, and in astonishment Mik almost dropped the plates. Bowing to Maloney, he launched into a long speech, accompanied by much nodding, with Maloney adding a word here and there.

Eventually, the conversation waned and Mik, still bowing, departed.

"Well," exclaimed Horis. "I never thought that you would speak the savage word, what on earth did you converse about?"

Maloney looked pleased with himself. "I talked of his tribe and of battles fought, for he was a warrior in the wars."

Horis only had the faintest idea of war, gleaned from news-sheets, but knew that the wars of the Western Isles were a horror story, of vicious jungle battles and silent death, any that survived were men indeed.

They had almost finished eating when a bell rang at the Captain's side, putting down his fork, he rose. "Excuse me gentlemen, I am wanted in the wheel-space," and with that he left.

Chapter 39

Shortly after they felt a change in the ship's motion as the engine was slowed, then stopped. Horis felt a dread, had they been found already? He sat, not knowing what to do when Mik came to them. He tugged at their sleeves and spoke urgently to Maloney in his native tongue. Maloney nodded and answered, it sounded like he was clearing his throat but Mik just smiled and bobbed his head. "Come Horis, we must go, now," said Maloney. "Mik says that there is danger to us."

Mik led them into the engine-space, to a small locker, whose entrance was in the shadows. They entered and the door clanged behind them. Unseen crewmen moved pieces of equipment and rubbish to hide the door.

In the wheel-space, Faustus calmly lit his pipe, watching from the starboard side as the *Rainbow* rolled lazily in the low swell. On answering the call and arriving in the wheel-space, he had found the vessel's way blocked by a Norlandian warship. Flags fluttering from her mast instructed him to heave to and be boarded. Fearing that Horis and Maloney were the subject of their interest, he had sent Mik to hide them, and his mate to prepare for boarding.

Now, he was relaxed as a small boat was rowed across, the occupants were two officers and six rowers.

"Ready the boarding ladder and guest warps," the mate called to his bosun, and the crew jumped to comply.

The mate led the two officers onto the wheel-space deck, where hands were shaken, the atmosphere cordial. The senior took the packet of ship's papers offered by Faustus and passed them to his junior to examine. Taking the steaming mug of char, he spoke, "Captain, where are you bound?"

Maloney and Horis remained in the locker for what felt like an age. Light came in from a grime encrusted porthole high up on the bulkhead. By clambering up on a pile of drums and squeezing between two metal beams, Maloney could make out the blurred shape of a warship off their beam. He passed this information to Horis, who was sat on the deck. "Do you think Terrance has the power to order the navy?" asked Horis. "Surely he has not." Maloney said nothing, He had used to wonder the same, knowing now what he did of the senior classes he had little doubt that Terrance was capable of that and more. He remained wedged in place, while the warship was in his view he kept watch. Horis said little, he was consumed with worry that his rescue was over before it had begun.

After what was only an hour according to Horis's timepiece they felt and heard the engine start with a hiss and a rattle. Maloney looked out again, "The warship has departed," he said and climbed back down to the deck. They heard clanging and scraping, as the crates and rubbish were moved and the metal locking pins knocked clear.

Not knowing what to expect, they tensed as light flooded in, but were relieved to see Captain Faustus in front of them. "It's alright, gentlemen," he said with a smile. "You may come out safely, for our glorious navy has taken its leave." They moved quickly through the noisy engine room, and into daylight. He led them up to the wheel-space, from where they could see the departing shape of the warship. "They were not after you," he continued when he was seated and had ordered char from the ever present Mik. "But I thought it wise to hide you. They were merely looking for a smuggler's ship, which is apparently similar to ours. I satisfied them with our official papers and they departed."

Chapter 40

The next day, they were approaching the port of New Tempest, about halfway to their destination, when they spied the *Swiftsure* coming in the opposite direction. Faustus called the pair to the wheel-space, and as the two vessels closed, he hoisted flags, which he explained meant, "I have a message to give you". The two vessels closed and a rocket line was fired from the *Rainbow*, landing on the deck of the *Swiftsure*. After a signal, the line was retrieved, returning it had a loop of rope attached to it. In what was obviously a familiar operation, this was fixed through a pulley on the mast.

A bucket was then pulled across the gap between the two vessels, containing a speaker handset, Faustus cranked it and the voice of Nabbaro could be heard. "Hail Willem, how goes it?"

"Hail to you, Hector. I am in good spirits, I have someone here who wishes to converse," and he handed Horis the handset.

Horis had been dreading this moment, even though he was separated by perhaps fifty yards of water, he had made a promise and failed. "Hello sir," he said in a whisper. "'Tis Horis."

"Ah yes, Grace's paramour," boomed Nabbaro, and Horis fancied he could hear his voice without the speaker. "Is she there with you?"

This was it, Horis took a deep breath. "I'm afraid not, she has been taken by the Ministry."

This time Horis could hear Hector's shout above the wind. "What! How have you let this happen? I will ensure you pay dearly if she is harmed." Horis dropped the handset in a panic; he was shaking from the force of Hector's words and tone.

Maloney picked it up. "You remember me? I am Mister Maloney. I must speak for Horis. I was there and there was little Horis could do, my friend was killed in the commission of the deed. You must not blame him; he has suffered every day since."

Hector was silent for a moment and then he spoke again. "Very well, I would have more words." Maloney passed the instrument back to Horis, trembling he held it.

"Now listen," said Nabbaro in a quiet voice. "I understand from Maloney that you are blameless and took all precautions to try to avoid this. I assume you are on your way to right the wrong."

"Oh yes sir," Horis replied. "She is held in Northcastle. We have the makings of a plan and some stout fellows to help."

"Very well then," said Hector. "Here is what I will do. The *Swiftsure* is due a repair break, it's a requirement of the law. Normally I would go to Aserol or some other place in the south, as it is warmer and the yards are better, but this time I will arrange to dock in Northcastle. When you have rescued Grace, which you will do, you can come to my ship and be safe. I will ensure that I have enough repairs to keep me in port for a while, but I will not arrive before another fortnight is past, for I have contracts till then. That should give you time to do your duty to her, and to me."

Maloney had overheard Hector's booming, and now took the mouthpiece from Horis. "That will be admirable and thank you," he said. "We have men in position already; after we arrive we will need but a few days to arrange our plan."

"I have a thing for you, to help you along," said Hector. "When we have finished talking I will send the bucket back with it."

Horis and Nabbaro said their goodbyes and Willem conversed with Hector for a while. Then the speaker was returned to the bucket and taken back on board the *Swiftsure*. The bucket returned swiftly.

When it arrived it contained a waterproof folder, containing maps of Northcastle Bay, along with the extent of the fence surrounding the Ministry compound. It also showed in detail the position of the main buildings, although not their purpose.

"Thank you," shouted Horis. "We will get her back," and he waved. He saw Hector return the wave, though whether he heard him, he did not know.

The meeting and relief that he had told Nabbaro calmed Horis but while they were alongside the stone wharf in New Tempest he faltered and was all for leaving the *Rainbow* and proceeding overland to Northcastle. Maloney advised against it. "Horis, we have ample time to kill, if we rescue Grace too soon before the *Swiftsure* arrives we will have to secrete her somewhere and then smuggle her into the docks. The least time she is visible the better."

Through his desperation, Horis could see that he was right. Even so he paced and muttered all the time the vessel was alongside, only relaxing when they departed.

As they continued their way north, the *Rainbow* was struck by another storm. Faustus was forced to reduce the speed and alter course to keep the weather on the bow, even so it meant for two uncomfortable days as the *Rainbow* rode up and over mountainous seas, the top-works were under water more often than they were not and Horis fretted that he had made the wrong choice. It was taking too long, and of course he had no way to communicate with the soldiers, who presumably had all arrived by now and were awaiting orders. Maloney tried to relax him, pointing out that they were used to plans going awry, and that they would spend their time keeping out of trouble, drinking char and reconnoitring the area.

The *Rainbow* was a vessel of similar size to the *Swiftsure*, but less well appointed, and considerably more abandoned in its motion. Horis, however, found to his surprise and pride that he coped well and felt little discomfort.

By the time they were in sight of Northcastle, he and Maloney had gone over the maps till they could draw them from memory, which pleased Maloney. "It's always an advantage to know your ground," he told Horis. "It may be crucial if things go awry."

Chapter 41, Northcastle

Since Ralf's successful flight, the engineers had been working day and night on the gas engine, creating and refining the design so that the latest version bore little resemblance to the one that he had last flown. Following the senior engineer's report to the Ministry, it had been decided that the project was of major importance and they had diverted men away from other things.

Ralf was in the main workshop, in a cave under the mountains. The space echoed with hammering and the roar of burning gas. The statics lighting was harsh and flickered, giving movement a jerky quality.

Ralf regarded the new engine, which was strapped to a heavy workbench. "Is that it?" he asked his artificer. He was surprised to see how much smaller the thing had become.

"That's all of it, sir," replied the man as he wiped the casing, his grease-stained head bobbing in acknowledgement. "We got rid of the big exhaust pipe, it was adding nothing to the engine's performance and the weight we saved meant we could add more gas tanks and landing wheels to the craft."

Ralf walked around the bench. "The propeller has been moved as well," he observed.

"Oh yes, sir. It's more efficient at the front, the power of this one is about three times that of the old engine."

Ralf realised that he could not see the hole for the starting clockwork.

"How will it start, where is the slot for the rotator?" he asked.

"We have put that on the side of the engine now," said the engineer, pointing to a bulge on the casing. "It's all built in. Not only that, by using the rotation of the fan we can rewind the spring after use. You can then take off anywhere you like, as long as you have gas. It works like this, watch."

There were two switches on the side of the engine. One was thrown and the propeller started to spin. The engineer lit the burner with the other switch and the propeller rotated faster and faster until it was a blur. The rattling of the straps and the bench revealed that the whole thing was straining to move forward. It howled as the cool air was sucked into the combustion chamber. Hot air blew out of the back, through a small pipe and the bench under it shimmered.

"Come, Ralf," said the artificer. "We have one ready to fly outside." He led Ralf out onto the flat roadway. There sat a new machine, sleek on a triangle of wheels. The brass-works shone in the weak winter's sun and it looked poised, ready to leap into the sky. It was painted in Brown and Green patches to match the countryside. The engine and propeller was sat in front of his seat, which was now enclosed by glass and steel.

"We have enclosed your seat," said the engineer, "we think you will go to fast to cope with the breeze on your face."

"What is that?" asked Ralf, pointing to a pipe that jutted out from the wing.

The engineer shuffled his feet. "Ministry orders," he said. "It's a powerful gas gun, a new invention. It fires a lead bullet every second with a range of a hundred yards, and it reloads itself."

Ralf walked around the plane, spotting a similar pipe on the other wing. "And would they stop a Drogan?" he asked.

"The gun has been tested on bovines," replied the engineer grimly, "and it stopped them."

Ralf performed his usual checks before and after climbing into the pilot's seat. The artificer climbed onto the wing and pointed out the new controls. On his left side he saw a lever marked "Start" and one marked "Burner", he guessed that they were the same as those on the engine inside the workshop. On his right was a lever marked "Brake", which the artificer told him was for the landing gear. He grabbed the control stick and almost pushed a red button on the top.

"Don't touch that yet," remarked the artificer dryly. "It fires the guns." The man jumped down and whistled. Two workers came over and each grabbed a wingtip. Ralf slid the canopy shut over his head. Now he could hear nothing from outside. At least he wouldn't get cold, he thought.

The men on the ground pointed to the wheels and signalled with his arms, Ralf guessed his meaning and released the brakes. The plane was turned to face the wind, the roadway stretched out in front of him. He lifted the brake lever and the plane was still. The men all backed away.

Ralf pressed the "Start" lever and then the "Burner", hearing the click-click of the igniter. In front of him the propeller started to spin and on a dial the speed of rotation was shown. He increased the gas supply and felt the craft straining at the brakes. Releasing the brakes he started to roll, finding that very quickly the tail lifted, leaving him moving on just the main wheels. The control stick felt light as a feather in his hands and he gently pulled it into his stomach. The rumbling of the wheels stopped, and looking over the side of the seat he could see that the ground was receding.

He reduced the gas and the propeller speed dropped back slightly. Pulling and pushing on the control stick and his rudder pedals he performed a series of manoeuvres, finding that the reduced weight made the plane easier and more responsive. It was definitely faster and before he knew it, he had reached the coast. He turned south, with the afternoon sun on his right and was soon over the fence that separated the camp from the rest of Norlandia. Remembering what they had been told, "Keep all behind the fence secret", he turned back to the north, but not before he had spotted that the fence was broken at the cliff edge, probably from a landslide. Glancing at the gas gauge he saw that he had hardly used any, the needle hovered just below full.

He passed over the Gudrun River, scene of his exploits in the first machines and wondered just how far he could go with the fuel he had on board. He flew past the warship at the river mouth and they waved and dipped flags as he passed. Deciding against flying up the valley he continued north, along the coast in the shadow of the tall cliffs. He raced across a wide sandy beach, looking for something to test his guns on. Ahead of him on the sand was a wrecked wooden fisher-boat, he lined the plane up and pressed the red button.

The plane shuddered under the recoil of the twin gas guns and Ralf watched fascinated as two lines of eruptions in the sand marked the strike of his bullets. Lifting the nose slightly they converged on the fisher-boat, which shuddered under the impact. Large chunks of wood were tossed into the air by the bullets. In a flash the plane had been turned from an interesting invention into a formidable weapon of war. Ralf's mind raced as he considered the implications of the machine he was in control of. He flashed past the boat and climbed over the cliffs, breaking out into sunlight. He was elated by the performance of the machine and longed to tell the artificer. He saw that his gas tanks were still half full; the plane had range enough for a lot more flying yet. Deciding that he had been away long enough he turned again towards the line of balloons he could see marking the river. Beyond them it was a short hop to the landing field.

Landing would be interesting, he thought, there was no reference to show how far below him the wheels extended, he would have to be gentle to avoid breaking them. He became distracted with thoughts of all the things this craft might do when he spotted a Drogan in the distance. He decided to test his abilities against this other master of the skies and headed towards it. At a distance he fired his guns, aiming over the beast to allow for the bullets' flight. The Drogan never flinched but swung its head in his direction as he approached. It flew across him, attempting to get into a position to attack.

Ralf tried to turn the plane and get the beast back in front of his guns; it was too quick. He tried to increase his speed, turning the gas to maximum but it kept just out of his reach. He tried stalling the plane, reducing the speed and lifting the nose but it merely flapped to a stop. It was playing with him, Ralf decided. It suddenly broke off from its manoeuvring and dove away to the ground. Below him Ralf could see another Drogan on the ground feeding on a carcass. Alone now in the clear skies and well west of the landing field Ralf pointed the plane away from the sun and headed home, following the fence.

As he crossed the roadway from the main gate, he saw a convoy of steam-lorries trundling towards the buildings. One was painted white, with the red markings of a hospital lorry on the roof and sides. Ralf wondered as to its purpose, there was an infirmary on the camp, why would they need one from outside?

If he had been worrying about landing, the event was easier than he thought. He swung the plane around until it was pointing into the wind along the roadway and reduced speed. The craft sank lower and lower as it ran along the line of the road until with a squeal the wheels made contact. Ralf stopped the burner and the tail sank as speed fell off. He gently pulled the brake and came to rest.

"You made that look simple," said the artificer as he arrived with the rest of his squad.

"'Tis easier than landing on water," admitted Ralf. "It is still for one thing, there is no swell to arrest your motion suddenly. And I have lots to tell about my flight today."

Ralf realised that there were bound to be other flyers that had also been testing the new craft but the engineer's next words surprised him. "There are several of you now who can fly this thing and land it safely, soon you will fly in a group and demonstrate this invention to His Majesty and senior politicians. So you had better start practising together. We can all share what we have learnt over char."

Chapter 42

The carriage containing Grace had arrived in Northcastle. It had taken nearly thirty hours to travel from Metropol City, stopping only twice. The mighty locomotive had been fed with coal by two teams of stokers, working in relays to keep the steam pressure high. The last thirty miles were through the King Oscar Tunnel, named after the Monarch who, before being usurped had ordered the joining of the north with the rest of the land by Rail.

The Ryde emerged into the afternoon of a northern winter's day, already the sun had sunk below the hills to the west and the shadows were long. The huge statics light on the front of the locomotive illuminated the long sweeping stone bridge over the Gurden River as the Ryde swept past. The bovine shredder was empty of debris and the soldiers on the roof relaxed now that the end was in sight. It had been a long and boring journey for them.

Slowing, the Ryde came to rest under the glass and steel canopy of the terminus and with a whistle the doors opened. Harris was the first to disembark, during the journey he had moved to sit in the carriage nearest the special one at the rear. The entrance had been guarded by a rail-master, who turned away any person approaching. From his position on the platform he saw a white steam-lorry in military hospital livery approach the carriage. Still under the influence of the sedation and strapped on the stretcher, Grace was put into the lorry. Harris guessed from the uniforms of the attendants that she was to be taken up the asphalted road to the Ministry facility. Terrance got into the lorry as well; he had been greeted as a friend by the driver of the lorry. Harris turned away, the first part of his task completed; now he had to find a base for the party.

The lorry made its way through the town and once on the road to the camp it picked up speed. Inside it was not the most comfortable of journeys and despite her comatose state Grace stirred and pulled at her bonds. One of the attendants injected her with a colourless liquid, via a bronze and glass syringe and she lay still for the rest of the trip.

Once past the guard houses at the camp entrance the lorry made its way towards the main accommodations and to the punishment compound. This was a low grey building, where political prisoners and other dangerous criminals were kept.

Grace was secured in a cold cell, still on her hospital stretcher. The straps and chains were removed and a thin blanket was placed over her. The warders left the cell and the door was locked from the outside. It opened briefly some time later, when a bundle was thrown into the corner but Grace was still asleep.

Much later she slowly awoke, she was cold and her head throbbed. Where was she? The last thing she remembered was the slam of the mobile's luggage hold door shutting out the view of Horis and daylight; how long ago was that?

She looked down; under the blanket she was wearing a hospital gown and little else. Rising to a sitting position revealed stone walls, they were wet with water and green moss. A small high window let dull light into the space and a solid wooden door, studded with nails, completed the scene. There was a pile of objects in one corner and a hole in another, behind the door. A brass pipe with a valve on the end dripped cold water. She climbed slowly off the stretcher and staggered as her muscles protested. Her stomach rumbled; she was famished. How long had she been unconscious?

The pile contained the clothes she had been wearing when Eavis had snatched her and she donned them, feeling better immediately. A slit in the door opened and a plate made of stale bread was pushed through. "Where am I?" called Grace, the only answer was the clang as the slit closed. The plate contained a dab of cold gruel and a small piece of boiled porker. Grace scooped the meagre meal up with her fingers and gulped it all down, eating even the stale plate and licking her fingers clean afterwards.

The light dimmed and she realised that it was late afternoon, she still felt weary and with nothing else to do she dragged the hard board from the trolley to the cold stone floor and laid down on it, covering herself with the blanket. Her thoughts as she fell asleep were of Horis and the night they had spent together in Aserol, how long ago it all seemed.

As winter was approaching it was cold in the cell. In the morning there was ice inside the window; it melted and dripped, seeming to mark the time. A bread-plate of food appeared and again she called, again there was no answer. She found a small pebble in the corner and used it to scratch a mark on the wall above her bed. There were many such marks; clearly this cell had seen many occupants and the thought of them made her shiver even more.

Grace was determined that the treatment would not break her spirit, and concentrated on thoughts of Horis, who she was sure was working towards her rescue. She resolved to rise above the privations of her captivity, and passed the long solitary hours singing and dancing to tunes in her head. She suspected that she was being watched, although she could not see any obvious spy-hole.

After four nights had passed, she was awoken on the fifth morning by the sound, not of a plate being pushed through the slot in the door, but of the door itself opening. Turning her head, she saw two guards, and a familiar face. "Come, my dear," said Terrance. "Let's talk and see if we cannot resolve this situation." She allowed herself to be led to a well-appointed room, with heavy velvet furnishings and a roaring fire. It was so warm, after her cell, that she immediately felt sleepy and relaxed. Catching herself, she remembered that Terrance was no friend, and that her words would have to be carefully chosen. He walked around a large desk and sat in a leather chair. The smell of food and hot char drifted across from the desk top. "Please sit," said Terrance, adopting the manner of a concerned rescuer. "Would you take char?" but Grace decided to meet him head-on. "Don't try that with me, sir. I know your motives, and will give you no satisfaction."

Terrance smiled, but there was no warmth in it. "Don't be foolish, you are here and no-one knows. Your hero will not be arriving to rescue you."

"He will come," said Grace, and Terrance shook his head. "He cannot possibly come to your aid. You are in the best protected place in all Norlandia. Strongman and his rabble will be no match for the guards here."

It was Grace's turn to smile, and hers was the smile of one who had faith. "He has right on his side, sir, and so will prevail; all I must do is to be patient."

"And in the meantime," said Terrance icily, "you will tell me everything I need to know of the events in Aserol. What does Strongman know and who has he told? Come girl, you may eat and drink your fill if you just tell me."

Grace's stomach rumbled and her mouth watered at the smell of the food, she could see it on the desk, steam rising from the fried porker and fresh eggs. Bread and butter were piled on the side of the plate. She was tempted to say anything, just to satisfy her hunger. But her loyalty for Horis overrode her pangs. "I will tell you nothing," she said. "And if you mean to use force, then start, I am not afeared." Grace tried to sound brave but her voice betrayed her, it croaked and whispered.

Terrance's face adopted a pained expression, though his eyes were cold and empty. He looked at a piece of parchment on his desk. "We are not yet at the point where I would cause you harm. Hopefully we will not get there. You will be left for a while to think before we take that road. It will be your choice how we proceed. But be assured that the next time your door opens, if you will not talk, no good will befall you."

He pressed a clockwork bell on his desk and the guards returned. "Take her back," he ordered. "And halve her rations." As she was led out he spoke again. "The next time the door opens, remember that."

Chapter 43

Terrance was now faced with a quandary. He was desperate to keep the information that Horis was alive away from Cavendish and the Club but had to report to Cavendish on his progress. He was fearful for his future as a man with influence, and indeed for his life, should his failure to keep control of the situation become known. He knew that Cavendish had broken men for less.

Feeling safer without face to face contact he called Cavendish as soon as Grace had been led away. To justify the call, he had information about the consignment of rocks from Aserol. He intended to dress it as good news if the call went badly.

There was little of the wait that normally formed part of such a call. The speakers out of the Ministry did not require an exchange, a new development had produced a mechanism that could place a call via a system of buttons on the speaker itself, when pressed in a distinct sequence for each recipient they found the appropriate connection by some technical means. Terrance was not a scientific man; to him such things were a source of wonder.

"Cavendish here, who calls?" the sound of his voice even at this distance made Terrance's stomach flutter.

"'Tis Terrance," he squeaked. "I'm in Northcastle."

"I know," replied the other. "You have taken one unconscious hostage with you, the girl I believe. I assume that means that Strongman is no longer a problem."

It was the moment of truth for Terrance. "Strongman evaded us," he whispered. "I know not where he is."

Cavendish was furious. "How in Bal's name did that happen, you assured me that it was all under control, and now he has vanished!"

"He had help, from a bunch of soldiers I think. At least that's how they were dressed."

"I got your thugs away from the Watch and you told me that they would finish this," said Cavendish, his voice returning to a normal volume. "What has happened at the mine? And what have you learnt from the girl?"

Terrance knew that Cavendish was probably aware of everything that had occurred; his replies would have to be honest. "The mine is resolved," he answered. "There were no survivors, the families were shown the bodies and have taken them for burial." He paused.

"And the girl, has she told you anything?"

"Not yet, but I am starving her and have put dire thoughts in her head."

Cavendish sighed. "And is this working?"

"Not yet, but give me time."

"Time is what we don't have," replied Cavendish sharply. "If I may suggest, treat her better and say it is on my instruction. Kindness may induce her to speak. If we knew that she was the only one left with any knowledge of the truth we could just dispose of her."

"Very well," replied Terrance, hoping that would be all. Then he remembered his news. "Wait," he said.

"What is it now?" answered Cavendish, in a voice that suggested that he was prepared for more bad news.

"The rocks are on their way from Aserol," Terrance triumphantly exclaimed.

"On the *Bold Cutter*," said Cavendish in a bored voice. "It left Aserol two days ago and is presently approaching Ventis."

Terrance felt deflated.

"And another thing," Cavendish continued. "Strongman and the soldiers are resourceful. I would not be surprised to find them near you. It would be easier to let them come to us. We can round them all up. Keep your eyes open. I will be coming to Northcastle soon for a demonstration. We will finish this once and for all."

The line went dead and Terrance replaced his handset wearily. He sighed. Cavendish was still a step ahead of him. Perhaps he was right about Grace. He seemed to be right about most things.

But he could leave it a while before he did anything, Horis had thwarted him and ill-treating Grace was his only way of retribution. He would leave her a while longer before changing her treatment.

Locked in her cell again, Grace lost herself in thoughts of freedom and Horis coming to her rescue. Two days had passed since Terrance had threatened her, and she was beginning to realise that he was playing a cruel game to wear her resolve. She could feel her clothes getting loose on her as the lack of food weakened and starved her. She had a constant headache from the lack of water, the pipe dispensed drips so grudgingly that there was barely a small cup with every meal.

Chapter 44

When the door opened again, she shrank back into the dark corner and the guards came into the cell and pulled her out. Making her body limp, she was dragged into the corridor, where she came face to face with her captor.

"Will you tell me what I wish to hear then?" asked Terrance.

"Never," she hissed, her head held high. "Do your worst then, I am ready for it."

Terrance realised that his way would not work at that point, all he had left was torture and considering what Cavendish had said, that might be a step too far to explain away. On her past performance it may not even work, Terrance could see that she was a tough adversary but he dared not risk her death. In a way he admired her spirit.

He sighed, Cavendish's way it was then. And he was right, Grace was incommunicado. If Horis came and was captured, all would be well.

"As you wish." He paused seeing if she would quail at the last but she did not. "You have a friend in authority," he continued, "and I have been instructed to improve your treatment."

"What do you mean?"

"I have been persuaded that I was wrong to treat you so, you will join the other prisoners in their daily duties, you will never leave here, but your life will be more comfortable and have purpose."

Grace was taken to a bathroom with a roaring coal fire and left to bathe and wash her locks. As she removed her clothes, which now resembled rags, and lowered herself into the tub she saw that her ribs were showing and her skin was loose. She relaxed into the warm suds and drifted in and out of sleep. Clean clothes and warm towels were laid out for her and after washing and dressing she went to the door of the room. It was locked and as she rattled the handle it opened.

A female guard with a severe face and a short whip stood outside. "Come on then, girl," she shouted. "You've made yourself respectable and you don't stink. That's your bath for the week, time to get to work." She prodded Grace with the handle of the whip and moved her along the passageway. Grace was led across the courtyard from the prison block, the sunlight hurting her eyes. There was a chill in the air and her wet hair blew in the stiff breeze. She could tell from the parade ground and the soldiers everywhere that she was in some sort of military camp but saw nothing to indicate where it might be. However, the low sun and temperature led her to believe it was in the north somewhere. In her mind it mattered little. Horis would know of her whereabouts and soon be arriving to save her. In her imagination over the last days she had seen him come and vanquish Terrance, removing her to safety. All she must do was keep patient.

Initially, Grace was put to work in the kitchens, where she helped prepare and serve food, under the watchful eye of the cook, who was not a prisoner, but a soldier. On first meeting her, he shook his head. "My dear," he tutted and shook his head. "You have been on gruel for too long, look not in a reflecting mirror for it will shock you." He was fat and always sweating, as all the cooks in her experience tended to be, but his food was good, better than the stuff that had previously sustained her. He made sure she had extra rations for the first few days and she filled out, regaining her previous colour. Her headaches ceased as she became more properly nourished and she felt able to cope once more.

Grace knew how to use many of the mechanical devices that the kitchen was equipped with from her time in the hotel in Aserol, a time that seemed so long ago. However, she found that they were all slightly improved on the ones she was familiar with. "These are the latest versions," the cook explained to her. "They are devised and made here. We test the improvements, finding any flaws before they are made available to the people."

Mealtimes were a busy affair, with hordes of soldiers at one end of the canteen, forming a long line to be served. At the other end, the artificers and scientists sat at better tables and were served their food. Off to one side, behind a partition, the senior staff had fine plates and wine to go with the food. But for all the division, Grace saw that they all ate from the same stove.

There was a small group of men who sat at the corner for meals. Generally ignored by the masses, they talked among themselves with much waving of hands and laughter. But beneath it they seemed intense and distant, and Grace asked one of the other serving girls about them.

"They are the pilots," was the reply, "and they keep to themselves."

"Ah," said Grace, "you mean balloonists."

"No," said the girl, who wore the same drab prison clothes as she. "They are true flyers. They have machines that move without a rope tying them to the earth. It's better not to talk to them, or form any attachment, as they very often do not return from their tasks."

Grace had never heard of such a thing and wondered if the girl was imagining it, after all balloons had been familiar for a long time and were safe as long as they were anchored securely. But then she thought of the new kitchen machines, who could say what else might be made here. The full realisation of the nature of the place started to come to her. She noted the group, and sure enough, at the next mealtime the number was the same but two of the faces were different.

After a few days, Grace was taken from the kitchens and marched to see Terrance once more. Again he asked her of events in Aserol and the depth of her knowledge. Once more she refused to say. This time however, he seemed less interested in her replies, as if he was only asking her to be seen to. Grace felt a worry enter her mind, perhaps they were no longer interested in her because they had Horis. The thought gnawed at her as Terrance sat, looking at papers on his desk.

Finally he looked up. "Your supervisor says you have worked

well," he said. "Perhaps you have realised that this is your new home. You will be moved away from the kitchens and given the job of steward for the pilots."

Grace gasped, she had not expected that. Now she was even more certain that she was alone, that Horis would not be coming to rescue her. Her shoulders slumped and she felt dizzy. Very well she decided, then I will carry on and make the best of it.

In her new role, she fetched the pilots their food and cleared their table. She found that she was also expected to run errands for them and was given a parchment pass to pin to her lapel. This allowed her free rein of parts of the camp in hours of daylight and in between her duties she used the freedom it gave her to walk among the gorse and heather and breathe the cold fresh air of the outdoors.

There were many wonders to behold. On one of her first walks she happened upon the river and saw the flying machines in the skies and the Drogans flying with them. She saw many Exo-Men and thought of Divid controlling one. But her thoughts always returned to Horis and the doubts she now felt.

She was watched by the guards in their towers and mobiles, and as she saw the number of them she realised that her thoughts of rescue had been just wild dreams, whether Horis was able or not. And if he was not then there was no-one else. Every evening at dusk, after the flyers had been fed and the tables cleaned, she was returned to her cell. The thought that Terrance might be using her growing despair to make her submit never entered her mind.

Chapter 45

In her new role as steward for the flyers, Grace remembered what she had been told and was careful not to become too friendly with them. The faces had stayed the same for some days now and they seemed a happier group. In truth it was quite easy to remain detached as most of them affected an air of superiority, certainly they considered a common criminal to be beneath them, their only words were, "more char" or "clean our boots, girl".

Except for one; she took a shine to Ralf, learning his name by accident when she heard one of the others calling him. He was different; he was polite and thanked her for her work. In return she made sure that he got the best of the rations and her attention, and every day worried that he might not return from flying or whatever else he did. When any of the others did not come back she had been sad but not as much as she would have been if she had been well treated by them.

They started to converse, initially with banalities about the weather or the food but one day when he was eating alone, he stopped and looked straight at her. "Grace," he said in an intense whisper, "pardon me but why are you here? You are not like the others. What wrong can one as sweet and kind as you have possibly done?"

Grace blushed; she hoped that this was not leading where she feared it might. Ralf was handsome it was true but she belonged to another, even if he was not alive she would keep herself to his memory.

"Oh sir," she replied, "you would not believe me if I told you, but rest assured, I am innocent." She realised how it sounded, she knew from her life in Aserol that that every guilty person protested their innocence, in a rush she continued, "My man is accused and I have been taken to ensure his silence. And I know not if he still lives." She dissolved into tears.

Ralf put his arm around her shoulders. "There, there girl," he said, softly stroking her hair. "I know of your pain. We are all hostages here, in one way or another."

"Are you toying with me," she answered him, "do not think you can talk your way into my affections."

"Madam," he said, his tone hurt, "I would not. I merely mean that you do not behave as the other women prisoners, you have elegance and pride and they do not appear so. And although they would all swear their innocence, I have heard that unlike them you have committed no crime."

Just then one of the female overseers came across. "No fraternising," she reminded Ralf, who released his hold.

"You see, Grace," he said, "we are the flyers and because of what we do you might think that we are special here, but we are also prisoners, just like you." The guard glared at him.

The next afternoon, Ralf came across and spoke to Grace, the other flyers gave them knowing looks but Grace cared not.

"I have important news which may help your cause," he told her. "In ten days there will be a flying demonstration for the government, His Majesty may also be here." Grace was puzzled, did he mean that she could somehow appeal to the King.

"How does that help me?" she asked.

"Well, I was about to tell you, on my flights I have seen a break in the fence. It is at the seaward end to the south and if you can get there you may escape."

"I see," she replied. "But again, how does that help me?"

"On the day no-one will be watching you for all eyes will be on me in the skies. You can steal away and will not be missed. It is a fair walk but there are places to hide out."

"That is interesting," she continued. "But I am not dressed for a walk across the hills, especially now that winter is almost upon us."

"I have an idea for that also," said Ralf. "I can get some warmer clothes and stout boots from the stores and leave them hidden for you."

Listening to herself, Grace saw that she had changed. She was putting every obstacle in the way of escape. She had become used to her imprisonment and was comfortable in it. And then she saw the truth, Terrance had made her compliant by his suggestion that she no longer mattered. The scales fell from her eyes. And if Ralf had heard that she was innocent then she should not just sit here and accept things as they were. Let them think she was tamed then, she decided, I can escape with this man's help. I just need to keep up my defeated appearance.

"Thank you, Ralf," she said, meaning it. "Make your plans, I will be ready."

Chapter 46

After Harris had seen Grace loaded into the lorry, he left the terminus to complete the second part of his mission. Sapper and the men would be arriving in Northcastle over the next two days and he had to find them rooms if they were to avoid sleeping in a field somewhere.

He walked out of the terminus and saw a town built of local stone, grey and imposing, dour as the people were reputed to be. But there was money here, the people looked prosperous, the camp consumed all they could produce and employed them in the port and in agriculture. The streets were wide and well cobbled, there was a steady stream of traffic, both equine and steam powered. Suited men strode around and there were ladies shopping and chatting.

There were many Drogan nets and watchtowers, all in good condition and well manned. The crisp air was moved by a light onshore breeze, smoke from the high brick chimneys of the Locals was drifting up the river in wisps and tendrils. Steam-lorries moved in a steady stream to and fro.

Harris had been to the town before and reckoned that the market would be a good place to start his search for lodgings for the group. He needed nine berths, eight for the soldiers and Horis, and a single room for Grace. A hotel would be the best plan, if not the cheapest. That did not concern him overly, he had funds and Maloney's instructions were to find somewhere safe and easy to vacate in a hurry.

He wandered the pannier market, set out in a large stone building with a glazed roof. The stalls were bursting with local produce, meats and roots and all manner of comestibles. He asked a butcher if he knew of accommodations but the man did not. He asked a fruiterer and received only a shake of the man's head.

He was about to ask a fish merchant when he was accosted by a woman who whispered, "Beware" in his ear before booming out to all around. "There you are, sir. How much longer must I wait for you?" She grabbed his arm and led him away to subdued laughter, still booming, "Come and purchase me this fine hat that I have found."

Harris and the woman were outside before he could realise what was happening and he was released. Turning, he saw his attacker was an imposing woman of middle years. Dressed severely in lace and black velvet she regarded him with intelligent eyes.

"What in Bal's name are you doing, woman?" he asked, he had fought the savage but this lady was something else.

"You could thank me," she replied fixing him with a steely stare. "You were about to talk to an agent of the camp's private watch. Any activity like yours, a large number of men arriving on some dubious purpose, will be suspicious to them. You would find yourselves in a cell very quickly."

"How did you know?" he asked in wonderment.

"Laddie, I have lived here a long time and have seen many things; that place up the road exerts an influence hereabouts and I like it not. Too many enter and stay for my liking. Since it came the Drogans have increased and life has more danger. I overheard you talking to the fruiterer. You were lucky for he has no sympathy with the camp."

Harris understood immediately. "In that case, I thank you," he said. "But in less than a day my mates will be arriving and we are no further towards a solution."

She nodded. "So laddie, you are looking for accommodations?" she asked in her northern lilt. "I will help you, in memory of my husband. He was a soldier and a fine one at that. You are military, I see it in your bearing and even if I know not your purpose, I sense it is just. How many of you will there be?"

Harris did not want to give out too much information. "Nine in total," he replied. "Myself and seven comrades and later a lady will be joining us."

It was as if he had given her the full tale, she nodded. "It will be a rescue then, how exciting. I take it that the lady is held in the camp?"

"Clearly," said Harris, "I will have to take you into my confidence, although you seem to know half the tale already."

She laughed at that. "Let's just say that you will not be the first to journey to Northcastle for that purpose. Allow me to introduce myself, I am Mrs Wring. Come to my house, it used to be a hotel but the powers that be closed it down. Have no fear. I will not betray your endeavours. You are safer with me than any other." Harris allowed himself to be led away.

The next afternoon, Harris was at the terminus, waiting for Sapper to arrive with Daniel and Wilson. He had survived the night at Mrs Wring's, her food was superb and plentiful. She had got most of the tale from him over stew and char. The rest had escaped his lips over porker and eggs this morning, then char at ten and a cold luncheon. He tore his thoughts from food to his mates. They should be bringing some gear with them, equipment for marching and reconnoitring. Harris wondered what reception his activities would receive from Sapper, who after all was his superior in the service. But I used my initiative, he thought, and if it had not been for Mrs Wring I would have been in deep trouble.

Chapter 47

The three alighted from the Ryde promptly, this one had clearly had a more eventful journey, there were parts of a tree hanging from the shredder and the carriages bore signs of attack, windows were broken and the soldiers' positions on the roof showed deep scratches and bright metal.

Harris greeted the three and took his pack, which Sapper had brought along for him. "Come on then," he said after handshakes. "Let's get to our accommodations."

"You had better have lodged us in an ale house," said Wilson. "I for one am in need of ale. There were two Drogan swoops on the Ryde and a gang of brigands blocked the line. When we slowed to clear it, they attacked with gas guns and projectiles. The soldiers fought them off."

"Mrs Wring will not allow ale," said Harris and there was a stunned silence.

"What are we doing there then?" asked Daniel. "I'm with Wilson, if there's no ale I want to stay somewhere else."

Sapper turned to Harris, sensing mutiny. "Well then, Harris, explain your choice of hostelry."

"It will be better if you meet our host first," Harris said. "Then you will understand."

They set off up the road, muttering.

Mrs Wring answered the door. "So Mr Harris, are these your men?" Her massive arms were folded across her midriff and she radiated authority. There were traces of flour on the skirts of her pinafore and a smell of bovine and pastry drifted around her in the doorway. Sapper felt that he ought to salute her, such was her bearing. He had seen less frightening Sergeant Majors.

"Good after, madam," he said. "I am Sapper, in nominal charge of this rabble, at least until my officer arrives. These two are Wilson and Daniel. We have two more arriving tomorrow on the Ryde and two at sea."

"Oh I know all about that," she replied a little impatiently. "Mr Harris has told me of your mission."

At this Sapper shot Harris a look of exasperation. Mrs Wring continued, "You must not blame him, I can be very persuasive."

Harris nodded glumly. "She saved me from the secret police and sort of winkled the tale from me," he admitted. Sapper could see how that would be.

"You can trust me," said Mrs Wring. "I have no love for the camp, it took what was left of Mr Wring, Bal rest him, and all I got was a message, they would not even let me collect his corpse for a decent internment." At that she looked about to weep, the hard exterior cracking for a moment. It passed and she gathered herself.

"Now, there's a fine pie in the stove for you and char brewing, if you're proper soldiers you'll be wanting char, come on and sit, I'll get the makings." She departed for the kitchen and they went into a sitting room and took chairs.

"See what I mean?" Harris said to Sapper. "She's like the tide or a brisk wind, you can't stand against her."

"And she knows it all?" Sapper prompted.

"I managed to keep some from her," Harris said, "and she says that she will help us, I think we have landed right."

"Very well then, it's too late now to alter things anyway, we must just hope she is sound."

Whilst they drank their char, Mrs Wring told them more of her tale. She had been a cook at this building when it was a hotel and on the death of the owner had bought it with her husband's war bounty. He had a year's service to complete and had been posted to the camp. Mrs Wring had hoped to see him occasionally but he was never allowed out, or even to send a letter, she kept the place running as a hotel and hoped that on completion of his service her husband could help her. Then one day, a message had arrived to say that he had been killed in an accident. No more details were given, nor was she allowed to collect his corpse, his wages had stopped and all her pleas for information went unanswered. So she had soured to the camp and all it represented.

She explained that when she had seen Harris about to fall foul of the camp's agent she had decided to save him. As he had told her of Grace's plight she had jumped at the chance to aid in her rescue. She made no mention of the mysterious rock that Horis possessed or of the name Terrance, so Harris had at least managed to keep some of the story secret.

After the pie, which was as glorious as the aroma had suggested, there was more char. Then the four settled in for the night, on the morrow Keen and Meek would arrive and they could begin.

Chapter 48

Once they were at full strength, the soldiers started to explore the area around Northcastle. Each morning they left one of their number to watch at the port for the arrival of Horis and Maloney while the rest took to the hills, reconnoitring the area and making maps. At this point they kept well clear of the camp and if challenged would claim to be on a training exercise.

After each of these forays they regrouped and exchanged intelligence. They had found that there were two roads from the town to the camp, one direct and straight, it had clearly been made for the rapid movement of large convoys of vehicles or marching men. It had a sealed surface of melted and cooled coal ash that had been smoothed by much use. The other way followed the river from the town to its mouth, passing the port and then turned up the cliffs to rejoin the main route at a junction about a mile from the gate of the camp. This way was smooth to the port and then it turned into a track, made of compressed rocks that had been roughly graded, the holes filled in with loose rubble. It would suit a lorry but would be hard going indeed for a mobile.

At these meetings, when everyone had discussed what they had found, the talk turned to planning how to infiltrate the camp and see what could be learnt of Grace's whereabouts.

"You're the expert in concealment," said Meek to Sapper.

"But you have been in the camp, Meek," he replied. "That makes you a better choice."

"True," replied Meek. "But I have never seen the lady. I would not recognise her if I saw her."

Sapper sighed, that was true. "Looks like me again then," he said. "You boys will have to keep busy while I'm gone." He went through the list of things that still needed to be arranged before a rescue was possible. Much had been achieved and he was confident that the mission could be accomplished. After dividing the work between them they sat down to another of Mrs Wring's majestic creations.

Clad in green and brown camouflage, Sapper surveyed the fence that enclosed the Ministry facilities through a spyglass. He had risen well before the dawn and had spent half the day, walking cross-country from Northcastle to get to this position, shielded by rocks and heather above the roadway into the compound.

Traffic was plentiful; there were equine-drawn carriages and many steam-lorries laden with goods hidden under canvas covers. There were open-backed vehicles of all kinds filled with troops. The main gate was guarded by about twenty soldiers, with some sort of large gas-powered gun set by the sides of the road. Heavy clockwork barriers stopped all traffic. The fence extended as far as he could see in both directions, to his left he could see it march over the folds of the ground, two lines of metal mesh, with a gap in between large enough for a steam-mobile to pass. And indeed one did, at regular intervals, manned by several soldiers. He could see straight away that his entry would be complicated. No matter, he had a week before the others would start to worry about his capture. Horis and Maloney had not yet arrived so nothing could be done.

Sapper decided to start from the end of the fence at the coast. He returned to his pack, which he had left among the rocks. After hitching it onto his back he started to move off to the east, towards the sea. He kept close to the fence, using the cover provided by the heather and gorse every time he heard a mobile approach. He saw that every so often the gap between the fences widened, to allow mobiles to pass or turn around. He realised that he was steadily moving uphill as he neared the coast, and as he crested a ridge he could see the sea in the distance.

From his higher position he could see a line of gas balloons, tethered in the breeze to the north, and as he neared the cliff edge, he could see that a recent landslide had foreshortened the fence, which was damaged and loose at the edge. He crept closer to the gap, tensed for the arrival of the patrol, but looking at the ground, there was grass growing in the tracks between the fences, indicating that this section was not regularly traversed by a mobile.

By lying down, he could wriggle under the damaged fence and after a moment of concentration he managed to work his way round the inner fence, where it hung over the edge of the cliff.

He was inside, now he had to make some distance from the fence in what daylight remained, he knew he must find a secure hiding place till morning.

Striking out in the direction of the balloons he found himself in a small valley and spotted a fold in the hills, which turned into a narrow canyon. The walls closed in until he found himself outside a cave. Deciding that it would make a good base, he crept on cautiously.

Inside it was dry and opened out into a good sized space. Risking a light, he lit his gas torch, force of habit made him shield the beam with his hand. There was evidence of habitation, the remains of a fire and a few lupine bones. There was a rough bed made from bracken and moss, covered in some sort of cloth, matching the grassland outside. The remains were old, there was evidence that small animals had gnawed at the bones and rubbish. It seemed unlikely that he would be disturbed. Still, he set himself up ready for surprises. He lit a fire in the entrance, using dry wood that he found on the cave floor. No smoke came from the blaze and it was enough to heat water to make char. While it was heating he laid his mess tins out on the path, tying them together with twine. Anyone approaching would tangle in them and wake him. He ate sparingly from his army rations and lay down on the bed, facing the door. Wrapping himself in his groundsheet, he settled himself for a sleep.

Chapter 49

Next morning, he awoke feeling refreshed. The fire had burnt itself out. Surprisingly, the bed had been comfortable and after some food from his pack, and a drink of cold water, he was ready to go on towards the balloons.

By mid-morning, he had reached a road, cutting arrow-straight through the wild moorland. Keeping out of sight of traffic, he followed it; making good time towards what he assumed was the centre of the camp. The balloons loomed larger as he approached them. They were manned; he could hear conversation on the wind although he was unable to make out the words.

Sapper found a side track and followed it, finding himself at the side of a wide, deep river valley, near to the anchor block of one of the gas balloons. The main road was curving away to his left, away from the river. Keeping to the cover of the bushes, he was surprised to hear a clearer voice, distorted through a speaker. He realised that it was balloonists talking to their ground station, which must be close by. "They are ready to launch," the mechanical voice said. "They have a green flag."

"Understood," was the reply from the ground. Peering towards the sound, Sapper could make out a small hut, blending in with the surroundings. Taking out his spyglass, Sapper swept the skies, but the undergrowth hid the balloon and any flag.

He wondered what they were launching, and moved past the hut towards the river. Reaching the last of the bushes he crouched down.

He didn't have to ponder for long, the voice squawked, "Away!" and he heard a roaring noise to his left. Turning his head, he suddenly caught a glimpse of a bright red machine, flashing down the valley, it was past him so quickly and was such an unexpected thing that he almost thought he had imagined it. He had never seen such a thing before and found it hard to grasp what he was seeing.

"Past and clear," reported the voice. "The flyer seems to be keeping his feet dry this time. Our flags have been acknowledged, winch us down." Sapper retreated back towards the road, hiding in dense brambles and ferns. He found it hard to believe that he had just seen a man flying.

"Very well, just give me a minute," answered the man in the hut. There was the sound of a chair being drawn back and as Sapper shrank down, a soldier emerged from the hut, in shirtsleeves and with leather braces holding up his uniform trousers. He passed so close to Sapper that he could make out the man's features, he was heavy set with a bristling moustache.

He was just about to creep away, when he heard the sound of a clockwork winch. Changing his mind he moved towards the hut, hand on his bayonet. But the room was empty. There was a small brazier, on which a charpot sat, apart from that there was only a single chair in front of a desk. A speaker set hung on the wall. Quickly he looked around him; there were a jumble of items on the desk. He picked up a small bag, opening it he saw that it contained an identification badge, attached to a parchment pass with a ribbon. Judging by the desk, the soldier was making them up, piles of the parchment and ribbon lay around. He scooped a handful of the bags up, shoving them into his pocket. They may well come in useful, he thought. Looking at the soldier's jacket, which was hung over a chair, it had one of the badges pinned to the left breast pocket under his name-tag and medal ribbons. Turning, he peered carefully round the door. The winch was still in operation and he could hear talking both from the ground and from the air. The balloon must be nearly landed, he thought, and ran quickly into the cover of the bushes. There was another path from the hut and he watched as two men in the heavy gear of balloonists trudged up it. Keeping to the side of the path, Sapper followed them, pinning one of the badges onto his lapel as he walked. The path joined the road.

Chapter 50

Chimneys came into sight long before buildings, and the frequency of passing steam-mobiles and lorries increased. There were several types, from large and tracked to small and wheeled. All were painted dull brown and blue, and marked with the Ministry crest. One fitted as an omnibus had stopped and picked up the balloonists. Sapper reached a hill and near the top he lay down. Crawling to the top he peered over. The main camp was laid out below him.

There was a large open space, around which buildings clustered. Off to one side was a row of houses, looking out of place with their small gardens. Large watchtowers stood at the corners of the buildings with strange objects mounted atop them. There was Drogan netting spread between the buildings.

The most important job would be to find Grace, to that end he needed to work out which building was the prison. He spent time looking at each building, trying to fathom the uses of each. Some were obvious, the Local and the coal store amongst them. And the row of barracks looked like any row of barracks in Norlandia, with its regimental flag fluttering. Sapper gazed through his spyglass, he thought he knew every regiments' flag but this one was a mystery to him. There was one building off to one side, with smaller windows, the only one showing bars. That must be the prison.

An idea began to form in his head as he crawled back out of sight. The autumn light was fading and he decided to look for a place to spend the night, his plan would have to wait for the morning. Once he was back over the crest he rose and made his way into a stand of tall trees.

As night fell, Sapper could see a glow in the sky over the hill, he realised that the towers held some sort of powerful statics light, which moved around, illuminating the complex. He had seen such lights on navy ships but never on land. Clearly this place was important. He was tired from his exertions and setting down his pack, he lay with his back against a tree.

Sapper awoke with a jolt; the earth was shaking under him. Day had broken. Bleary eyed and slightly apprehensive, he crawled to the edge of the glade and looked around. The earth resonated to a steady thump, thump and animals crawled through the undergrowth all around him, even the earthworms were awoken, scurrying and slithering as they took flight.

A line of Exo-Men was coming across the moorland, striding quicker than any he had seen before. He had a clear sight of them and it took a moment to realise that they were not connected to any generators that he could see. Normally, there was the snaking steam hose attached to the rear of the Exo at mid-back level, but these did not possess any such appendage. He rubbed his eyes, scarcely able to believe what they were showing him. They were in perfect time, feet rising and falling as one. It was this stepping down that had awoken him. As they came closer, Sapper could see that they were twice the size of the Exo-Men in common use, and appeared to be self-contained, having a chimney on top of the body. The implications for the future were astounding; in both war and peace the things he had seen since he crawled under the fence could change the world.

Now was the time for him to get closer to the buildings, and perhaps find Grace. Judging by the size of the place it was unlikely that everyone knew everyone and he had his badge from the balloonist's hut.

He took out his uniform jacket and trousers, which he had folded into the bottom of his pack. They were slightly creased but would serve better than his camouflage. He changed quickly, remembering to add a badge to his lapel. Hiding his pack in the trees he adjusted his cap and confidently marched off towards the camp.

Sapper approached the parade ground, keeping his eyes open for signs that his presence was unexpected. There were enough soldiers moving around to render him inconspicuous and he marched towards the building he had marked as the cell block, the one set apart with the small barred windows. As he passed each soldier, he took a closer look at their cap badges, they were many different ones; all unfamiliar to him, but his elicited no response.

He was almost at the building when a voice rang out, "Stop that man!" Sapper stood and slowly turned around. Across the other side of the parade ground a burly soldier was surrounded by a group dressed in black. The voice rang out again, and Sapper realised that it was not directed at him, the burly soldier was being admonished for incorrect dress or some other misdemeanour. Breathing a sigh of relief, Sapper entered the door to the cell block. He was met by a guard, gas pistol ready, who eyed him suspiciously.

"And where are you going?" the guard asked in a bark.

Sapper noted the security measures, the locked doors and reflecting mirrors which gave a view all along the corridors. "I'm new here," he answered. "Trying to find my bearings, is this the cookhouse?"

The guard looked at his badge and laughed. "Balloonist eh!" he observed. "Does it look like the cookhouse? This here is the place for all the wrong 'uns. The cookhouse is outside and to your right. Now clear off back to your balloon."

Sapper left, it was clear that he would not get in there easily, even with the badge.

He was lost in thought as he rounded the end of the building and bumped into a woman coming the other way. She kept her face lowered, averting her eyes. "Beg pardon, sir," she muttered and tried to pass. Her tone was familiar to Sapper.

"Grace?" said Sapper. "Is that you?"

Her face turned up. Sapper could see the thinness of her features, and the red eyes from crying but her curls were still distinct under the kerchief. On realising who he was she broke into a smile. "Sapper," she said as she looked wildly around. "Where is Horis, am I to be rescued?"

"I would love to rescue you," replied Sapper, "but I am alone."

Her face fell and she slumped. Sapper put his arm around her shoulders.

"Fear not," he reassured her, "Horis is on the way but not yet present, I am reconnoitring so as to make a plan."

"Thank Bal," she replied, moving away and almost dancing. She held his hands and looked longingly at him. "When can I be rescued?"

"Within the next few days, we are nearly in readiness," he said and her joy was evident.

"Listen, this may help you, there will be a flying demonstration here in five days, at noontime," she said. "There will be so many extra folk about the place that I would not immediately be missed. And I am free to move around, as long as I perform my tasks, looking after the flyers' needs."

"That sounds useful. We will aim to be here then, depend on it," replied Sapper, calculating his options. There would be just enough time to get back to Mrs Wring's and return as a group. If Horis and Maloney had arrived by then they could assist. If not, Sapper supposed he would have to manage somehow.

Just then one of the warders approached, flicking her whip. "No fraternising, I've told you before," she shouted. "Now get back to your duties, girl. And you," she spat at Sapper, "if it's girls you're after, get you to the commissary."

"I will see you again," said Sapper as Grace was led away with flicks of the whip. He knew not if she had heard him. He only hoped he could deliver on his promise.

Sapper moved across the parade ground. His work was done, now he had a plan and a time, all he had to do was get back to town with the knowledge. But first he must retrieve his pack.

Chapter 51

On the morning of their arrival at Northcastle, Horis rose early and went to stand in the wheel-space of the *Rainbow*. In the dawning sky he could see the rocky outline of the coast and nestling in its shadow the tops of cranes. Faustus handed him a spyglass and looking through it he saw the entrance to the Gurden River with the port breakwaters on the northern side. Slightly behind them was a small town, spreading out from the river banks up the hills in an untidy cluster of dwellings. All were made from dull grey blocks which sparkled in the morning damp and low sunshine. Smoke from the Locals stained the blue of the sky.

The harbour pilot boarded up a rope ladder and took charge, easing the vessel down the buoyed channel and through the breakwaters. Here tugboats made fast at each end and the vessel was turned and laid alongside a stone jetty, fendered with wooden posts. Almost before the crew had secured the mooring ropes, a gang of longshoremen boarded over the rails and started opening the vessel's holds. The pilot departed with a handshake and a bottle of Malt from the ship's stores for his trouble.

Faustus excused himself. "I must go and greet the customs man," he said and Horis who had quite forgotten his criminal status felt a sudden panic. Faustus saw this and reassured him. "Fear not, I know the man from old. After a few glasses of Malt he will not care if the ship is full of Drogans. Get you both ready to go ashore."

Horis and Maloney were all ready to depart as soon as the customs had finished their business. They had to present themselves in front of the officer and have their identities checked. Faustus had worked his magic for they were barely noticed as the bored and slightly inebriated officer glanced at them and their identity cards. Collecting their gear they walked down the gangway. As they crossed the wharf, dodging the steam-mobiles and swinging cranes they spotted Keen, who had been chosen to spend the day waiting for their arrival.

On the way to the rest of the group, Horis could not contain himself. "Have you had word on Grace?" he asked.

Keen tried to sound unconcerned. "We have not," he answered. "Sapper went off a few days ago. But that is not a problem; he can remain invisible and evade capture for longer than that. He'll be gathering as much information as he can before he returns."

After a brisk walk in the sunshine, they arrived at a large stone building. Keen walked up the steps and opened the door with a key. "What's this?" said Maloney. "You have found us somewhere grand to stay then."

"We have," he replied, "and it's fortunate we did not decide to camp. Since we arrived the weather has turned for the worse. Not so much rain but cold, in short we would be freezing anywhere else whilst we waited for developments. When Harris arrived in town he met Mrs Wring. That is a tale of fortune in itself. She persuaded him to come and stay with her."

"Well," said Maloney, "she must be a formidable lady if she can sway Harris."

"After sampling her hospitality he had no hesitation, he was at the terminus next day with the good news when we arrived."

"Who have you there?" The voice echoed along the hall. "Mr Keen, pray introduce your companions."

Mrs Wring appeared from a side room, her hair swept into a large bun atop her head, making her appear taller. As usual when talking, her muscular forearms were crossed under her ample bosom. She radiated a powerful presence.

Horis could see immediately that she was a lady to be reckoned with, not unlike Sour Face back in Aserol. Only this lady had a kindly air about her, like a favourite aunt.

Names and handshakes were exchanged and Horis was impressed with the strength of her grip.

"Come," she said, "I have a hot meal ready for you all."

Entering the dining room, they greeted the rest of the group. Horis was relieved to see them all and started to believe that now they were here the rescue of Grace was possible. All that was needed now was the return of Sapper.

After the meal, a rich stew with unspecified but delicious contents, Horis felt drowsy, it was probably a reaction to the stress of his journey. Excusing himself he went to his room and fell fast asleep.

Chapter 52

He was awoken at some early hour of the morn by a commotion downstairs and the booming voice of Mrs Wring. Rising and dressing he went out onto the landing, from where he could hear a familiar voice.

"I declare, it's good to see you," said Sapper, on sight of Horis. "And I have good news for you."

Horis practically shook him. "Tell me without delay."

"In good time," said Maloney. "We should all sleep, for I feel we may have to move quickly now."

But Horis would not be moved. "Sapper, I implore you, ease my mind."

Sapper grinned. "The lady is well, if a little thinner and awaits rescue. She has been reasonably treated and has furnished me with news that will help our plan."

Horis was so relieved to hear the news that he embraced Sapper. "Oh thank you for your bravery," he exclaimed in a heartfelt tone. Sapper, embarrassed, gently disentangled himself. "And there is more," he said. "On my walk I have thought of a way in, and a means of escape."

"How so?" enquired Maloney, all thoughts of waiting till morning seemed to have deserted him.

"Well," replied the other, "they use a particular type of steam-lorry for all transport to and fro. They all have a small parchment device in the front, behind the window, this is checked every time one enters or leaves. It is the same as the one every soldier wears."

"So we need to copy one of them?" asked Maloney.

"Oh no." Sapper rummaged in his backpack. "I have some here."

He produced a handful. "I got them from the maker, after I went in for a little look around. There is no guarding to speak of; they place all their trust in the fence. Once inside it, you are assumed to be on some legitimate purpose."

"So we can just borrow a steam-lorry and drive in?"

"Well, some of us can, but the rest might be advised to go in the long way round. And now I'm tired, we have time to spare and I must sleep."

And Horis had to leave it at that.

The relief of knowing that Grace was safe meant that Horis slept soundly, and had to be awoken by Maloney, who brought a steaming mug of char to him.

The sun was just clearing the hills to the east, shining dully through thin clouds and the even thinner curtains at the window. After another enormous fast-breaker they spent the morning refining a rescue plan, Sapper reported all he had learned, from the fence to the disposition of troops. Horis made him relate his meeting with Grace several times. And they thrashed out details.

"We have the rough basis of a plan then," said Maloney at last. "And it's set for three days from now. The special event in the compound is a stroke of luck; it will cause enough of a distraction to help us in our work. Sapper has found where she will be on that day, and has passes for us to get into the facility. All we need is a steam-lorry and Keen can get off and arrange that now. Sapper and three others will set off overland, he knows the way in. They will extract Grace from her duties and escort her to the lorry which you and I will take inside."

"But I have no uniform," said Horis.

"None needed, you have a suit and a Ministry identification, and you will be with me, I will be in uniform so it will appear that I am under your command."

"But what if we are stopped? Suppose my name is on some list of undesirables," said Horis.

"Just brandish it and shout if you have to," replied Sapper, "act as if you own the place."

~~~

Keen returned with the lorry in mid-afternoon, it was painted in the Ministry colours and had a gate pass affixed in the front window glass. Keen said not where he had obtained it and Horis thought it better not to ask. He took Sapper and the rest as close as he could to the fence before returning in darkness.

After going over the plan again, there were two days to wait; everything was in place save the *Swiftsure*. Next day, Keen went to the port offices and found that it was expected on the next day and should remain for at least a week. This good news allowed them to relax a little, it would be easier to take Grace direct to the ship than bring her to Mrs Wring and then move her through the town. They spent a relaxing day and had an early night, after mugs of Mrs Wring's malted milk to aid their slumbers. Tomorrow would be a busy day.

In the morning they left in the lorry, Keen was driving in full uniform, with Maloney and Horis sitting on the seats behind him. The lorry was poorly sprung and rattled over the cobbled roadway through the town. Once they were clear of the narrow streets they joined the smooth roadway to the camp. It was busy with traffic, mobiles full of soldiers and grander vehicles of the rich and powerful were all converging on the place for the flying demonstration.

Sapper and his companions had had plenty of time to march in and lie up. The hope was that everyone would be in position at the same time.

They approached the main gate and slowed in a long line of traffic. The guard came from his box and saw the pass in the window. Turning to his companion, he shouted and raised his right hand in a salute. The barrier raised and they drove through. They were clearly overwhelmed by the numbers arriving and were passing everyone, Horis need not have worried.

The main parade ground was packed, with raised seating on one side, ready for the throng to behold the flying machines. Keen drove carefully around the back of the structure and parked the mobile in its lee, he left the engine running and the rhythmic rattle of coal dust into the furnace set Horis dozing. He awoke to see that he was alone and panic gripped him. Slowing his breathing helped to steady his thoughts and before long Maloney and Keen reappeared, with mugs of char. "Oh you're awake now are you?" Keen cheerfully exclaimed, passing Horis a mug. "We didn't want to disturb you, you looked so peaceful."

Horis tried not to look embarrassed. "I don't know how I could doze," he said, "when Grace is still not safe and I am surrounded by enemies."

"We have had a quick turn around the place," said Maloney. "There is a small fenced compound by the side of the seats, it looks like it will be where Grace will be held."

"And we have found Sapper and the others," added Keen, "so we are all ready."

With an hour to go till the display an official party arrived. Cavendish was in the lead and took his seat in the front row, next to the camp commander.

"Where is Mr Terrance?" asked the Commander. "He left this morn; I thought he would return with you."

"I know not," replied Cavendish. "We conversed yesterday and I expected to meet him here."

"He went out this morning," repeated the Commander. "I assumed he had gone out to greet you."

Cavendish was clearly annoyed at Terrance's absence. He looked around at the open space with a look of puzzlement.

"Tell me, Commander, why are there no balloons flying, and I see that the towers and nets are struck."

"Mr Terrance wanted the area clear for the flyers," he answered. Cavendish shook his head; this was more of Terrance's slovenly planning.

"And what of the Drogans? We know they are attracted to large gatherings of humans."

"We have had no Drogans for months," said the Commander, with confidence. Had he known what Ralf had seen and reported he would not have appeared so, but secrecy was so tightly enforced around the camp that the message had not been passed.

Chapter 53

Since seeing Sapper, Grace had more of a spring in her step; her despair had gone, as had her doubts. In the absence of proof that Horis was coming she had been ready to follow Ralf's plan. Of course she realised that once she was outside the fence she had no plan for what she would do next. Now that she knew that Horis was on his way and there was a plan for her rescue, everything had changed. At the same time she was careful to temper her elation with caution, as she did not want her captors to have any cause to change their treatment of her. If they guessed from her demeanour that she may be rescued, then she could find her movement around the camp restricted. With the passing of time she had been given more freedom and she suspected that she owed a debt to Ralf for that. She had not seen Ralf, or any of the flyers since she had seen Sapper; they had been separated from the rest of the camp. There had been a lot of flying, with groups of three of the planes practising over the parade ground all the hours of daylight.

The days until the flying display could be marked with the progress of the building works on the parade ground. A large wooden frame was bolted together, to which seats were added in tiered rows. Flagpoles were raised all around the frame and bunting strung. The Drogan nets and watchtowers were struck. All the male prisoners were put to work on the task and the job continued after dark, under statics lanterns mounted on portable tripod masts. The noise was a constant backdrop to sleep, although Grace and the others were too tired to be kept awake by it.

On the day of the display the morn was bright and clear. When she was let out of her cell, Grace could see that preparations were well underway. As she went about her tasks, the parade ground was hosed down and swept. Unexpectedly the flyers came in for fast-break, they were subdued and ate in silence. Grace caught Ralf's eye and he smiled and beckoned her over. "Today is the day," he whispered as she served him porker and eggs from the trolley. "I will do my part to aid your escape, when I do you will have but one chance, take it and head for the coast. I have told you of the break in the fence by the cliffs."

"Thank you," said Grace, she did not want to tell him of Sapper and her impending rescue. "What will you do?"

"You will know it when it happens," said Ralf, "watch for my dive. There is a cache of clothes and other useful things for you," he continued, "left by the rear door of this building, behind the swill bins. Good luck to you."

The flyers finished and left and as Grace cleared the table she saw a steady procession of people start to arrive and seat themselves. There were many grand mobiles and she saw faces that had only been seen as pencil drawings on the news-sheet, whispers were exchanged on the identity of some, and of the companions that they had with them.

There would be a great crowd, that much was evident and in the same way as it would cover her under Ralf's plan it would do the same for Horis. She wondered how he would arrive, would he walk in like Sapper had done and expect her to walk out, or would he arrive by mobile, like any senior official would? She decided that if she could, she would attempt to use the clothing that Ralf had left for her, it would make her less conspicuous, whichever way rescue came. And if she needed to walk, the overalls and boots would be easier to move in than her rag of a gown. She spent the rest of the morning packing luncheons into baskets, pies and apples and small bottles of wine for the guests, together with glasses and napkins, they were taken out as fast as they were assembled and handed to the arriving throng.

When the task was complete, Grace and the rest of the kitchen staff were allowed to take a few morsels from the leftovers and were sent to stand at one end of the seating in a small group, watched by three soldiers. The mood was relaxed and convivial.

The crowds were all assembled, lunch had been eaten and the agreed time for the display was upon them. Cavendish looked about him from his position in the front row. He was facing the hills and although he knew what was coming he had never actually seen the flying machines.

His ire had not faded, where was Terrance and why had he removed all the protection from the parade ground? Didn't he realise that most of the government was here? He rose from his seat and walked to the middle of the parade ground. All the soldiers had been assembled in ranks, their buttons gleaming. The soldiers had no weapons; the government were not that trusting of the generals. All the rifles and pistols were stored in a secure place, well-guarded by trusted men. Turning to face the seated throng Cavendish cleared his throat.

"Citizens," he began, "we are here today to witness the next glorious chapter in our country's story. Unfortunately His Majesty cannot be here to see it," he paused and there was a groan, the Monarch was popular, the best figurehead the Club had picked so far.

"But rest assured," he continued, "I have spoken with him recently; he is well aware of the achievements of our scientists here and you are all in his thoughts." Again there was a cheer and hats were waved.

"And now, let us see what has been done here." He waved his arm and the word was passed to the flyers, behind the hill on the roadway.

Ralf and his colleagues were poised. They had trained and practised almost without ceasing since news of the display had reached them. They had been kept apart from their fellows. There were six flyers that were good enough at flying in formation and performing the manoeuvres. Ralf had chosen the two who were to accompany him in the first flypast. After a delay of a few minutes the second three would join in. The rest sat in a group by the spare planes.

"Off you go, boys," said the artificer, as the message was passed to him. "Good flying." The engines were started.

The first three planes ran down the roadway spaced fifty feet apart, Ralf in the lead. As their speed increased they lifted off the ground and climbed into the sky. As arranged, they formed up in a line abreast and turned towards the parade ground. As they flashed close over the hilltop and saw the parade ground beneath them they flew low over it in formation. They passed over the heads of the crowd with a roar and a wind that dislodged caps and ruffled crinolines; then as one they climbed into the sky, turning for another pass.

Ralf was now ready to create his diversion. He intended to ignore the planned manoeuvre and fly straight towards the end of the seating where he knew Grace would be, pulling away at the last minute. He would explain it away afterwards as a temporary problem with his controls. His hope was that the plane being so close would startle the guards and divert their attention, allowing Grace to run. But as the three swung around and lined up they saw a terrible thing come over the hills.

They had been followed by Drogans; there must have been twenty or more darkening the sky. Where they had come from was impossible to tell but they now fell on the helpless crowd beneath, there was little they could do about it. All the defences had been struck and there were no nets or watchtowers. All the soldiers on the ground were unarmed. They had only their planes guns to defend the government.

Chapter 54

On the parade ground Cavendish had just regained his seat when the planes could be heard. The crowd looked up and saw the three come over the hills flying in formation. There was a gasp, turning to a cheer, as they passed low overhead and heads turned as they rose again behind them. Then someone looked back and saw the Drogans appear. Their first thought must have been that they were more flying machines. "Look!" was the cry, "there are more of them."

"No, they are Drogans," shouted another and the cheers became a scream.

The whole crowd moved as one, like a wave breaking, to avoid the dive of the beasts.

Even though all three aircraft had the new gas guns fitted into the wings the pilots were loath to use them for fear of hitting the crowds. In a ragged line abreast they did the first thing they could think of, they flew into the melee, attempting to disrupt the Drogans' attack.

Ralf saw the flyer on his left misjudge his dive and crash into the crowds, with a whoosh his gas tanks erupted in flames, adding to the pandemonium. At this point the three other planes arrived; the artificer had seen the Drogans and had sent them off to assist.

The crowds had ceased to care about the planes, they milled about under the flapping wings of the Drogans and their razor tipped claws, screaming and dying under the assault.

Cavendish turned to the Commander, "unlock the guns," he screamed. "Arm your men."

A Drogan appeared in front of him and he flinched. Suddenly his face was soaked in the blood of the Commander, whose head had been bitten off by the Drogan. Cavendish's calm deserted him as the body fell at his feet. He staggered over it and ran towards the troops, "Fire on them," he shouted, "get your weapons and fire on the Drogans."

The soldiers had already moved to comply but they were hampered by each other.

Suddenly, the end of the seating platform, by the only stairway, collapsed under the extra weight of panicked humanity. This added to the chaos and provided easy pickings for the Drogans to land and feast on.

Even over the roar of the engine Ralf could hear the screams. A Drogan appeared in front of him and he pressed the red button on his control stick.

The Drogan shuddered under the strike of the lead bullets and fell to earth, landing on its comrades. They ignored its throes as they concentrated on their prey. Another pilot had witnessed the demise of the Drogan and did the same, swooping behind a beast and loosing off his guns. The range was so small that the effect was to almost cut the body in half. The Drogans that still flew realised that they had a new enemy. They bunched together and flapped protectively over those on the ground. Ralf and the others now flew leisurely and shot at the flying Drogans at will. The troops had started to regain order and were receiving arms from the store. They formed up and started firing at the grounded beasts. The worst might be over, thought Ralf, but it was still dangerous, a Drogan's wing slashed at one of planes and the pilot collided with the beast as he tried to evade it. The propeller sliced great chunks of Drogan flesh away before it shattered. The plane and the Drogan fell to earth in a bloody mess. There was another explosion.

Sapper saw his chance. He had spotted Grace at the other end of the seating to the stairway and with Wilson and Daniel in tow had worked his way towards her before the planes had appeared. Now he could not see her in the crowd of milling bodies. "Split up," he said to Wilson and Daniel. "She is here somewhere." Ignoring the Drogans they forced their way through the crowds.

Grace had taken the chance to slip away when the Drogans first attacked. The soldiers guarding the group had run for weapons, leaving them to fend for themselves. Most of them stayed where they were, cowering under the seats but Grace moved off with a purpose. She was not frightened but intent and she moved quickly to the rear of the mess-room. Finding the things left by Ralf, she crouched behind the bins and removed her gown. The overalls were too long for her but when she had rolled the sleeves and legs up they looked presentable. Tucking her hair under the cap which had also been left she laced up the stout boots, re-emerged and made for the place she had been. She saw Sapper and went towards him. "Hello Sapper," she said and at first he did not realise who she was. She pulled the cap off and her curls tumbled free, recognition dawned on him.

"You had a gown on, not a minute ago," he said and she laughed.

"I'll explain later, is this part of your plan?"

"A bit more than I had expected," he said with a chuckle. "Come on."

Sapper grabbed Grace as all around there was screaming and the flapping of leathery wings. The squawks of the Drogans mixed with the panicked cries of the humans and there was the snap of teeth. He forced her through the crowds toward a steam-lorry.

Grace found herself hoisted into the load-bed of the lorry under its canvas cover, the tailboard was slammed shut and Sapper shouted, "Hold tight!" as he ran to the door. Grace saw there was another in the gloom and realised it was Horis.

"Oh my love," she cried and they embraced. As he held her he was shocked at her thinness. "How I have longed for today," she muttered in between kisses. The lorry rattled as it stood and they fell entwined to the floor.

Sapper was leaning through the front window, talking to Maloney. "Me and the boys will hike out," he said. "The pass will get you out alright."

"I'll get them on the *Swiftsure*," Maloney said, "then come back to Mrs Wring's to wait for you, we can all leave this place together." Maloney waved his arm out of the window as they accelerated away.

Chapter 55

Grace and Horis sat in the rear of the steam-lorry as it drove towards the gatehouse. Overhead, Ralf and the other surviving flyers were still attacking the Drogans. There was the rattle of small-arms fire as the soldiers, under Cavendish's command, mounted resistance. Keen stopped the lorry at the barrier pole. The soldier checked the parchment disc in the windshield and had wound the barrier halfway open when a luxurious steam-mobile approached from the direction of Northcastle, the driver sounding his horn continuously. The soldier stopped winding, sighed and said, "One moment if you please, sir. I'll just sort this out."

The driver of the mobile got out and approached the gate at a run. "You must let me in, I'm late," he panted. It was Terrance and looking across he recognised Maloney. His face registered shock for a second, then surprise.

"Stop that lorry!" he yelled at the soldier. Maloney and Keen saw Terrance at the same time and Keen pressed the accelerator to the floor. With a belch of smoke the lorry lurched forward. There was scarce enough room for the cab to squeeze under the pole, but the lorry was building up momentum, the pole hit the roof of the cab which splintered as they raced through the gap and onto the road away from the camp.

Alarmed at the sudden movement, Horis and Grace looked out of the join in the canvas cover. They saw a scene of confusion. Terrance had got back into his mobile and was trying to turn it around but was jammed by the press of traffic, a soldier had jumped into it and another was shooting the fixed gas rifle at them, one of the explosive projectiles hit the ground under the lorry and it lifted off the ground from the blast.

Inside, Horis and Grace were tossed around like dolls, but the lorry kept upright and continued down the hill. As it swung around the first bend the gatehouse was no longer in sight.

Maloney opened the partition. "Are you alright in there?" he called; both Grace and Horis were shaken but managed to reply in the affirmative.

"We are discovered," he said. "Now we must keep moving as they will soon be after us, if we can get to the docks unseen we may be able to complete our plan."

They reached the fork and without hesitation Keen took the unmade road. "We will do better here," he explained, seeing Maloney's quizzical expression. "I've been down here on foot. We can go faster than a luxury mobile on this unmade road."

They bounced down the road with Horis looking over the rear of the lorry. The blast from the projectile had blown a hole in the floor and the road could be seen through it. He expected to see Terrance gaining on them at any moment, but the road was twisting and rutted. The high suspension of the lorry had saved them from the worst of the blast and now it meant that they could travel faster than a low slung mobile, which would scrape the ground as its wheels hit the potholes. Added to that, the road wound around the hillside and there was never a long straight section on which to build up speed.

Suddenly Horis and Grace were thrown to one side as the lorry cornered sharply. Then they were flung forward as they came to a halt. "What are you doing?" Horis called through the partition.

"We have turned off and are hidden down a track," replied Keen, opening the door and getting out of the cab. "We cannot be easily seen here." And with that he ran back towards the road, Maloney and the others following. Sure enough they were in a small depression, surrounded by trees. They hid behind the trees nearest the road and watched as Terrance's mobile came towards the turning and drove past. Terrance and a soldier armed with a gas rifle were inside and their speed was slow, they bounced and jarred on every obstacle. Even so, they showed no sign of stopping as they passed the hiding place.

Chapter 56

The lorry was shuddering and hissing as pressure was vented from its boiler. Grace and Horis stayed at the edge of the trees and peered at the road. "Keep your heads down!" shouted Maloney as he and Keen wrestled with the canvas cover on the back.

On the other side of the road from their hiding place the cliffs sloped steeply down to the sea and the harbour was visible.

"I spotted this place when I was scouting," said Keen. "There were a gang of labourers loading a lorry here when I passed. I reckoned the place might come in handy as a refuge and a place to disguise us."

"Well done," congratulated Maloney who was using his false arm to try and lift the canvas cover and its frame clear of the lorry. The drive over the uneven road and the impact of the gas bomb under the lorry had twisted the struts. "Hey Horis, come and give us a help here," he called.

Between the three of them, they removed the cover from the rear of the lorry and the metal frame that carried it. The appearance of the lorry had been altered but Keen was not finished. Beside the lorry was a large pile of cut logs. "There were more here then. Still, there's enough to fill the lorry up," he said and Maloney nodded.

"Good plan, Mr Keen," he said.

As they lifted the logs onto the load-bed, Horis called out to Grace, who was still watching the road. "Grace," he said, "'Tis a pity Divid is not here with his Exo to help us." At the memory of her brother Grace sniffed a tear away. "Poor Divid," she said, "I must get a message to him, he will be worried by now."

"Plenty of time for that," called Horis, "we will be back in Aserol soon."

"I hate to disappoint you, Horis, but you and Grace can't go back to Aserol."

"What do you mean, Maloney?" asked Horis, he had thought no further than getting away and spending the rest of his life in Aserol with Grace.

She had not heard Maloney's words, there were other things on her mind though, she had spied the *Swiftsure* alongside but there was a troubling development.

"Maloney, have you your telescope?" she called. "In the cab, girl," he answered. "What's amiss?"

She did not answer him but went to the cab and retrieved the telescope. Gazing at the *Swiftsure* confirmed her suspicions. "Mr Maloney, we must rush to the port," she gasped.

"What do you mean, Grace?" said Horis, breathless now from the unaccustomed exertion.

"Uncle Hector is flying the sailing flag," she said. "It means all crew to return, the vessel will sail on the tide."

"We have enough logs," Keen decided. "We will pass for a merchant now." The pile in the lorry was respectable and the three roughly secured it with a rope and the tailboard.

"Come on then," said Maloney as they all climbed back into the cab. He removed the parchment pass from the window as Keen turned the lorry around. The soldiers had removed their uniform jackets and now looked like any lorrymen. Horis was in his shirt and braces, grimy and sweat stained. He and Grace sat in the back seats holding hands.

They eased back out onto the track and proceeded slowly down the hill. Grace explained the significance of the flag as they jolted over the rough road. "It's flown for six hours before sailing," she said, "so the crew can know to leave the ale houses and their girls and get back on board."

They were passed by several army vehicles, in both directions but were paid little attention. They saw Terrance in his mobile heading back towards the camp; he was looking for a covered lorry and sped past. Each time a vehicle approached, Keen or Maloney shouted a warning and the two in the rear ducked down.

They reached the paved road and increased the speed. "How will we get into the docks?" asked Horis. In the excitement he had quite forgotten Maloney's remark.

"Leave that to us," was the reply. "Now lay down." They both did so and a large piece of sacking was thrown over them. "Don't move till I say," said Maloney.

At the dock gate they stopped at the customs post. A burly officer strode towards them. Keen wound down the side glass. "Logs for the *Swiftsure,*" said Keen, jerking his hand over his shoulder.

"Where is the paper for this load then?" asked the officer, holding his hand out.

"We have none," admitted Maloney. The customs man tensed. "We saw that the *Swiftsure* is to sail and we were in a rush," he continued.

"That's the truth," said Keen, "and we only have half a load and all in our haste. We will get no profit unless we can deliver this."

The officer nodded in understanding. "'Tis true, the order for the ship to sail came as a surprise, very well then you may go in," and he waved to his mate who lifted the gate.

"You can get up now," said Maloney, prodding the sacking. They emerged looking red-faced.

"Bravo Mr Maloney," said Grace in an admiring tone. Maloney blushed. "But what did you mean about Aserol not being safe?" she continued, "Horis just told me."

"Well," he said, "I'm sorry but I thought you would have realised, you cannot go there, everyone will expect you and that's where they will await."

"But why?" she said.

Horis answered her. "I'm afraid, my dear, that we have defied the government, we have proof of things they want hidden. I fear they will not rest till we are recaptured."

"I want to go home," said Grace with a catch in her voice. "I want to see Divid and drink in the *Drogan.* I want to grow old there with you. Why rescue me if we can't be together?" Horis held her as she sobbed.

"I see the truth of it, Maloney," he said. "Grace will come to understand. We will be safe on the *Swiftsure* until then."

"I will pass a message to Divid through my boys," Maloney assured them, "he will be comforted that you are alive and safe."

They rounded a cargo shed and saw the *Swiftsure* in front of them, its gangway unwatched. Keen stopped the lorry by it and they disembarked.

Chapter 57

Terrance had driven all the way into town without sight of the lorry. Desperately, he returned to the camp. He scanned the traffic for the steam-lorry with a damaged cab and ripped roof but saw none matching that description. Only one vaguely resembled his quarry, it had a damaged cab, but as it passed it was only a woodsman with a load of logs in an open load-bed.

At the camp the soldiers had restored some sort of order; the Drogans had been driven off with a barrage of fire from the soldiers and the flyers. Many of the beasts lay dead. There was a row of bodies in front of the collapsed seating, some without heads where the beasts had bitten them off. Under the woodwork there were more and a pool of blood surrounded the lower steps like a frozen lake. Others had been the unfortunate victims of the flyers' gas guns. The pyre of the flying machines and their human victims still smouldered. The remaining flyers had run low on gas and bullets and had returned to land and refuel. The smell of blood and death hung in the air as Terrance alighted and walked over to his senior.

"Where have you been?" Cavendish asked Terrance, as the latter surveyed the scene of carnage with shocked eyes.

"I was delayed in town," Terrance answered, in fact he had been organising the clearing of a berth for the ship from Aserol. On completion of that chore, he had taken an early lunch with one of his lady friends, one thing had led to another and he had fallen asleep. Cavendish did not need to know that part.

"Strongman was here," he blurted out.

Cavendish laughed. "Oh really, did you see him?"

"I saw him going out or at least I saw his henchman, that oaf

Maloney from Aserol, the ex-soldier. They were in a lorry. I chased them but they evaded me somehow."

Cavendish called for the Guard Captain. "Find the lady," he ordered.

"Yessir, which one, sir?" the man asked. Cavendish turned to Terrance. "Describe her." He barked.

"Grace, the flyers' stewardess," Terrance answered.

Cavendish looked at him with disbelief. "She is the flyers' stewardess?" he said.

"You told me to treat her well so that she might talk," Terrance replied sullenly, he was fed-up with running around doing this man's bidding; he always felt he was doing the wrong thing.

Cavendish sighed. "I said treat her well, not give her the run of the place, and while I'm trying to make sense of your actions, why did you remove all the towers and nets?"

"It seemed safer for the flyers," Terrance started, realising the enormity of the events that had taken place. And of his part in them.

"They could have just flown OVER them," said Cavendish. "At least the crowds would have been safer."

The Guard Captain returned, his face was red and he was out of breath, he saluted Terrance. "Beg pardon, sir, but we cannot find the girl, no-one has seen her." He held up a gown. "We found this by the swill bins."

"That's hers," said Terrance, grabbing the garment.

"She has got away then," observed Cavendish. "With your junior and the soldier Maloney. I found out about him after the events in the city. You called him an oaf, not so. The man is resourceful, a highly decorated senior from the regiment of pioneers."

"Where can they go?" said Terrance.

"They will have made a plan, and there would have been others involved; that much is obvious. Captain, we need to seal the town and the port. Stop the evening Ryde to the city." Quickly Cavendish gave orders and the man ran off to comply.

At mention of the port, Terrance remembered his reason for

being late. "Cavendish," he said, "the rocks from Aserol will be arriving in the port tonight, which is why I was late, I had to clear a berth for the vessel."

"At least we can salvage something from this shambles then," said Cavendish. "If we are not too late we may yet round everyone up." He looked at Terrance with his cold eyes. "For your sake I hope so. When things have quietened down you will have some explaining to do."

He gestured at the line of bodies. "Half the government is lying there, largely due to your actions. You are not the man your father was, by a long distance. Oh yes, there will be a reckoning."

Chapter 58

Nabbaro was pacing the deck by the gangway, there was definitely something going on, he had expected to be here under repairs for at least a week but just after luncheon a port official had come on board and ordered him to leave on the tide. There was no reason for it that he could see and the official gave none. So he had to agree, and had hoisted the departure flag, hoping it would spur action. In truth he knew that it was probably futile, but he hoped. He had no way of knowing how close Grace was to rescue, so he paced. There had been a lot of noise from the distance and the stevedores had said that there were crowds in the camp. Hector with his keen sailor's eye and telescope had watched Drogans in the distance, more of them than he had seen in one place before. There was definitely something going on.

He knew that the pilot would be arriving soon and had arranged for a delay in readying his engines if needed. He could blame the repair work although it was not strictly true. He knew that it would not be wise to mess the port about too much though, as they would simply tow him to sea with tugboats. It might also spoil his standing for his next call.

He saw a lorry loaded with logs stop by the ship and knew that it was in the wrong place. Then he saw who emerged from the cab and his heart filled with pride. The man from the Ministry had done it, just as he had said he would. Grace and Horis ran up the gangway and Hector greeted them, wrapping Grace in a hug he was shocked at her thinness.

"Hello, my dear," he muttered through his joy. "We must get you fed." To Horis he turned and clasped his hand, pumping his arm. "Well done, sir," he said. "You have restored my faith in you. Now get inside out of sight, we are about to sail."

Maloney coughed, he had followed the pair on board. "Mr Maloney, I'm sure we all have you to thank," Hector boomed, "and I do."

"It was my pleasure to be part of it, sir," replied Maloney, "but you must be aware that the pair will not be safe in any port in Norlandia."

Nabbaro nodded. "I thought as much, sir," he answered thoughtfully. "They will be safe enough here though until such time as the fuss has died down. And what will you do now?"

"I will keep watch on Grace's brother," said Maloney, "and shield him if I can. Please let Grace know that. Then I can try to go back to my life of anonymity."

"I will," affirmed Nabbaro. "You have been a stout friend to them both and I thank you for it." Again they clasped hands.

Just then the harbour pilot came on board. "Captain?" he asked and Hector nodded. "Are you ready to depart? Single the moorings and ready the engine."

Maloney turned to go. "I must see to my men, Captain. I'm glad to have been of service."

"Good day to you, Mr Maloney," said Hector, "and safe journey for all of you." He turned to follow the pilot, "Bosun," he shouted, "lift the gangway and stand by to let go moorings."

The *Swiftsure* passed the breakwaters and reduced speed, preparing to drop the harbour pilot. In the wheel-space Grace and Horis were watching as the ocean opened up ahead of them. Nabbaro was talking to the harbour pilot. "Tell me, sir, why the rush to sail us?" he asked.

"Well," the man replied, "we had orders from the Ministry to receive a special shipment of goods from Aserol. The vessel had been damaged by storms and had taken refuge in some bay to make repairs." Nabbaro nodded, he had been forced to do the same once or twice. The pilot continued. "There was no room in the port but as it was an important and urgent cargo we were instructed by

Junior Minister Terrance to make room."

At that name Horis's ears pricked up. He nudged Grace and listened more intently.

"And your ship was the unlucky one chosen to make way for it," the pilot continued.

As he spoke he pointed to another vessel which was making for the pilot boat, bobbing in the swell a half mile ahead. "That must be it now," he said, reaching for the ship's telescope. He regarded the other vessel for a moment. "She is the *Bold Cutter*. Yes, that is that one," he said, his tone perplexed. "I'll be aboard her presently, but it's strange."

"What's that?" replied Nabbaro. He took the telescope from the pilot and inspected the other vessel for himself.

"Well, it is supposed to have a full cargo for discharge," said the pilot, "yet it sits high in the water, the goods on board must weigh next to nothing."

Horis and Grace said nothing but Horis fingered the rock in his pocket and allowed himself a small smile as Northcastle dropped astern.

Keep up with Richard Dee at richarddeescifi.co.uk

If you enjoyed this, then try the first Chapter of Freefall

Freefall is the story of Dave Travise, an interplanetary trader with a past. Trying to forget, whilst being constantly reminded is no way to live, but sometimes letting go is just too painful. His ship is his past, so that's part of the problem.

So when excitement comes back into his life, in the shape of a dead girl and a stolen disc, his world turns upside down. Events take control of his life, and before he knows how, he's at the centre of a galaxy-wide conspiracy, chasing the answers that explain the past and may hold the key to the future.

The story moves from the civilised centre to the edge of exploration. A cast of pirates, smugglers and legendary explorers all play their part in a story that's older than us.

Chapter 1

I do like a nice sunrise, and I've seen a few. There's a beautiful binary on Wishart, and the Red Dwarf of Jintao, with its rosy glow lighting the mist rising off the grass sea. But any of them, even the boring ordinary ones, look so much better from orbit. There's no warning, one minute space is black, the planet's edge may be fringed with a haze of atmosphere, instantly a line of brightness appears and grows quickly into a disc. It has the viewport polarizers working flat out to take away the glare before you go blind. But for that moment, I get a surge of well-being, a feeling that it all starts again, and maybe this time, things will be different.

Captain Dave Travise, ship-owner and trader, is what it says on my papers, and the grand title makes it sound much more than it is. In reality I'm just a driver with a past, trying to forget whilst everyone insists on bringing it up and reminding me. Sometimes I think that the old me is someone else, and sometimes I wish that it was.

Traders, or whatever you want to call us, are the lifeblood of the colonies, without us there would be just a collection of worlds, isolated in space. We deliver the mail, shift livestock and produce, and just occasionally if we stray the wrong side of the odd regulation, well most things in the universe are legal, somewhere. At least that's always been my defence. As I said, the name's a bit of a hangover, most of us don't actually trade any more. Now we just move stuff around for other people.

So here I am, hanging in upper orbit, while the customs do their thing, all coded between my computer and theirs, it's really just checking that we both have the same story, my agent should have done all the hard work, that's why I pay him.

Naturally, as far as my body is concerned, it's the wrong time of day for me to be alert, hence the value of the semi-intelligent comms link.

The one thing that's never mentioned, in all the books or films, is that no two planets keep the same time. And it doesn't matter when you arrive; it's always at the opposite time to your body clock. So if you've just eaten lunch, it will be the middle of the night. Although most planets' days are in the twenty to thirty-two hour range, travellers use standard hours in conversation and trade, and rely on the wristband to do all the hard work.

Ah, the wristband, how did we ever manage without it? To think that mankind developed space travel and colonised the galaxy without one. The concept all started from the annoying job of having to adjust your watch every time you went somewhere.

And like the old communicators that everyone once had, more and more functions were added to it, until only those who had never lived without one could use it properly.

I could feel mine, on my left wrist. It's not big or heavy and the energy cell is sewn into the strap, considering its functions it's a marvel of design. You can get all sorts of colours and shapes, but this one is a plain grey. Apparently practical people wear them on the left, and the more cerebral on the right. I don't know about that, it just feels comfortable there.

At its most basic, it's a piece of tec that shows planet time, season and all sorts of useful information, and converts local to standard, all via radio from satellite. All the data is displayed on a small holopanel that hovers in mid-air, and can be positioned where it's convenient to read.

The wristband also interfaces with just about anything else you might want to control or access. It's such a common device that people forget the good old days, when things were achieved with less tec than we now use to clean our teeth.

Meanwhile, the two computers chatted away, exchanging cargo

details and allocating docking facilities, maybe even talking about the weather for all I knew. My wristband told me that it was a late spring day where I was headed, and without looking, I knew that probably meant rain.

There are all sorts of planets, as many types as you can think of, and then some. There are water worlds, ice worlds, deserts and a mixture of all the above. And unfortunately there are the disasters; the quarantine worlds where humans have experimented and fouled up. Like Prairie 7, which was going to solve all the grain shortages the early colonists endured. But the genetically modified crops took over the ecosystem, caused mutations in the pollinating insects, and forced the settlers to get out fast. At least the damage could be confined, but no-one has been back for a long time, so who knows what's developed. Before the corporations were reined in, there were a rash of planets contaminated, and even now, the odd experiment still goes out of control.

There are about 200 inhabited planets in the Federation; the number varies depending on who you ask, and who is in charge at any particular time. The whole arrangement is very informal; planets join or leave all the time, whenever they think they can make a better deal with the independent worlds, which of course doesn't suit the Senate, the group who like to think they are in charge.

'Order is Strength' is the motto of the Federation, but about the only thing that unites people is their dislike of attempts to order them. Although they are not as heavy-handed as they used to be, the Federation Guards still manage to overreact to most things, and instead of leaving the planets to sort themselves out, prefer the remote faceless bureaucracy model of overbearing government. But there are places where you can escape, where locals are happy, and space is free. After all, it's a big galaxy. And I'm lucky enough to be arriving at one of those places today.

The customs check seems to be taking longer than usual, but the wait would be worth it. In my mind I can taste the fresh food; I've been living on concentrates for the past week. I hadn't been able to take much fresh food on Wishart and it ran out after four days.

I've always liked New Devon (that's the name the locals call it, as far as the Federation is concerned it's Nova 5, not a very romantic name, but then the Federation is not that sort of government), it's not rushed and the people don't seem to be stressed all the time. And it's not pretentious in the way that the newer colonies are. I think the inhabitants are more comfortable with themselves, they feel secure in their place.

And they have a healthy disregard for the Federation. The guards are tolerated, but the locals make it clear they are in charge. Outside interference is not wanted.

Looking out of the viewport, I could see the deep blue of the ocean below, and swirls of cloud marking the weather systems. The sun also reflected off the customs satellite, drifting in its geo-stationary orbit, its solar panels making it look like a golden moth. I wondered if it was manned, if there was someone there as excited as me at the thought of a return to solid ground.

They say New Devon is named after a place on Old Earth, I can't say that I've ever been, but then so few of us have, but it's a historic fact that the first colonists came straight from there. That's one of the things with exploration, you have to find a name for everything, and I guess it comes from the need to feel in a familiar place, even when you're half the galaxy away from familiarity.

I expect that the amazing scenery must have influenced the naming as well. New Devon, like its namesake has got the lot, rolling hills, cliffs, blue seas and golden sands. Quite surprising really that it's no tourist haunt, only the dedicated know and appreciate it, the most popular of the vacation destinations seem to be the ones least like Old Earth. This suits the locals down to the ground because, although I find them friendly, they aren't all over you, a slow thoughtful approach is the New Devon way.

As I said, I like the place, I've always been happy with my own company, and I think most traders are. It's probably something to do with all the time spent in a small steel bubble. Life tends to pass you by, you get very confused as to where you are, planets have different customs and it's easier to say little than to keep putting your foot in it.

Once you get used to it, the tec is fairly unobtrusive, and after a bit more electronic chatter between the customs and the ship, the soft voice of my computer said, "Clearance has been granted, Dave, and I have the entry plan, shall I proceed?"

No matter how many times I hear the voice – it's Myra by the way, it reminds me of the happy times. When she had put her voice print on the computer she said it was so she could order me around. It must be fifteen years ago but I sometimes look over my shoulder expecting to see her in the hatchway. You can still see the faint dent in the panel if you look closely, I try not to. The paint was worn there; I rubbed it every time I passed.

I could always use the wristband to control the ship, but I prefer the voice activation, it lets me think that I can still speak to Myra, and the responses are varied enough to maintain the illusion. And it keeps me from feeling lonely.

"Okay, Myra," I answered, "let's go to work." After a short delay, the thrusters fired and the nose dropped. There was that moment when the black of space turns red, then blue as you start to slide through the atmosphere and the hull heats from the drag.

There's always that instant, just before the plasma envelope cooler kicks in, when I wonder if it's going to work, but, like I said, it's all controlled by the computer, less chance of a mistake that way. It sometimes seems a pity that we rely so much on the tec, but there's a reason, it doesn't go wrong.

There was the usual rumbling and bumping from re-entry, the ship stood up to it as well as ever, but if I looked out behind me, over the rear of the catwalk I could see the hull flexing and moving under the strain. The presence of cargo damped out the worst of the movement, or at least the sight of it but the rattling of lashings and noises from badly packed containers added to the picture.

It was a testament to its design, the ship was older than it had a right to be, an old Federation Sprite class supply vessel, named *Freefall*, they had been retired from service when the Sprite 2 class were developed. This one lay gently rusting in a field until rescued and refitted by Myra and yours truly. I had changed the name, even though Myra had said it was bad luck. I sometimes wondered if she hadn't been right.

Anyway, today I'm landing in New Devon City, or Capita as the Federation would prefer, it's the only really large population centre on the bigger of the two continents. The locals have been debating for years whether to give it a grander name, among others there's the Plymouth faction and those who don't see the need to remind everyone of the past. They would rather call it something else, something newer.

Dropping through the cloud layer, I skimmed over the ocean, it covers a large part of the planet, and accounts for all the rain, quite surprising but after all the years of thinking that Earth was the only inhabited planet, the discovery that water rich planets were quite common spurred on the advance of technology.

Within 100 years of the discovery of several water rich planets we were sending ships to them, quite slow ones at first, but these were overtaken by the discovery of trans-light drives. Of course, these crews actually arrived before the sleeping crews on the first ships. And that made for some interesting meetings. And a field day for the shrinks.

The Gaians would tell you that the progress of space flight was very logical, deep space travel became possible when we had found somewhere to go, just the same as every other advance, we couldn't do it until either we needed to, or had a reason to.

New Devon was one of the Five, the first planets to be settled, all those centuries ago. It was found to be very Earth-like, with an oxygen atmosphere, and carbon based plant and primitive animal life. And it has not suffered from the arrival of the ancestors of the settlers, like a lot of the colonies. Its seas became a home for the endangered species from Earth, and its red soil grew crops and nourished animals from the old world.

In fact I could see a pod of whales below me as I chased my shadow over the ocean, sounding in the clear blue waters. They had adapted very well to the oceans on several worlds, and even enjoyed eating the local fish and plankton.

On Nova 5 there were mainly blue and humpback whales, other worlds had selections of different species, all of which had either been captured from Old Earth's polluted waters and transported across the galaxy in vast tanks, or brought in as embryonic creatures, and reared locally.

It's funny, but in all the worlds that we found so far, there's quite a similarity in the life forms, there's plants and trees on most of them, and fruits and grains, even a few vegetables and varied animal life. Some worlds have mainly fish or birds and some have a lot of mammalian type creatures, but nowhere have we seen any evidence of advanced intelligent life. Of course these have been added to by the things that the first settlers brought with them from Old Earth, and a lot of interbreeding has taken place, not all of it intentionally.

I could also see one of the giant sailing vessels that carried planet-wide trade, it was moving briskly through the water, using a combination of the wind and solar power generated from panels sewn as part of the sails. New Devon was very proud of its use of renewable energy.

The tall cliffs below me marked the start of the Big Land, there are only two island continents, each referred to as the big one, depending on which one you are on the other is considered smaller. The official name is Primus, don't ask me why it has a Latin name, but it's the rocky, wooded and less agricultural one, it's where the Science and Technology corporations do all their work.

The abundance of running water solves all the electricity needs of the planet, everywhere has its own hydro generators, and with the wind and solar and tidal plants, more power is produced than is needed. The corporations developed ways of storing this surplus, in portable energy cells, and the ones that they produce here are generally reckoned to be the best you can get. They sell everywhere where there's no easy way to produce or store power, on new colonies or for emergency systems, and a good part of my load was exhausted ones for recharge.

Crossing the shoreline, there was a brief updraft caused by a bit of anabatic air, but the trimmers coped with only minor disruption to my stomach and a splash of coffee on my overall leg. It was hot.

"Sorry, Dave," said Myra, and I thought that I detected a faint amusement in her voice.

Freefall is available as an eBook or paperback from Amazon and Smashwords.

Lightning Source UK Ltd.
Milton Keynes UK
UKOW02f1315060716

277803UK00001B/54/P